THEODORE TERHUNE STORIES

Work for the Hangman

A THEODORE TERHUNE MYSTERY

BRUCE GRAEME

With an introduction by J. F. Norris

 Moonstone Press

This edition published in 2021 by Moonstone Press
www.moonstonepress.co.uk

Introduction © 2021 J. F. Norris
Originally published in 1944 by Hutchinson & Co. Ltd
Work for the Hangman © the Estate of Graham Montague Jeffries,
writing as Bruce Graeme

ISBN 978-1-899000-32-6
eISBN 978-1-899000-33-3

A CIP catalogue record for this book is available from the British Library

Text designed and typeset by Tetragon, London
Cover illustration by Jason Anscomb
Printed and bound by CPI Group (UK) Ltd, Croydon, CRO 4YY

Contents

INTRODUCTION

Bruce Graeme, the Mixologist Mystery Writer

Readers who first met Theodore I. Terhune in *Seven Clues in Search of a Crime* will be thrilled to learn that *Work for the Hangman* is a legitimate detective novel. All action is confined to Bray-in-the-Marsh and its environs with none of the first book's globetrotting adventures. This is no eerie thriller as in *House with Crooked Walls*, with the spirit of an evil monk haunting the story and skeletons waiting to be uncovered. No courtroom transcripts to pore over as in *A Case for Solomon*. We get some inventive detective work in this fourth of the eight Terhune books. Julia MacMunn really shines this time. Her nascent detective talent, first explored in *House with Crooked Walls*, was until now limited mostly to library research. Much to Terhune's surprise Julia does lots of offstage legwork and delivers some of the choicest moments and damning evidence against the prime suspect.

Personally, I was happy to see that Graeme was giving more stage time, as it were, to Julia over the other woman in Terhune's life, Helena Armstrong. Helena, the secretary to Lady Kylstone, another recurring character in this series, seems only to be used as a foil, and a rather weak one, for Terhune's affections. Julia—tart-tongued, brash, unscrupulous and often extremely selfish—is complicated, conflicted and much more interesting than Helena. Yet beneath her haughty facade there lies hidden a woman of substance, of insight and of feeling. Her mercurial temperament and fluid moods are well suited to those of a competent actress, and she makes use of that burgeoning talent at one crucial point in the novel.

Convinced that Robert Shilling is a murderer, she wants to trap him into revealing he is not the decent man he presents himself to be. During a tour of his lavishly furnished home Julia subtly picks at the character of Veronica, Shilling's second, much younger wife. After hearing him compare the differences in their tastes in home decoration, Julia warns Shilling that men should always be careful of whom they marry as men are more proper, less fickle and less indulgent than women. She says a woman will pull a man "down to her level instead of trying to raise herself to his". And that is the trap she needs to reveal Shilling for who he really is:

> If he has an ounce of decency in him, she reflected, he will bundle me out of this house neck and crop for insulting his wife like that. He is frowning. Is he going to tell me that I am the most insulting guest he has ever had the misfortune to have in the house? If he does I shall respect him a little. I may even begin to wonder whether he is the cold-blooded murderer all of us believe him to be.

Work for the Hangman may be a more traditional detective novel than the previous Terhune books, but it is not without some deliciously creepy moments. Graeme's love for psychic ability and superstition come into play at a charity fete where Terhune and Veronica Shilling visit a palmist's tent. The palm reader is a rather clever intuitive detective herself and stuns the easily impressed Veronica with pronouncements about her marriage, her husband and Terhune's identity. Then both of them are astonished when the fortune teller gets the name of Veronica's first love correct but will divulge nothing else, for she sees darkness in Veronica's palm. Nevertheless, this scene ends with a stunning revelation that paves the way for the twisty denouement.

Astute readers in tune with genre history will soon begin to notice that this mystery novel is a melding of two types of story, two subgenres within the overarching category of detective fiction. Terhune is investigating suspicious accidental deaths that might be murders. All is presented as an old-fashioned whodunit for about the first third of the book. Then the narrative veers away from his viewpoint and we follow another character. Graeme has subtly transformed his story into an "inverted" detective novel. When evidence starts to pile up the reader may be savvy enough to recognize that the story appears to be morphing into one of the earliest "murder by proxy" crime fiction novels.

Graeme was not the inventor of this now oft-used motif, of course; there is one book that that most people think of when the topic of murder by proxy comes up. Patricia Highsmith's classic debut *Strangers on a Train* (1950) is the apparently groundbreaking book many people seem to think was the first novel to deal with a scheme to switch murders in order to hide motive and identity. However, that novel did not appear until 1950, well after many prolific crime writers had already made use of this convention, some employing much more ingenious methods. Genuine aficionados will tell you that many of the greats used some form of this plot device in books published in the heyday of the Golden Age of detective fiction, including *Murder by Proxy* (1937) by Peter Drax, *Antidote to Venom* (1938) by Freeman Wills Crofts and *Counterpoint Murder* (1940) by G. D. H. and Margaret Cole. Graeme ought to get some credit for his story in *Work for the Hangman*, originally published in 1944, as he certainly beat Highsmith to the punch along with the colleagues listed above.

Detective fiction fans of the work of Freeman Wills Crofts and Christopher Bush may also pick up on the convention of alibi-breaking, a favourite motif of those two Golden Age mystery writers. As the case progresses it is imperative that Detective Inspector Sampson determine exactly where Shilling and Ronald Strudgewick were at the time of Strudgewick's uncle's death, a supposed accident that Terhune and Julia believe to be a cleverly arranged murder. The two men were apparently together but it is hard for Terhune to accept this as true. It's too convenient, and he works to tear apart this ostensibly iron-clad alibi. The alibi not only links the two suspects but also reveals a criminal plot that calls to mind the "murder by proxy" motif. In the final chapter our detective heroes prove their case and deliver a final bit of evidence that also shocks one of the villains of the novel.

Graham Montague Jeffries (1900–1982), better known as Bruce Graeme, was married and had two children: Roderic and Guillaine. Both his son and daughter went on to write books and interestingly also used their father's alter ego surname for their own pen names. Guillaine Jeffries, as "Linda Graeme", wrote a brief series of books published between 1955 and 1964 about a girl named Helen who was a ballet dancer in theatre and on TV. Roderic Jeffries followed in his father's footsteps and turned to writing crime fiction, using his own name and the pseudonyms Roderic Graeme (continuing his father's series about the thief turned crime novelist Blackshirt), Peter Alding, Jeffrey Ashford and Graham Hastings. In addition to more than sixty crime, detective and espionage novels, Roderic wrote a number of non-fiction works on criminal investigation and Grand Prix racing.

Late in life Graeme gave his Elizabethan farmhouse in Kent to Roderic and his wife. Graeme moved up the road to a bungalow and would have lunch with his son and daughter-in-law once a week. According to Xanthe Jeffries, Bruce Graeme's granddaughter, he remained in Kent while his son's family moved to Majorca in 1972. They remained close even while apart, and Graeme would visit in May every year, on his birthday.

When I asked for any family stories she might share with Moonstone Press readers, Xanthe very politely complied with an anecdote-filled email. I learned that her grandfather kept a couple of marmosets as pets and had inherited a Land Rover from his son when Roderic moved away. She also wrote of his annual visits to Majorca: "If the weather was not to his liking," she reported, "we never heard the end of it. On his last trip to us he became very worried about having to travel back to the U.K. via Barcelona." Apparently he was concerned about Spanish customs law. "When asked why he told my parents that his walking stick was in fact a swordstick!" Clearly, Graeme was something of an adventurer himself.

In *Work for the Hangman* readers will get to know better many of the recurring characters who populate Bray-in-the-Marsh and its environs. Julia MacMunn, especially, is richer and livelier than ever, proving herself as capable at detective work as her friend Theodore Terhune. Once again we have an amalgamation of subgenres, with the traditional aspects of detective fiction intersecting with those of the "inverted" detective novel. In the coming volumes Bruce Graeme will continue to experiment with formal conventions, find new interpretations of the bibliomystery and adeptly blend subgenres like a skilful bartender concocting new refreshing and flavourful cocktails. Let's raise a glass to this mixologist of mystery writers and toast to yet another welcome reprint from Moonstone Press. Cheers!

J. F. NORRIS
Chicago, IL
March 2021

A NOTE FROM THE PUBLISHER

While a reader does not need to have read the earlier novels to enjoy this one, *Work for the Hangman* is the fourth book in the Theodore Terhune series and as such contains some spoilers for earlier books in the series, particularly *Seven Clues in Search of a Crime*.

Chapter One

Sunday morning. A clear, sunny morning to make one happy just to be alive. A blue sky, with just a wispy cloud here and there to give it life. A gentle breeze, fragrant with Nature's perfumes. A morning to make houses and buildings seem superfluous and depressing.

From the window of his dining-room Terhune looked down upon Market Square. It was not quite deserted. A car stood outside the house of Brian Howland, the dentist. It was Howland's own car, and he and his family were piling into it. Every member of the family carried something—Howland himself a wicker luncheon-basket; the others, brown-paper parcels, bottles, collapsible seats. It looked as if they were off for a picnic.

Two men were strolling towards Higgins's opposite, to buy Sunday newspapers, no doubt. Terhune did not recognize their faces, and as they were both in hiker's clothes he concluded that they were guests at one of Bray's three inns—the *Wheatsheaf*, probably, for they were coming from that direction. Doctor Harris, who lived in one of the old Georgian houses which bordered the Square on the west side—he lived a few doors away from Brian Howland—was ambling absently towards the southeast corner, exercising his dog. Collis, the grocer, stood outside his shop, smoking a pipe. His hands were thrust deeply into his trousers pockets, and although the expression on his face was fixed, Terhune received the impression that, mentally, Collis was completely relaxed. Two dogs, tentatively sniffing at Doctor Harris's animal, completed the picture.

A picture of laziness, taken all in all. Just the sheer, happy, blissful laziness of a warm June Sunday morning. A Sunday morning, mark you! for by 8.30 a.m. on any other morning the Square would be showing every sign of preparing for, and even starting, a day's hard work. In point of fact, save on market days —Thursdays—the inhabitants of Bray-in-the-Marsh did not work hard by the standards of a commercial or industrial town or city, and it is true to say that practically no one in Bray would willingly have changed places with any city worker. But any city worker having changed places, even with 75-year-old Thomas Hobby—who no longer worked as hard as in his youth—would have been whacked long before sunset brought a welcome relief from the sustained physical labour to which leisurely methodical diligence lent a deceptively easy air.

But Sunday is Sunday, especially one which already promised to be a scorcher. So Bray-in-the-Marsh presented the appearance of a forgetting, forgotten corner of the world. Which, in effect, it was—except when the little Kentish market town became a newspaper headline on account of its one and only bookseller, Theodore I. Terhune—or Tommy for short. By a series of coincidences, three times in as many years, Terhune—whose only real interest in life consisted in buying and selling books, and, more latterly, in writing them—had become involved in a local mystery or crime, in consequence of which he had established the reputation of being an amateur detective. He detested this reputation; not only did he know that it was not genuinely deserved, but he wanted no hand, nor had he ever wanted a hand, in hunting down a criminal. He was quite satisfied to do that in his books.

But on this lovely Sunday morning Terhune thought neither of his books nor of detection, amateur or otherwise. His only reflection was: What should he do today? A hike? That was his favourite pastime, but hiking on a scorching hot day—well—! A visit to the Rectory in the afternoon to play tennis with the Rector's young son and two nieces—sixteen, seventeen and nineteen respectively? Young scamps, all three, but jolly and companionable. The trouble about playing with them was that they made his not-so-bad efforts at playing tennis look like feeble pit-patting. Doreen, in particular, had a backhand drive which left him gasping.

Perhaps a cycle-ride to Dymchurch or Hythe for a day's laze on the sands, sun-bathing and swimming? The more he considered this last suggestion the more attractive it became, but before he had reached a definite decision the telephone bell rang.

As he hurried downstairs intuition warned him that one of two people was calling him—Helena Armstrong or Julia MacMunn.

His intuition was not at fault. As he picked up the 'phone he recognized Julia's low, assured voice.

"You were a long time answering, Theo, my sweet," she began sharply.

He grimaced, believing that Julia was suffering from the aftermath of one of her periodic tussles with her mother, Alicia, and Julia in 'one of her moods' was not very companionable. True, he had a knack of restoring her humour, he more than anyone else, but there was no joy for him in the doing thereof.

"I was in the dining-room—" he began.

"Haven't you had breakfast yet?"

"Not yet. Have you?"

"Fifteen minutes ago." Without pause she continued: "What are you doing today?"

"I was just trying to decide."

"In that case you can come with me to Beachy Head."

"Why on earth do you want to go there?"

"Is there any reason why I should not?"

"Of course not, Julia."

"Well, then, just because—"

"You are not planning to commit suicide by throwing yourself over the cliff?"

"If that is your idea of a joke, Theo, it isn't mine," she told him in her chilliest mood, that notorious haughtiness which affronted the women of the neighbourhood—the men, too, for that matter; mentally they took care to pull on their thickest gloves before deliberately seeking her out. Which is not to say that Julia was unattractive, for her slim figure, lustrous black hair, gipsy-brown complexion and expressive eyes first provoked, and then held, the male regard. But Julia was individual, and frankly intolerant of the mediocre or the commonplace, so few men troubled to cultivate and keep her friendship.

"Will you come, or won't you?" she continued, impatiently.

"Yes," he replied briefly—one had to make up one's mind quickly when dealing with Julia. "Have you any particular itinerary in mind?"

"No. Have you?"

"I think the day calls for a swim—"

"I'll bring my costume. Can you be ready by nine-thirty sharp?"

"Yes."

"I'll be with you then. See you later, Theo." Without giving him a chance of speaking further, even of saying 'Good-bye,' she disconnected.

Actually it was already a few minutes past the half-hour when Julia's car turned right into Market Square from the Ashford-Willingham Road, and then left, to come to a shuddering halt outside the shop-door. So Julia was driving on her brakes—still more evidence, if any were needed, that something had upset her. He hurried downstairs, but even before he could let himself out of the private door, which faced a side-road leading off the Square, he heard her car horn blaring loudly.

She did not take her hand off the horn button until he was standing on the pavement beside the car.

She greeted him with: "You might have been down here by the time I arrived."

He ignored her tantrums, and grinned at her. "What's the hurry?"

"I'm not in a hurry, but you know I hate waiting. For heaven's sake climb in."

He ran round the back of the car, opened the off-side door, and jumped in. He had scarcely time to slam the door before the car was leaping forward with a shrill whine. While he settled himself in the yielding seat Julia turned to her left, past the Georgian houses in which Dr. Harris and Brian Howland lived, then right again back on to the Ashford road.

As long as she was within the limits of the small market town Julia restrained herself, and held the speed of the car down to around the forty mark—which was still ten miles an hour above the legal limit. But with the last house left behind she lost patience, and pressed her foot down hard upon the accelerator. The car sped forward at a speed which would have alarmed Terhune had experience not taught him that she was a skilful driver, and possessed comfortingly steady nerves.

Presently the road forked. She turned off the Ashford Road to her left, along the Rye Road. As they neared the humped bridge over the Canal she slowed down, for at the speed at which they had been travelling the hump presented an obstacle which even Julia hesitated to ignore—it might have flung them into the reedy water or against the old trees which bordered the Rye Road on the far side of the Canal. As soon as danger from the bridge was past Julia speeded up. The occasional farmhouses, cottages, and isolated bungalows flashed past: more than one chicken had to half-run, half-fly for its life.

"Well?" Terhune said later.

"Well, what, my sweet?"

"Get it off your chest."

"Your grammar is deplorable—particularly for a writer. Get *it* off my chest! Really, Theo!"

"You've had a row," he accused.

"With Mother." The lines of her mouth set sullenly. "I dared to suggest a voyage."

"A voyage!" For an unaccountable reason her words startled him. "Abroad?"

"Where else can one voyage to?" she asked tartly.

"Why are you so suddenly anxious to go abroad?"

"Don't be ridiculous, Theo. What is so sudden about my anxiety to go abroad? You know very well that I have always wanted to travel, and that only Mother's stuffiness has prevented our going."

What she stated was a fact. She had never tried to conceal her resentment at having to live in a quiet, almost forgotten corner of Kent. Of course, had she insisted, she could have travelled by herself and her mother neither would nor could have prevented her, but a queer sense of loyalty prevented Julia from deserting Alicia, and as Alicia was completely happy spending at least three hundred and thirty days of the year at Willingham, and refused to indulge Julia's passion for travelling to other countries, it thus happened that, where travelling abroad was concerned, Julia had her own way only rarely—Julia, who otherwise almost always obtained whatever she wanted.

No wonder she was sulky and irritable, Terhune reflected. Yet he remained puzzled, having received an impression—wrongly, as it now seemed—that Julia had been happier of late to remain put, as it were.

"I know, but you haven't spoken so much lately about wanting to leave Willingham," he commented weakly.

It was a silly remark to make to a girl like Julia, as he realized almost before the words were spoken. "Do you believe that I have no private thoughts of my own?" she snapped. "What do you expect me to do? Cry on your shoulder every time I meet you? There are times, Theo, when I think you are becoming as brainless and superficial as all the rest of the silly people who live in the neighbourhood."

"Then why did you ask me to come out with you?" he asked calmly.

"I am beginning to wonder!" After a pause she continued, in a changed voice: "You are lucky, Theo."

"Me, lucky! Why?"

"Because you are a man, and a bachelor, and have nobody but yourself to consider. You have nothing to consider but your own whims—"

"What a blithering lot of rot you are spouting," he interrupted cheerfully. "I have a business, haven't I, upon which I rely for the best part of my livelihood? A fine living I should draw from it if I began to do anything I wanted to do, instead of getting on with some of the things that I have to do to keep the business going."

"Yes, I know, but if ever you wanted to sell the business in order to live elsewhere, there is nobody to stop you, is there?"

"But I don't want to sell the business, and I don't want to live anywhere else."

"You are impossible this morning!" she snapped. "I'm sorry now that I asked you to come. I should be happier on my own."

He did not make any response to that remark, and for several minutes neither spoke. But at last she said, in a milder voice: "Of course, I didn't really mean what I said, Theo."

He grinned. "I know that. If I had thought you really meant it I should have got out of the car and walked home. Which would have been a reversal of the accepted procedure," he added.

The quaint inflection in his voice, and the mental picture produced by it, made Julia smile. Soon afterwards her ill-humour evaporated, for though she knew that he was teasing, yet she realized that she would be the sufferer were such a ridiculous thing to happen. For they were still within a walkable distance of Bray, especially for Terhune, who was an enthusiastic walker. The distance, therefore, would cause him no dismay, but the prospect of having to spend the rest of the day by herself certainly would have dismayed Julia. In her present mood Terhune's mixture of youthful good humour and whimsical philosophy made him just the right companion for her—how right she dared not admit even to herself.

It did not take Terhune long to discover the change in Julia's mood. Thereafter, the morning brightened, and soon both were attune with each other, laughing, chattering cheerfully, and enjoying the coolness of the salty breeze which blew hard against their faces, ruffling their hair to glory, and tempering the increasing heat of the morning.

They broke their journey at Cooden Beach to enjoy a swim. There they stayed, alternately swimming and sun-bathing, until both Terhune's appetite and his watch warned him that it was time to eat. They reluctantly dressed, and moved on to Eastbourne for lunch. They lingered a while over the meal, lazily and happily content just to enjoy the feeling of complete abandon to the mood of hot sunshine and blue skies. It was not until the waiter's anxiety for their departure had become acute that they realized that they had overstayed their welcome. They returned to the car, and moved on to their destination.

Beachy Head was glorious, but they did not stay there very long. Julia wanted to swim again, with which demand Terhune was fully in agreement, so they continued along the coast as far as Shoreham-by-Sea. The afternoon passed as the morning had done, ideally and all too quickly. They swam and sun-bathed until the first chill of approaching dusk brought that part of the day to an end. They dressed and returned to the car. As Julia pressed the self-starter Terhune said—not without deep regret: "Home, James."

"Why?" she asked unexpectedly.

"Aren't you ready to go home yet?"

"It is still early, Theo. Shall we dance out the finish of this glorious, glorious day?"

Terhune was always ready to fall in with suggestions of that nature. "I'm game," he agreed promptly. Then a doubt worried him. "Your mother—"

"She won't worry. She knows I am with you. Do you know, Theo, my sweet, you are one of those rare men to whom almost any mother would temporarily entrust her daughter? You are so terribly sweet and honest."

He grinned. "Any regrets on that score?"

"Not really."

Her answer astonished him. "You mean you—you do sometimes have—regrets—"

"Why not? May not a woman have desires occasionally?"

"I'm not much good at—at that sort of thing, Julia—"

"Of course you are not," she interrupted sharply. "If I thought you were I should not have said what I did. Besides, I should probably detest you if you were like many other men I know." She laughed gaily, and changed the subject. "Where shall we dance? Brighton, Eastbourne, St. Leonards, or Hastings?"

He paused uncertainly, having no preference. "Let's toss."

He took out a coin. "Heads, Brighton; tails, Eastbourne." The coin fell tails uppermost.

"What about the other two places?"

"I'm coming to them. Heads, St. Leonards; tails, Hastings."

This time the coin indicated St. Leonards.

"Here goes for the final. Heads, Eastbourne; tails, St. Leonards."

Eastbourne won. Julia revved up, and skilfully steered the long sports coupé through the over-filled car-park into Old Fort Road. Then to the crowded main Worthing-Brighton road and right for Brighton and Eastbourne. The engine of the car purred with a contented hum as it filled with superior pride at the knowledge that the slightest pressure on the accelerator would send it flashing past the sedate saloons, and tourers, and babies which stretched away ahead like an undulating multi-coloured ribbon.

Soon the crimson glow in the western sky turned to a slate-grey: and presently they saw coming towards them a car with its wing-lights glowing. This was later followed by a second, and a third, and then all the cars had their small lights on, but by then Julia and Terhune were approaching the outskirts of Eastbourne.

Just as daylight gave way to the soft, velvet-grey of a cloudless summer night they entered the ballroom of a large hotel, facing the promenade, which advertised a dance-cabaret for that night. A few couples were already on the dance floor, but the hour was still early and the majority of the empty tables displayed a Reserved card.

Terhune's cheerful smile secured for him a small table for two which was sufficiently far from the orchestra for him and Julia to talk in comfort. They decided to finish eating before beginning to dance, so Terhune told the waiter to serve the meal right away. When they began to eat they discovered that their healthy luncheon appetite was still with them.

"I haven't eaten so much for ages," Julia confessed as she finished the ice-cream. "Theo dear, can't we do this more often?"

"Why, do you want to eat more and become fat?"

"Don't be a pig. You know what I mean. It has been a heavenly day. I have never enjoyed myself more."

"So have I, Julie, but the sun usually has that effect upon me."

"Thank you for the compliment," she murmured drily. "You haven't answered my question yet. Wouldn't you like to take me out more often?"

"No," he told her frankly.

Her eyes began to sparkle. "Really, Theo, that is not a very diplomatic answer."

"But it is the truth. You are not often as cheerful as you have been today. In fact, like the little girl with the curl in the middle of her forehead—"

"When she was good, she was very, very good, but when she was in a bad mood she was a nasty-tempered vixen," she completed mockingly. She placed her fingertips on his hands. "I know what you are trying to say, my pet. If we were to meet too frequently the novelty would wear off, and I should be more often vixenish than good. Isn't that so?"

"Well, not quite—"

"But almost. Don't try to prevaricate, Theo, for it is true. I know I am peppery at times, but most people bore me so. Have I really been worse lately?"

"You have, Julie."

She stared across the ballroom. "I think boredom is mainly responsible for my bad moods," she said presently. "Country life gets on my nerves. I wasn't born to rusticate, or to stay in one spot all my life. I want to travel, to see different lands and different people."

"Why don't you find yourself some work to do?"

She laughed scornfully. "Can you really see Mother allowing me to work! Besides, Theo, I am a perfectly useless person. There is no job I could do properly even if I wanted to work. I am just an ornament—"

"A very nice ornament."

"I don't like you when you make pretty compliments," she commented acidly.

"Couldn't you do something for the cottage hospital?"

"I could *not!*" she asserted firmly. "And you know why."

Terhune did know why. The dear, fussy souls who did voluntary work for the hospital linen league, or sat on the main or subcommittees—well, they were certainly not the type of women with whom the impatient, intolerant Julia could work amicably.

"Let's dance," she went on abruptly.

He rose instantly, but before she could follow his example a man passing by the table halted unexpectedly, and held out his hand.

"It is Miss Julia MacMunn, isn't it?" he asked.

Terhune glanced irately at the newcomer, but did not recognize him.

Chapter Two

Julia glanced up at the newcomer; for a moment she was perplexed, but presently came recognition. She nodded and took his hand.

He chuckled. "I'll bet a bob you don't remember my name."

"I happen to have a good memory for names, Mr. Shilling."

"So you have. I think we both have good memories, don't you, considering the time—how long ago was it when we met? Two and a half years if it's a day."

"About that." She glanced at Terhune. "Theo, this is Mr. Robert Shilling. Mr. Theodore Terhune."

The two men shook hands. "Glad to meet you," Shilling acknowledged jovially.

"Mr. Shilling was a guest at the hotel in Las Palmas where Mother and I stayed when we visited the Canary Islands," Julia explained. A note of mockery entered her voice. "Mr. Terhune was indirectly responsible for our taking the trip," she added.

Terhune was annoyed with her for that unnecessary and cruel remark, for there was just enough truth in it to make it hurt. His indirect responsibility for her trip lay in the fact that he had exposed as a murderer the man whom local gossip had decided she would marry. Whether or no this deduction was a true one, the fact remained that, as soon as the trial had finished and the murderer had been sentenced to death, Julia and the Hon. Alicia had sailed for the Canary Islands, Julia for once having persuaded her mother to travel abroad.

Shilling was not interested. "Indeed!" he murmured. Then, eagerly, snobbishly he went on: "How is your mother, Miss MacMunn? Still well, I hope. We all thought her so entertaining, and so lively. You know, she made me promise to visit her when I returned to this country, but you know what holiday invitations are—one can never be certain—"

If—as Terhune suspected—Shilling was hoping for confirmation and a renewal of Alicia's invitation his tactics met with no success.

"Mother is quite well, thank you, Mr. Shilling. And Mrs. Shilling, is she well, too?"

"Blooming, Miss MacMunn. Blooming—" He paused abruptly. An extraordinary expression passed across his face. "You mean Mary?" he stammered.

"Yes."

"Well—Mary—you see Mary—she—died about a year ago."

"I *am* sorry to hear that, Mr. Shilling." Julia was unusually sympathetic. "I liked Mrs. Shilling so much."

An awkward pause followed. Shilling pulled a handkerchief from his pocket and nervously wiped his plump round face, and forehead.

"I don't like to talk about her—her death. It came as a bit of a shock to me. We were—pretty—happy—together." He swallowed. "Well, I mustn't keep you two young people from dancing. It was nice meeting you again, Miss MacMunn."

"Good-bye, Mr. Shilling."

Shilling turned, but as he did so a fourth person joined the group—a blonde wisp of a girl with no bust, thin ankles, highly rouged lips and cheeks, and plucked eyebrows.

"Hullo, Bob, darling. Met some pals, I see."

Shilling's face sagged—he looked far older when his round face was not smiling.

"Yes, old girl—but they want to dance—"

"So do we, don't we? But there's no harm in introducing them, Bob dear."

"This is—" He seemed to find difficulty in enunciating properly. "This is Miss MacMunn. And Mr.—Mr.—"

"Terhune."

"Terhune," Shilling repeated. "Now, my dear—"

"What about me, Bob? Aren't I to be introduced?"

"This is Veronica," he said gruffly. "Now will you come?"

She did not move. "Veronica Shilling—Mrs. Shilling. Bob's wife."

Shilling stared helplessly at Julia. Terhune, too, glanced quickly at her, anticipating some caustic insult which would send the Shillings hurrying away, embarrassed and flinching, or perhaps angrily vituperative.

But Julia always unpredictable, smiled sweetly at Veronica.

"Are you with friends?"

She shook her blonde curls. "No. Me and Bob are just on our lonesome having a good time. Aren't we, Bob darling?"

He eyed Julia with a wary, suspicious glance, and nodded.

"Why not join us and make a party?" Julia went on.

Shilling's relief was almost comical. "That suits me fine," he answered boisterously. "What do you say, Vee?"

Veronica smiled pertly at Terhune. "It would be lovely."

"Get two more chairs, Theo, my pet," Julia murmured.

Terhune went in search of a waiter. He was astounded almost to the point of confusion. He couldn't believe that Julia, of all people, had really asked Veronica and Robert Shilling to sit at her table— Julia, who was usually so intolerant of mediocrity and vulgarity. It couldn't be that Julia genuinely hoped to enjoy the company of the bumptious, well-fed Shilling; still less, his young sophisticated bride. Or was he, Terhune, prejudiced? Was Shilling a passable fellow on closer acquaintance, and had Julia experienced a liking—a romantic holiday-inspired liking—for the man?

As Terhune returned to the table, followed by a waiter carrying two chairs, he noticed that Julia was trying to convey a message to him. On raising his eyebrows to suggest a query, Julia's gaze moved and rested significantly upon a bottle of wine which stood upon a neighbouring table.

Drinks! That was it.

"Mrs. Shilling, may I offer you something to drink—a port perhaps—"

Shilling broke in loudly: "Not so fast, young man. This is my shout." He raised a hand to stop any expostulation on Terhune's part. "No argument now. We are going to enjoy ourselves. It's not going to be port for my little lady, or for any of us. We're going to have a bottle of bubbly. 'Tisn't every day we run into old friends, is it, Vee?"

"No," Veronica said, shortly, glancing at Julia with puzzled eyes.

"Hi! waiter."

A waiter approached. "Yes, sir."

"A bottle of—no, make it a magnum—of the bubbly we had last night."

"The Bollinger, sir?"

"That's the stuff." Shilling turned to Julia. "The stuff is a hell of a price, but it's worth it. The old boy who took the order told us its history last night, didn't he, Vee?" He did not wait for her reply but went on: "During the war somebody in the Champagne district managed to blow up the main entrance to a cave full of privately-owned Bollinger of the nineteen thirty-seven vintage. During the whole of the German occupation of France the Huns never once suspected the existence of the cave or its contents. Every now and again the owner of the stuff managed to sneak into the cave by a smaller cave which was hidden in a forest. Then he and his family used to turn the bottles over, and re-cork, and do all the rest of the palaver that is necessary to make champagne. When the war was over and the stuff was ready to travel the owner came over to England, and sold the whole caveful to a man in the wine-business whose brother owns this hotel. What do you think of that for a story?"

"I am surprised that it has not all been drunk by now," Julia answered.

Shilling chuckled. "Ah, but you see the wine merchant is also a partner, and it pays him better to sell the champagne retail in this hotel than to sell it wholesale to the trade, so he allocated the whole bang shoot to this hotel. That is what I call business. There's still enough in the cellars below us to last another couple of years. By that time they should be able to renew their stocks from the new wine coming over. What about a dance, Miss MacMunn?"

"I should love to." Julia rose and accompanied Shilling to the dance floor.

Veronica giggled. "I'm sorry for your friend. Bob's a lousy dancer, though he's quite sure he's another Fred Astaire." She added, significantly: "Do you trip the light fantastic?"

"A little. Would you care to dance?"

"What do you think?" she replied promptly.

They stepped on to the floor. After a few tentative steps Veronica sighed a little, and snuggled closer to him. "You can dance right enough, I can tell that already. You're a nice change after Bob. Not that Bob hasn't a heart of gold, even if he can't dance," she went on defensively.

"I can see that for myself," Terhune lied.

"That's what I like about Bob. He's got such a cheery face. And a cheery manner which makes everybody who meets him like him. You wouldn't believe the number of friends Bob has. Do you live near here?"

"Not very."

"Where do you live?"

"At Bray-in-the-Marsh."

She giggled loudly. "You're teasing me."

"I'm not. You can ask Miss MacMunn."

"Does she live there, too?"

"Quite near. At a village called Willingham."

"Where is Bray-in-the-Mud anyway? I've never heard of the place."

"Bray-in-the-Marsh," he corrected. "It's near Ashford, in Kent."

"Ashford!" She seemed vaguely pleased. "Then you don't live so very far from us. We're at Tunbridge Wells. Perhaps we shall meet again one day."

"I hope so," he agreed, without enthusiasm.

She chattered on: "When did you first meet my husband?"

"A few minutes ago."

"Oh! Then it was Miss McMunn he knew?"

"Yes."

"Long ago?"

"More than two years ago."

"That was before Bob and I had met, nearly nine months ago. I was in London, staying at the Savoy with my mother. One day in the ballroom he introduced himself to us, and asked whether I would dance with him. I said I would, so we danced. And that was that! You know what I mean," she enlarged, skittishly. "We clicked. Three weeks later he proposed to me. We were married on the first of December."

She paused, as if hoping he would say something, but Terhune was too bored even to simulate politeness. Besides, he guessed she would continue without any prompting.

He was right. When he said nothing she went on, once more defensively: "Did you know that I am not Bob's first wife?"

He nodded. "Miss MacMunn had met her."

"I thought so," she said in a flat voice. "That is why Bob didn't want you to know that I was his wife. He seems ashamed to admit that he has married a second time. I don't know why, I'm sure. Lots of film stars and stage actresses have married more than three times. But perhaps it's because she only died a year ago, and Bob doesn't like people to know he married so soon. I think he is a silly goose, don't you? There's nothing to be ashamed of, is there, in a man missing a wife so much that he marries again? Not that he married me just because he was missing Mary."

"Of course not," he murmured. "Mr. Shilling has good taste." He could not analyse the impulse which prompted him to add that inane remark, but it bore good fruit. He could feel by the added vivacity in her movements that his flattery had pleased her.

She squeezed his hand. "I like you," she told him naively. "Do you ever visit Tunbridge Wells?"

"I've been there about twice in the last few years."

Apparently there were no reservations in her code of manners. "What for?"

"To buy books."

"Stuffy old books. I never read books. Only women's magazines. Are you in the book business?"

"Yes."

Having obtained the information she wanted, she seemed no longer interested. "My husband's in business, too. At least he is if you call being a director of a firm of builders business. He used to be a big builder in Exeter, but soon after his wife died he sold the business to a rival builder, and invested the money in a London firm. Now the only business he does is to go to Town about once a fortnight."

Her chatter flowed on in an unending stream, bemusing him and rasping his nerves. Perhaps he could have borne her monologue more easily if her accent had been less studiously cultivated, or if her voice had been deeper, but it was high-pitched, and freely interspersed with nervous giggles. Besides, she spoke so quickly, and swallowed the tail of her words so often that he found it necessary to concentrate in order to hear what she said. He hated to concentrate mentally while dancing; he was beginning to feel sleepy from the effects of the sun and the swimming, and he longed desperately for the soothing coolness of Julia's impersonal company.

After innumerable encores—how Terhune cursed the obliging conductor—the dance finished. The four people returned to the table, where the magnum of Bollinger awaited them, chilling in its silver-plated cooler.

Shilling laughed full-throatedly. "Who's ready for a drink, boys and girls?"

As he watched the golden, frothing liquid filling the shallow glass Terhune discovered that he was more than ready for something to drink. As soon as all three had raised their glasses to their host he took a sip. The wine was just at the perfect temperature, and dry enough for the gaseous bubbles to prickle his palate as they cooled his hot, dusty throat. He thought he had never tasted nicer champagne, but perhaps that was due to the infrequency of his opportunities.

Presently Shilling turned to Terhune. "You have a first-rate partner in Miss MacMunn, my boy, and I hope you realize the fact. Vee is not so bad, but she can't hold a candle to Miss MacMunn. Do you know that, Vee?"

Veronica pouted. "It's mean of you to tell me so."

"Of course it is," Julia interposed quickly. "Besides, it is not true. I noticed how you were dancing with Theo, and I can judge for myself how good you are."

"Mr. Terhune isn't so bad himself."

"Not too bad," Julia admitted drily.

"Miss MacMunn is the daughter of the Hon. Alicia MacMunn," Shilling announced to his wife in a voice loud enough for people at the surrounding tables to hear if they so desired.

Veronica was impressed. "That means something, doesn't it?" she asked naïvely.

"Of course it does, my dear. It means that she is the granddaughter of a lord."

"Oh!"

"It isn't every day your old man has the opportunity of buying champagne for the daughter of a lord," Shilling went on. "Perhaps your ma won't have so much to say—"

"Please, Bob!"

He chuckled. "All right, my dear. I wasn't going to say anything about your ma." He looked round the table. "Drink up, boys and girls. There is plenty more in the bottle still to be drunk." He refilled the glasses.

"Here's to all of us," he toasted. "Here's wishing us all everything we want."

Terhune was convinced that Julia could not ignore such a lovely opening for one of her subtly caustic inferences, but again she surprised him. To his astonishment she said nothing, but drank a deep sip as if seriously joining in the toast. Just then the music restarted. Terhune saw Shilling's glance moving round towards Julia. Quickly, before the other man could speak, Terhune said swiftly:

"Julia—"

"I'd love to." She rose swiftly, and with a half-smile towards the Shillings joined Terhune.

They had completed more than a circuit of the floor before Terhune spoke.

"What in the name of Old Harry is the idea, Julie?"

"I'll tell you later, in the car."

"By the way, as you will be driving you won't drink too much champagne, will you?"

"Don't be absurd," she said, coldly. "Have you much money on you?"

"I shall still have that reserve five-pound note I always carry with me when I go out on the spree."

"After paying the bill here?"

"Yes. Why?"

"Will you do me a favour and buy another magnum of champagne?"

"Another! Good lord! But why—"

"Please, Theo."

"Of course, I will, but I wish I knew what was going on behind those expressionless eyes of yours."

"You shall know—later."

"That's something to look forward to. How did you find your last dancing partner?"

"Perfectly odious. And yours?"

"Pure Neo-Kensington."

They laughed in concert.

"She could talk a donkey's hind leg off," he went on.

The hand which held his stiffened.

"Is she talking a lot?"

"She's been giving me her life history."

"Has she been talking as though it were a welcome change to have an outlet?"

He did not reply.

"Well?"

"Now that you've put it in these words, Julie, I believe that is the impression which I had, without realizing exactly what it was. How did you guess?"

"Perhaps because Shilling talked so much that he scarcely gave me a chance of interrupting."

Terhune grinned. "Did you want to?"

"No."

"Did he, too, relate his autobiography?"

"He spoke of everything and everybody save himself."

There was a significant undertone in her voice which made him glance at her.

"Does that fact astonish you?"

"Doesn't he look like the type of man to talk about himself?"

"I should have said that he was," Terhune admitted.

He waited for her to continue, but instead she said: "Let's forget the Shillings, Theo, and enjoy the dance."

The dance finished all too soon; comparing it with the one he had had with Veronica, Terhune could not believe that both had lasted an equal length of time; he wondered if the band leader had discovered a personal dislike for him.

Between dances the four people finished the first magnum, and then the second which Terhune ordered. The wine made Shilling increasingly cheerful. Not so the rest of the party, for the more wine he drank the louder he insisted upon dancing most of the time with Julia. This pleased neither Veronica nor Terhune, both of whose faces grew steadily more glum as the evening progressed. Julia's expression of calm detachment never changed, however. It was impossible to tell, from glancing at her, what was her opinion of the course of events.

At last—at blessed last!—the evening came to an end with *God Save the King*. Shilling, by now cheerfully maudlin—having switched over to whiskies and soda—tried to persuade Julia and Terhune to stay the night at the hotel, and it was with some difficulty that they were able to escape his persistent attentions, which were rapidly becoming unpleasant. Then they did so only by exchanging addresses, and promising to arrange a future meeting.

Eventually they found themselves in the fresh air, purring along an almost deserted, moon-lit road.

"And now—" Terhune said presently.

Chapter Three

"And now—" Julia mocked.

"You know what I'm asking for, Julie. An explanation of why you permitted the ruin of what might have been a delightful couple of hours by willingly hobnobbing with the Shillings."

"Perhaps the evening wasn't ruined for me."

"You won't make me believe that in a hurry. I have known you long enough to know that you must have had some very sound reason for not freezing them off right at the start."

She relented at last. "So I had, Theo, but before I give you that explanation, be a nice man and answer some of my questions. Tell me, first of all, what is your impression of Shilling?"

"He's just a bumptious self-made man—no, not exactly a self-made man, but the son of one."

"What made you correct yourself!"

"Well, he has a veneer—a thin veneer—which probably comes from a middle-class education, say, at one of the minor public schools. The bumptiousness I put down to an inferiority complex. Actually he was a builder in Devon until a year ago. He sold out to a rival, invested the capital in a firm of London builders, and is now living on the interest, in Tunbridge Wells. As a director on the board of the London builders he visits Town about once a fortnight."

"Did you get all that information from his wife during your first dance with her?"

"Yes."

"Tell me, was she quite so confiding during subsequent dances?"

He carefully considered the question. "No," he admitted presently. "She wasn't."

"I believe he warned her to hold her tongue. When you and I were dancing together for the first time I noticed that he was talking rather earnestly with her, and that she was looking somewhat sulky."

"Why doesn't he want her to talk? Because he is a snob?"

"Undoubtedly he is a snob, Theo, but I do not think that that explanation applies in this instance."

"Why not?"

"In the first case because he has changed since the first time I met him in Las Palmas. His vulgarity wasn't so insufferable. He had himself under better control, perhaps because he did not drink to the same extent. Two years ago one could at least put up with him, but now——"

"What was his first wife like, Julie?"

"Ah! Perhaps in the change of wives lies the explanation for the change in character. By the way, at what age do you place Shilling?"

"In the late 'forties, or even the early 'fifties."

"The early 'fifties is probably the more correct. He has the type of face which ages slowly. And how old is Veronica?"

"About twenty-three or four."

She laughed softly. "How blonde hair deceives a man. If she is not thirty this year I am sure she will be next. But even at thirty she is still far too young for him."

"Veronica seems quite satisfied."

"Satisfied! Why not? He is comfortably wealthy, and very much in love with her. No doubt she twists him round her little finger on most occasions, though I should say he could be obstinate when the mood takes him. Mary Shilling was quite a different woman. She was the daughter of a small Devon farmer, and never pretended to be anything else. She was nearer his own age. I liked Mary Shilling. Mother did, too, but then Mother makes friends so easily. She counts any one a good friend who will listen to her without interrupting."

Julia went on: "Mary Shilling was a good wife. She was a good cook, a good needle-woman, and she loved her husband. But she was certainly not a striking woman where appearance was concerned. Perhaps Nature had not been too kind to her, but she was chiefly to blame. She had let herself go to seed, not from carelessness, nor from mental or moral slackness, but solely because she was a woman to whom the spirit meant all, the flesh nothing. I'm not being too dramatic, Theo?"

"Of course not. It sounds as if Mary Shilling was another Miss Amelia."

"Yes, that's right," Julia confirmed quickly. "She was just a simple, nice, homely woman. Just the kind to act as a restraining influence on her husband, by example rather than precept."

"Was Shilling fond of his first wife?"

Julia stared at the broad splash of white light which clearly illuminated the curving, hedge-bordered road. A line of cars was approaching from the opposite direction, so she dimmed her headlights and did not speak until the last red tail-light of the short procession was disappearing behind them.

"I don't know," she confessed at last. "That is a question I have been asking myself for the past hour, without arriving at a really satisfactory answer. In Las Palmas he appeared to regard her with affection—but was that affection of the kind which lasts only so long as it is never put to the test? I did not see enough of him to judge."

A short silence followed. Terhune gazed through the side windows with a slight feeling of irritation. Why were they wasting so much time on the Shillings? The perfect day had been followed by a perfect night, warm, balmy, and music-laden—the soft sigh of the fresh breeze through the telegraph wires, the drowsy rustle of tree-tops, crickets, the distant lowing of a late-calving cow. Low in the north-west the brilliance of a crescent moon dulled the surrounding stars, which, elsewhere in their blue-black velvet background, twinkled with febrile agitation.

The night demanded silent homage of its sombre beauty, but they were ignoring it on account of two uninteresting and boring people they were never likely to see again. As there was a pause in the conversation he decided that the subject should not be renewed by him, anyway—but it was curious why Julia should be so interested in them, for normally she possessed a superb indifference towards the mediocre and the vulgar.

In spite of his resolution to ignore it, his niggling curiosity persisted, so, after all, it was he who reopened the subject.

"Just now, when we were speaking of Shilling's possible warning to his wife not to talk so much, you said that you did not think his snobbishness was responsible. You didn't say why."

"I began telling you how he has changed since our first meeting. When I knew him in Las Palmas he had no inhibitions concerning himself, his wife, his work, and his life-history. Now, even a second magnum of champagne, to say nothing of several whiskies, is not enough to break down his reserve. I tried to get him to speak of Mary, but he wouldn't. He said it still made him sad to think of her."

"That could be true, Julie."

"It could be, but if her death had upset him to that extent why did he so soon afterwards marry a chit of a girl not much more than half his age?"

A chit of a girl! Terhune's eyes twinkled. He doubted whether Veronica was younger than Julia. Then instinctively he hastened to defend his own sex.

"I can imagine a man's having been so grieved by the loss of a wife that he hastens to marry again."

"But then you are an incurable romanticist, Theo, my sweet. If he just had to re-marry, why could he not have chosen some nice widow of his own age?"

"Because contrast would be likely to cause less unhappy memories than similarity."

She became cross with him. "Now you are being ridiculous," she snapped. "You've been reading too many of those romances which I saw on your library shelves last week. But speaking of Veronica, what did she tell you about herself?"

"That she first met Shilling in the ballroom of the Savoy, where she and her mother were staying—"

"Don't trouble to tell me the rest, Theo. I shouldn't believe a word of it. If that girl has ever stayed at the Savoy, it wasn't with her mother."

"Well, make allowances for Neo-Kensington, and substitute any small second-rate hotel for the Savoy."

"Well?"

"They met there, soon after the death of Mary. He became infatuated, couldn't wait for a decent period to elapse, proposed marriage, was accepted—"

"Snapped up."

"Snapped up, then, and—but that is the whole story."

"I still don't believe a word of it. The probability is that she was his secretary before she became his wife."

"Maybe." Terhune did not feel disposed to argue, because, on that point, he half-agreed with Julia.

"What chiefly interests me is, was she his secretary before the death of his first wife? I am convinced that she was, hence his reason for not wanting Veronica to speak too much."

"But why shouldn't she speak of having been his secretary before the wife's death? There's nothing for either party to be ashamed of if a man marries his secretary. Besides, we are only guessing, Julie; we don't know that she was his secretary."

"No?" she exclaimed drily. Her mood changed. "Oh! let's forget those stupid people! Look at that glorious moon."

"I have been looking at it ever since we left the hotel," he pointed out.

So, at last, they talked of other matters, and the Shillings became just a memory.

The following Thursday morning Terhune read an advertisement in *The Times Literary Supplement*.

FOR SALE, by tender or private treaty, a large, private library of books, antique and modern. The library numbers more than 2,150 volumes, and includes many complete sets of first editions, also limited and illustrated editions, and a fine collection of volumes on gardening, antique furniture, and reproductions of Old Masters. Serious purchasers only should send a remittance of 2s. 6d. for a complete, annotated catalogue to:

> Messrs. Hinchcliffe, Martin and Rogerson,
> Bank Chambers, High Street, Saxhawley,
> Yorkshire.

He gazed reflectively at the advertisement. More than two thousand volumes! The proposition was too big for his serious consideration, especially in competition with all the biggest book-buyers in the country. Even at the average price of 2s. per volume the cost of purchasing the library would amount to more than £200, and he had not that amount of cash available, having paid out £75 the previous week, and £89 the week before that, in each instance for a private collection of books. Besides, it was not to be expected that the average price would be as low as 2s. if the library were a well-chosen one.

Resolutely he turned over the page, assuring himself that it was not worth while his wasting two shillings and sixpence on a catalogue of books which he could not possibly afford to buy, particularly as he was sure the list would cause him heartburning not to buy it— and probably even more of heartburning to sell many of the books, just as he hated to sell some of those already on his shelves. That was the worst of being a book-lover as well as a bookseller.

Although it was Market Day—which meant that for several hours he had scarcely time to think—the memory of the advertisement haunted him for the remainder of the morning. Eventually he succumbed to temptation. As soon as he had finished his midday meal he hurried round to the Post Office and bought a postal order. Before the shop had opened for the afternoon a request for the catalogue was on its way to Saxhawley.

The catalogue arrived on Tuesday, by the late afternoon delivery. With mild excitement he slit the wrapper open and began to read the mimeographed list. From the first moment his attention was held.

Item One: Jourdain (M.), *English Decoration and Furniture of the Early Renaissance* (1500–1650). (Batsford). 1924.

Item Two: Latham (Charles), *In English Homes*. Plates and illus., 2 vols., folio (Country Life). 1904–8.

Item Three: Jekyll (G.) and Hussey (C), *Garden Ornament*, profusely illus. Folio. 1927.

Item Four: Mollhausen (B.), *Diary of a Journey from the Mississippi to the Coasts of the Pacific*. Plates and maps, 2 vols., 8vo., half calf. 1858.

Item Five: Birkenhead (Earl of), *Last Essays*. First Edition. 8vo. 1930.

Item Six: Symonds (R. W.), *The Present State of Old English Furniture*. 116 photographs, 4to. 1927.

Item Seven: Hope (Anthony), *The Prisoner of Zenda*. First Edition, Cr. 8vo. N.D.

Right away Terhune realized that the person who had compiled the list knew little, either of the books listed, or of a suitable method of cataloguing them. There had been no attempt to systematize or classify the two thousand-odd volumes. Anthony Armstrong's *Village at War* stood cheek by jowl with the 1890 edition of the sixteenth century classic, William Painter's *Palace of Pleasure*; Oscar Wilde's *Ballad of Reading Gaol* rather inaptly preceded Pufendorf's *Law of Nature and Nations*. In fact, it seemed very much as though someone had stacked all the books on the floor, higgledy-piggledy, and had then proceeded to list them by the simple method of noting down the particulars as they stood, stack by stack.

Nevertheless, Terhune's enthusiasm mounted as he studied the catalogue. More than fifty per cent. of the books were, he estimated, immediately saleable—he could almost name the purchaser of many. For instance, John Bowling, of Newcastle, would most certainly snap up Talbot Hughes's *Old English Costumes;* Sir George Brereton would buy W. E. Hodgson's *Trout Fishing*, although he possessed already a large and comprehensive collection of books on angling; Nicholas Harvey, the retired bank manager who lived at Great Hinton, would be tempted by G. A. Phillips's *Delphiniums* if the price were right; Silas Murdock, of Long Island, U.S.A., would surely cable an offer (and it would be a good offer, too) for Long's *Voyages and Travels of an Indian Interpreter and Trader*, which he would want to add to his library on early American history—

Before he was half-way through the catalogue Terhune's enthusiasm became despair. As he had anticipated, the price which would eventually secure the library would almost certainly be far beyond any sum which he could offer. Why, Long's *Voyages and Travels* would probably sell for fifty dollars, so it was not to be expected that an offer of a few shillings would buy it. Mollhausen would sell for at least five pounds, Jourdain's book on furniture more than thirty shillings, Jekyll and Hussey's *Garden Ornament* a like amount.

He read on, grimly, though he presently became aware that, generally speaking, the second half of the catalogue was worth less than the first—after all, he reflected drily, there had been some sort of system in listing the books: like the greengrocer, the cataloguer had put his best wares on top. Even so he doubted whether any one could buy the library for less than £350.

Three hundred and fifty pounds. He laughed sourly. The odd fifty was probably the limit of his cash resources. For the first time he regretted not having more capital behind him. If only he had a spare three hundred pounds or so to buy the library he would probably recover the outlay in less than six months, and still have a considerable part of the stock left from which to make his profit. And that he would sell at least eighty per cent. of the titles without much difficulty was certain; during the past few years he had collected a first-class mailing list of book-buyers who trusted him and paid fair prices for his books.

Ah, well! He hadn't the money, so that was that. The library must go to one of the big firms—a concrete example of money begetting money. He closed the catalogue, wistfully, reluctantly. If only—

And then he thought of Lady Kylstone. Lady Kylstone's income was larger than her modest needs. For years now her capital had been increasing, not because she was miserly—the mere thought was a libel upon that very dear person—but because she did not choose to spend money uselessly.

Would she loan him the money to buy the library? He believed she would. She liked him; as much as he liked her, he believed. If he went to her in a forthright manner, with a straight business proposition—

He wasted no time in speculation, but hurried to the telephone. Within a few seconds Lady Kylstone's warm American voice was answering him.

"This is Theodore speaking, Lady Kylstone—"

"Good afternoon, Theodore. Do you wish to speak to Helena?"

"Not for the moment. I wanted to speak to you."

There was a faint suggestion of surprise in her voice. "Well, young man?"

"May I come over to see you tonight?"

"Of course you may. Shall we expect you for the evening meal—"

He interrupted her. "I want to ask a favour of you, Lady Kylstone. A very big favour," he explained frankly.

"Is that a reason why you should not eat with us?"

"Well, you see, I—I am hoping to borrow some money for a business proposition."

She laughed deeply. "You will still be welcome, Theodore. We shall expect you at the usual time."

As he disconnected Terhune glanced at his watch. In a little less than two hours he would be expected at *Timberlands*. Before then there was work to be done. In spite of a retiring disposition which made Lady Kylstone content to lead the quietest of lives, she was business-like and efficient. However willing she might be to lend him the money, he was convinced that she would require to know, as much for his own sake as hers, full particulars of the precise amount he would need, and what profit he might reasonably hope to make as a result of her lending him the money. If she considered it undesirable for him to shoulder the financial burden she would not hesitate to exert an influence upon him by refusing the loan.

For the next seventy minutes he went through the catalogue, marking against each item the minimum price he might hope to obtain for it. He reached the last page with very little time to spare, but then observed a foot-note which had previously escaped his notice.

It is understood and agreed by the buyers that all tenders submitted for the purchase of the library will be subject to confirmation after inspection of the volumes. The highest tender will be provisionally accepted, and facilities will be made available for the books to be seen before the sale is completed. The library is at present housed in a residence one mile south of Saxhawley, Yorkshire.

He finished pricing the last page, then totted up the items. He grimaced. The total came to £346 17s. 10d. A large sum to add to his existing liabilities. Was it, after all, worth while hanging such a financial millstone round his neck just for the sake of making an extra three or four hundred pounds during the next two years? Yet the question was not a fair one, he reassured himself. Any profit he might make from the deal would matter less to him than the pride and pleasure he would obtain in handling the collection.

He quickly washed and changed, then cycled to *Timberlands*. Lady Kylstone and Helena awaited him on the verandah, beneath a thick vine. After a few preliminary words Lady Kylstone said:

"The sherry is on the table in the corner, Theodore."

Two bottles of sherry stood on the silver platter: a Solera for the ladies, a Manzanilla for himself. He poured out three glasses, distributed them.

"Now then, young man, tell me about the business deal," Lady Kylstone began in her forthright but kindly manner. "Of course, it has something to do with books; I can see that by the light in your eyes."

He nodded, and passed over the copy of *The Times Literary Supplement*.

As soon as she had read the advertisement her steady gaze regarded him questioningly.

"I tried to ignore the temptation of sending for a catalogue—" he began.

"Why?"

"I knew I had not enough money to buy the library, but I tried to assure myself that no harm could come of sending for the catalogue. It arrived by this afternoon's post—"

Lady Kylstone chuckled drily. "You wasted no time in telephoning me, young man." He looked embarrassed. "Now don't look like a scolded child. I take it as a compliment that you had the nous to come to me. How much money do you need?"

"About three hundred and fifty pounds."

"Humph! That is a lot of money to lay out for additional stock. Are you quite sure you will not be doing yourself more harm than good in buying the library?" He smiled. "Does the question amuse you?" she continued sharply.

"Yes, because I guessed you would ask it." He passed over the catalogue. "Against most of the items I have put the price one can afford as a buyer, and the minimum sum for which they should sell. Those with a cross against them I should hope to sell very soon, either because of the demand for the title, or because I have a client interested in the subject. Those not marked in any way I should have to sell for prices ranging from one to three shillings. Lastly those marked with a query mark are titles which might not sell for years."

Lady Kylstone glanced at him over the top of the catalogue. "It seems evident that you and I understand each other, Theodore." She glanced quickly through the catalogue, then passed it back to him "I am satisfied that you are a sufficiently good business man not to make an offer for the library unless you are satisfied that you can resell it. Helena, dear child, run and fetch my cheque book."

Terhune began to protest. "But, Lady Kylstone—"

"Well?"

"We have not discussed terms yet."

"We do not need to: you would feel insulted, and rightly so, if I were to offer to loan you the money free of interest, so you will pay me three per cent. per annum."

"If my offer is not accepted I should not need the money."

"Then you can tear the cheque up."

Terhune argued, but in vain. Lady Kylstone had an obstinate nature—either he accepted the loan of the money on her terms or the deal would not be completed. So Terhune gratefully accepted the cheque.

The next morning he submitted his tender to Messrs. Hinchcliffe, Martin and Rogerson.

Nine days later he received a telegram:

> *Your provisional tender for library accepted. Please make arrangements to inspect as soon as possible.*
>
> *Hinchcliffe, Martin and Rogerson.*

Two days after the receipt of the telegram Terhune arrived at Saxhawley, and booked a room at the *Saxhawley Arms*.

Chapter Four

Early the following morning Terhune visited the office of Messrs. Hinchcliffe, Martin and Rogerson, which was less than a hundred yards farther up the High Street from the *Saxhawley Arms*. Upon making known his name to the rather elderly spinsterish female who sat near the door in the outer office he was told that he was expected, and that Mr. Martin would see him at once.

Mr. Martin, Terhune found, was a tall, thin-faced man with bowed shoulders, sparse, grey hair and the peering gaze of a near-sighted person. With old-fashioned courtesy he rose from his equally old-fashioned table, and advanced half-way to the door to greet his visitor.

"Good-morning, Mr.—er—Terhune. Welcome to our little town. Did you have a pleasant journey yesterday?"

"Quite, thank you."

"I am glad to hear that. Ah! yes, quite!" He waved his long-fingered hand in the direction of a stiff-backed leather-seated chair which stood at the far side of the table. "Will you sit down while I explain the situation, Mr.—er—Terhune?"

Both men sat down. Martin picked up from the desk a copy of the catalogue of books.

"The name of our client who is selling the collection of books for which *you* have made an offer is Mr. Strudgewick—Mr. Ronald Strudgewick. Until a few months ago the books were the property of their collector, Mr. James Henry Strudgewick, Mr. Ronald's uncle. Upon the death of Mr. James last February the books, which were part of the estate, came into the possession of Mr. Ronald, who was the principal heir and residuary legatee of his uncle.

"Unfortunately—" Mr. Martin made a vague gesture with his hands. "If I may be permitted to use that personal expression of regret—unfortunately, Mr. Ronald is a traveller, a globe-trotter, a cosmopolitan. He never remains long in any one place, or even in any one country, certainly not in his native land." Mr. Martin sighed dismally. "A pity!" he murmured absently. "Surely no man can be happy if he is away too long from the country of his birth. He loses touch—and—sympathy—"

He paused. "But, dear me! I should not be wasting your time like this, Mr.—er—Mr. Terhune. It is no business of yours or mine, is it, where a man chooses to live? The only point which need concern us is that Mr. Ronald does not intend to keep up his uncle's residence. He is therefore disposing of the house and its contents, which naturally include the library." The old solicitor coughed. "I have made this explanation, my dear sir, to account for the —er—circumstances in which you will find the books. You see, Mr. Ronald is abroad at the present time—in Athens—and all instructions have come from him by mail. He has left it to his uncle's old manservant, Burton, to prepare the catalogue of the library. It is Burton whom you will find at the house, and who has been instructed to offer you every facility for inspecting the books. I trust, sir, that you will not think that our ordinary business is conducted on such haphazard lines—" Martin paused.

"Of course not, Mr. Martin," Terhune assured the other man. "I quite understand. If you will give me the address, and details of how to get there—"

"Of course! Of course!" Martin's fluttering hands adjusted the glasses more firmly on the bridge of his nose. "The address is: Tile House—not an unusual name for a house, I believe!—Tile House, Hawley Green. A taxi will take you there for the sum of two shillings—"

"The house is only a mile from here, isn't it, Mr. Martin?"

"A mile and a quarter, to be precise."

"Then I should prefer to walk. I shall enjoy the exercise, and, at the same time, have the opportunity of seeing the local scenery."

"An excellent suggestion, Mr. Terhune, particularly as the country-side between here and Hawley Green is extremely beautiful, if I may be permitted to say so. If you wish to return by taxi Burton will ring through for one to fetch you."

"Good! How do I reach Hawley Green from here?"

"Walk down the High Street as far as the *Saxhawley Arms*—but perhaps you are staying there?" Terhune nodded. "Yes, of course. Most visitors to our little town prefer the *Saxhawley Arms*. A wise choice, I may say! Did your bedroom overlook the Main Street or the side road?"

"The side road."

"Ah! Well, that is the road which leads to Hawley Green. You will know it is time to look for Tile House when you reach *The Dog and Duck* inn. Two hundred yards past the *Dog and Duck* you will see, on your right, a pair of ornamental iron gates opening on to a gravelled drive. They are the gates of Tile House. There is no longer a caretaker in the lodge, so you have only to push open the gate and walk to the house. There Burton will take care of you."

Terhune nodded.

Martin went on, rather more hesitatingly: "Are you proposing to stay another night in Saxhawley?"

"Yes. I shall catch the one-twenty-three, which connects with the two-seventeen."

The solicitor looked relieved. "In that case we shall be able to complete our business tomorrow morning, Mr. Terhune, if that will be convenient? Say, at ten o'clock?"

Terhune agreed, and as there appeared little else to be said, rose to his feet. Martin quickly did the same, to escort his visitor to the door, where the two men shook hands.

From Bank Chambers Terhune returned to the *Saxhawley Arms*, where he turned right for the road to Hawley Green. Before long he was beyond the outskirts of the small town, and facing the countryside, which fully justified Martin's praise. Of the type particularly agreeable to Terhune, it was undulating and wooded, offering a succession of hedge-framed vistas in almost every direction: miniature vistas of picturesque dells, grass slopes, irregular copses, and scattered dwellings, mostly of the kind which went with small holdings, but mercifully mellowed and inconspicuous.

It was not long before he became aware that the curving road was rising in a gentle but none the less steady slope. It was fortunate that he was a good walker, he reflected, for while a mile and a quarter on the flat was easy enough, the same distance uphill was a pull.

Twenty minutes after leaving Saxhawley he breasted the long rise, and came to a halt for the downright enjoyment of the view which presented itself. A mile or more away the altitude of the land was the same, or perhaps a little higher, than the spot at which he stood, but in between lay visible one of the most delightfully picturesque valleys. Like the countryside behind him, much of the land was wooded, particularly the upward slope on the far side, but through the bed of the valley rippled a wide, shallow stream which was bordered on either side by a line of weeping willows, and beyond by meadowland, in which sheep and cattle grazed drowsily in the warm sun. Somewhat to the right of where he stood, about half a mile down the slope, stood a small cluster of grey buildings, of which a square-towered church was the most prominent. Below the main square more farmhouses and cottages bordered the road down to the river's edge, and the hump-backed stone bridge which spanned it. There the village ceased abruptly, as though some power had decreed that no one should build on the far side of the water. Not for some distance to his left could he see any sign of farmhouses on the other bank, and none at all to the right. On the contrary, over the gently-waving tops of intervening trees he saw the grey sheen and expanse of still water. Beyond the lake, and to the right of it, the land—here heavily wooded—rose more steeply than elsewhere. In fact, just that part of the valley reminded him to some slight extent of the Lake District in miniature.

He continued walking, and wondered what sort of a man this Ronald Strudgewick could be. An ingrate, surely, for who, having the opportunity of living in such a natural paradise, would willingly desert it? Good lord! What wouldn't he give for a similar chance, especially as he had an idea that he would find Tile House by no means an insignificant residence? A lovely house, money, plus scenery fit for a king—and Ronald Strudgewick spurned the lot! Some people could ask too much of life.

Presently he rounded a corner and saw the *Dog and Duck*—it was much the sort of place he had imagined it would be from the moment of breasting the rise above. Low, small, curtained windows, a mossy tiled roof, whitewashed walls, creeper, a rose-covered porch, musical with the noise of clucking hens and a noisy pig, the *Dog and Duck* fitted into the picture with the precision of a piece from a jig-saw puzzle. He was sorry that he had not the opportunity of seeing the interior, particularly as he had developed an enviable thirst. But perhaps—later—luncheon, maybe—.

He soon saw the iron gates of Tile House, and the lodge, looking sadly desolate with its closed door, bare windows, and uncared-for garden. There was no sign of the house, though the curving, gravel, tree-bordered drive was visible for some distance. He pushed open the right-hand gate, which squeaked agonizingly, and continued along the drive.

On all sides there was evidence that, not long ago, the bordering woodland on either side had been landscaped. There were clusters of flowering shrubs, fine specimens of topiary art, short avenues leading to moss-covered garden ornaments, and thousands of choice bulbs.

But already neglect was beginning to obtrude its ugly presence, and the effect was depressing.

At last he saw the house itself. This, too, fulfilled his expectations. It was severely square, handsome, Georgian, and framed by a chequered green and brown background of rising woodland. A friendly, inviting house. A house to inspire the poet, and delight the romanticist. Unhappily, the lawns and gardens immediately surrounding the house were in sad need of attention. Weeds flourished unchecked, and choked the smaller flowers. A fish-pond was green. A roller beneath a tree near-by was badly rusted. A wooden rustic seat had collapsed. The lawns were knee high.

He reached the front door and pulled the bell-handle. In the far distance he heard a bell jangle—it had a mellow, homely note. A door closed somewhere. Presently the door opened, and he saw facing him an elderly man dressed in a black jacket and striped black trousers.

"Mr. Terhune?" the man asked, before Terhune could speak.

"Yes. You are Burton, I take it?"

"Yes, sir." Burton's sombre features dissolved into a smile of welcome—a smile which instantly made Terhune feel that the servant was a man in whom one could safely confide one's intimate secrets. "Mr. Martin telephoned to say that you were on your way here. Will you come in, sir?"

Terhune stepped inside the house, to become immediately conscious of an enveloping atmosphere of warmth and friendship, an atmosphere which he had often found associated with houses long occupied. While Burton relieved him of his hat he took a quick glance about him. The hall furniture was solid, genuinely old, of good quality. The carpets had a heavy, rich pile. Everything was neat, tidy, in its proper place—but dusty. Not terribly dusty, perhaps, as though no cloth had touched the place for weeks, but dusty enough to make him believe that none of the furniture had been touched for a couple of days at least.

"The library is on the first floor, sir, if you will follow me—"

With quiet dignity Burton led the way up a flight of stairs, turned to his right, walked the length of a corridor, and opened the last door on the left. Terhune entered the room, and warmed to it as quickly as he had to the house itself. This was to be expected, for every wall was occupied by crowded bookshelves, and the air was permeated with the musty odour peculiar to a large collection of old volumes. But even apart from the presence of books, almost the whole of the south wall was occupied by a tall window which afforded a magnificent view of the valley of Hawley Green, the shallow stream, the rising woodlands beyond, and the road which curved up to the brow of the hill opposite. This handsome window, the view from it, the thick pile carpet on the floor, and the dignified architecture and decoration all combined to make the room invitingly serene.

"Is there anything you require to know before I leave you, sir?" Burton enquired.

Was there a note almost of pleading in the manservant's voice? It seemed to Terhune that the old fellow sought an excuse to stay and talk. Well, why not? He would not be in the way, and might even be useful.

"Are you in any hurry?"

"No, sir."

"Would you care to remain, if you have nothing more important? You might be able to help me."

Burton quickly entered the library and closed the door behind him. "I should be glad to help, sir. What would you like me to do?"

"Sit down on that chair over there by the window."

"Thank you, sir." Burton sat down, respectfully upright. Terhune stood in the centre of the room, gazed lovingly at the bookshelves, and wondered where to begin his inspection. His inclination was to look first for special titles, but realizing that this course would prove a waste of time, he decided to restrain himself and proceed about his task as systematically as possible. He approached the books closest to the window, and therefore farthest from the door.

"Did you prepare the catalogue of books for sale, Burton?"

"Yes, sir. I did it while Martha—my wife, sir—spring-cleaned the shelves."

Terhune pulled out the first volume and began to inspect it with critical eyes. Its condition was excellent.

"Do you know much about books?"

"Nothing, sir. Although the master first started collecting books about the time Martha and me entered his service I never became one myself for books. Leastwise, sir, not of the kind the master collected. Now and again I used to read a Western, or a detective novel, but I prefer walking or looking after the kitchen garden during my hours off."

The quivering eagerness in Burton's voice confirmed Terhune's surmise that the old servant was keenly anxious for the chance of a gossip.

"How do you know the size, shape and style of books so well?"

"But I don't, sir. I got all those particulars from the master's records. He kept a record of nearly every book he bought, so it was easy to make the catalogue. Would you like to see the master's records, sir?"

"Later, perhaps."

As Terhune continued with his task of examining the books his joy increased. If the rest of the books were in any way comparable to the few he had already examined then he had made one of the finest bargains of his life. In making his offer to the solicitors he had allowed for the condition of the library to be no more than average, but already it was evident that excellent was the more correct adjective to use. Every book he handled appeared to have been well cared for, and even loved by its late owner.

"Did you help Mr. Strudgewick to keep his books clean?"

"I did that, sir. Many's the hour I've spent in this room helping the master to dust the books, or re-arrange them, or classify them. I've even helped him by doing some easy research work."

"For what purpose?"

"He was by way of being a writer, sir, but only for his own amusement. He's written more than four books in his time, but none of them has been published. Not because he couldn't get a publisher to print them, but he was not interested in having them published. As soon as he finished writing a book he had it typed and bound. Then he put it in a safe and started another one."

"What has happened to the manuscripts?"

"Mr. Ronald took them away with him; he said he was going to give them to an agent who would try and get them published—as a memorial to the master, Mr. Ronald said, but it's my belief—" Burton checked himself abruptly.

"Yes?"

"I was going to speak of something that isn't any concern of mine, sir," the servant pointed out respectfully.

Terhune naturally did not press the man. For nearly half a minute there was silence, then Terhune said: "This is a charming room. Did Mr. Strudgewick spend much time in it?"

"Nearly all his time. He scarcely used the rest of the house except for his meals, or to sleep in. But he wouldn't allow any of the servants to enter this room but me—except during spring-cleaning. The master employed seven indoor servants, including Martha and me," Burton continued proudly. "And three men and a boy outdoors."

"What has happened to the staff since your master's death?"

"Mr. Ronald discharged all the others as soon as the property became his. Me and Martha will be going, too, as soon as the furniture is sold up." There was a note of bitterness and regret in the man's voice which made Terhune feel sorry for him.

"Have you been here long?"

"Nigh on thirty-five years now, sir, and me and Martha was hoping to spend the rest of our days in this house. The master always promised us that we should. He said he was going to make provision in his will for us to stay on after his death, but he kept putting off making his will, so in the end he—he died without doing so. Now me and Martha will be leaving here for good, before the end of the year."

Terhune glanced at the old man, but seeing the tears well up in Burton's eyes he turned away to avoid embarrassment for them both. For want of something better to say he asked: "Was your master an old man, Burton?"

"Not so old that couldn't have lived several years longer than me, sir. He would have been sixty-four next October," Burton answered chokily.

"Did he never marry?"

"Yes, sir, when he was a young man of twenty-five or so. But Mrs. Strudgewick died two years later while giving birth to a child, and the master never married again. He gave all his love to books instead. He used to tell me that he loved books because books couldn't die."

"Then the child died too?"

"It was stillborn."

Terhune was silent, not anxious to pursue a subject which, as a stranger, embarrassed him. But Burton continued, as though it was a relief to talk.

"The master was always a lonely man, sir. He didn't make friends easily, though anyone who got to know him thoroughly—like Colonel Vance—used to love him. He hadn't many relations either, only one other besides Mr. Ronald. That was his sister Margaret. She was a Mrs. Willouby, and the master was devoted to her. He liked her husband, too."

Remembering that Ronald, a nephew, was apparently the sole heir to the intestate estate Terhune wondered what had happened to the sister. As soon as he put the question tears began to mist the old man's eyes again.

"Mr. and Mrs. Willouby were killed in a road crash about a year ago. That is why Mr. Ronald came back to England."

"To attend the funeral?"

"Not him, sir. If he had wanted to attend the ceremony he could have got back in time by flying. He came by slow ship instead, and wasn't here until three weeks after the funeral."

Not for the first time Terhune gained an impression that Burton disliked Ronald Strudgewick. Well, there seemed good reason for that dislike. After all, it couldn't be pleasant for the old chap to be turned out of a lovely home in which he had had every expectation of living until his death. At the same time, Terhune was not anxious to be made party to servants' gossip, so he tried to bring the conversation back from the nephew to the uncle.

"What did your master die of, Burton?"

"Accidental death is what the coroner's jury brought in."

Terhune was startled. "Coroner's jury!" he exclaimed unthinkingly.

"Yes, sir. The master was found drowned in the lake. The coroner said the master fell in, but I don't believe he did." Burton leaned forward in a strangely rigid attitude. "I believe he was pushed in, and I shall believe that until my dying day."

"*Pushed* in! But that would be murder."

"And that's what I mean, sir. Just plain murder, and nothing else." And the old servant relaxed as though with a sense of relief at having released emotions too long pent up.

Chapter Five

Terhune turned away to pull out another volume from the shelves, and smiled. It was strange how melodramatic people liked to be. For instance: women who revelled in attending or watching funerals; women who burst into tears upon hearing of the death of someone round the corner whom they scarcely knew; mild-tempered men who delighted in giving themselves up to the police for murders which they had not committed; ordinary men who sought to introduce a little colour into drab lives by dramatizing every insignificant incident. During the past year—in fact, ever since he had achieved unwanted local notoriety as an amateur detective—he had been made witness to several manifestations of this strange psychological phenomenon. Every now and again he had found himself being taken to some quiet corner, to be told, usually in hushed, but thrilled whispers, some vague, often rambling story of how Mr. Jones had been acting 'most queer-like this past month,' or how 'us has been saying that that clever Mr. Terhune should be told as how they Brown family has been carrying on o' late, paying Old Hobby one and six an hour to dig a large hole in the two-acre meadow; a hole well-nigh big enough and deep enough to be a grave,' or: 'D'you know, Terhune, in my opinion it's dashed queer why Percy Robinson always insists upon buying aviation spirit for his car. Now if I were an amateur detective I should ask myself—' And not an accidental death took place within a radius of ten miles but what somebody hinted that it might be well worth his while to investigate why this—that—and t'other— Oh, yes, indeed! He was well acquainted with the very human foible of dramatizing the commonplace.

Of course, old Burton had been sincere in his forthright accusation—but then most of the dramatizers were sincere; it was from the very depths and intensity of their sincerity that they devised their mildly masochistic pleasure. Still it couldn't hurt to humour the old chap by letting him talk—it was possible that, having got his suspicions off his chest, he might subsequently forget all about them.

"What were the details of your master's death?" Terhune asked in what he hoped was an interested voice.

"Can you come over to the window, sir."

The request surprised Terhune. He turned and looked at the servant. Perhaps his astonishment revealed itself on his face, for Burton went on to explain: "I want to point out a house to you, sir."

Terhune mentally shrugged his shoulders—he had time to spare—and walked over to the window. As he approached Burton jumped eagerly to his feet.

"Do you see that red-brick house on the far side of the river— the one to the left of the church tower?"

Terhune could see at least three houses on the other side of the water that were red-bricked, and on the left of the church tower. He said so.

"That one with the row of poplars behind it, sir."

This feature enabled Terhune to identify the particular house. He nodded his head.

"That is Colonel Vance's house. Colonel Vance was the master's closest friend. They had served together in the Boer War, and again in the First World War. One of the reasons Colonel Vance had for settling down in Hawley Green after the First World War was the fact that Mr. James—the master—lived here."

Terhune made an unintelligible noise to indicate that he was listening.

"Well, sir, for many years past Colonel Vance and the master have visited each other every Thursday night. One week the master went to *The Poplars*—that's Colonel Vance's house—the next, Colonel Vance came here. They've carried on that arrangement ever since nineteen-twenty. And what is more, they always walked to each other's houses unless the weather was very terrible. If it was, the Colonel used to drive here, or if it was the master's turn to be the visitor, then the Colonel used to send his car over to fetch Mr. James. The master didn't have a car."

Burton waved his arm to the left. "Do you remember the little stream you passed over on your way here from the road?"

"Yes. It reminded me of the streams one finds in Wales and the Lake District."

"That's right, sir. As a matter of fact, some folk about here call this valley Little Windermere. Well, that stream comes from a spring up on the hill to the north, flows through the master's land, and falls into the lake." His pointing hand moved again. "About there, sir, beyond the trees which hide it.

"It's not much of a fall in quantity, as you can guess, but it's pretty and quite high. About fifty feet, or thereabouts. Just before the fall the banks are quite steep; to get from one side to the other it is necessary to cross a plank bridge a few yards this side of the fall."

The old servant took a quick glance at Terhune's face as if to make sure that he was receiving sufficient attention. Satisfied, he went on: "The quickest way to get from this house to the Colonel's is by taking the footpath just below this window, which leads from a side door into the woods, crossing the plank bridge by the fall, taking another path down to the bridge, and then the side road as far as the *Poplars*. Colonel Vance always used to come and go by that way except when it was dark. Another, longer way to get from one house to the other is to use the main road as far as the bridge, but that means a longer journey—nearly fifteen minutes longer."

Terhune wondered what this long explanation was leading up to, but he did not interrupt, not wishing to disturb Burton, who had again become tense with emotion.

"The master never used the footpath to reach the Colonel's house except on a few rare occasions when he was accompanied by somebody. He always went, and returned, along the road. And do you know why he wouldn't take the short cut, sir? Because he was afraid to cross the plank bridge."

"Afraid?"

Burton's attitude became apologetic. "He had been afraid of the bridge ever since he was a boy of seven. You see, when he was that age he fell into the lake from the highest branch of a tree overhanging the water, and his father only saved him from drowning just in time. From that moment he was always afraid of going near any high place overlooking water, although I don't believe he feared anything else in the world."

At last Terhune began to pick up the thread of Burton's story. "Did your master fall into the lake from the plank bridge?"

"Yes, sir. Leastwise, that is the verdict which the coroner's jury brought in." The old chap became vehement. "But I don't believe he did fall in. I'm just as sure that he was pushed over the bridge as I am of my own name."

Terhune shook his head. "But haven't you yourself given the explanation of his falling in? I suppose he suddenly became giddy while crossing the bridge, lost his balance, fell into the lake below, and was drowned. Could he swim, by the way?"

"No, sir, he couldn't. But he wouldn't have gone on to the bridge by himself. He hadn't done so ever since I have known him—"

"So far as you know," Terhune interrupted.

"That's right, of course," Burton admitted. "But he has often spoken to me of his fear. He despised himself for it, and some years ago he tried to cure himself, but he didn't succeed."

"Then he might have been accompanied at the time of his falling."

"You don't understand, sir," Burton explained patiently. "He was on his way back from Colonel Vance. Besides, no witness came forward at the inquest to say he had been with the master."

Despite his previous good-humoured tolerance towards what he believed to be a dramatized distortion of an unfortunate incident, Terhune began to take an interest in what the old servant was saying.

"Suppose you begin at the beginning," he suggested.

This Burton did with an eagerness which made Terhune suspect that the old chap had been leading up to this very point.

"The master died on a Thursday. He had visited Colonel Vance as usual in the late afternoon, and I expected him home between ten-fifteen and ten-thirty, which was his usual time for returning. As he had not arrived home by eleven-thirty I became alarmed, and telephoned the Colonel to know whether Mr. James had left. The Colonel told me the master had left the house about the usual time, nine-thirty-five, which meant that he should have arrived home some time after ten-fifteen, for it takes about three-quarters of an hour to walk from the *Poplars* to here."

"What is the distance between the two houses?"

"About a mile and a half by road, and a little more than a mile by the short cut through the woods."

"Forty-five minutes to do a mile and a half?"

"It's uphill nearly all the way from the *Poplars* to here," Burton explained.

Terhune nodded. He had overlooked that fact. No doubt the reverse journey took about thirty minutes.

"What happened when you heard that Mr. Strudgewick had left the *Poplars*?"

"Well, sir, both the Colonel and I were alarmed—you see, the master was always so regular in his habits that we were quite sure he hadn't called in anywhere on his way. The Colonel suggested that

I should go out and look for the master, and said he would dress and do the same.

"Immediately we had rung off I put on my overcoat—this took place on the 18th of February—and went out to look for Mr. James. I took a torch with me, but I didn't have to use it because the moon was bright enough for me to see for quite a fair distance. I got as far as Hawley Green bridge without seeing any sign of him, and there I met the Colonel, who also hadn't found Mr. James.

"I didn't know what to do next, but the Colonel said he would return with me to this house, and if the master hadn't returned by the time we got back he would telephone the local police. Mr. James hadn't returned, so the Colonel 'phoned as he had promised. Later on some police arrived in a motor-car. Some of them searched the road all the way back to the *Poplars*, while others searched the woods."

Overcome by the memory of those tragic hours Burton turned away so that Terhune should not see his tears. But he continued his story, his voice husky with emotion.

"You can guess what happened next, sir. As the master hadn't returned by nine o'clock the next day the police inspector gave orders for the lake to be dragged. Just after three o'clock in the afternoon the master's body was pulled out of the water. Meanwhile police detectives had decided that Mr. James must have changed his habits for once, and returned by the short cut as far as the plank bridge, where he had turned giddy, and had fallen into the lake below."

"Was that possible? Is the plank bridge so near to the actual fall that anyone could fall directly into the lake?"

"Yes, sir. It is only two yards away from the drop, so that if anyone were to fall full length forward the upper half of the body would fall over the edge, and pull the rest of the body with it."

Terhune nodded, understanding. "But surely that is a dangerous position for a bridge to be in? Wasn't there a rail or something to prevent anyone from falling?"

Burton nodded his head sadly. "I suppose some people might call it dangerous, sir, but it isn't really dangerous for the normal person. I think Mr. James's grandfather put the first bridge at that point because of the view one has from it. Even if it were two yards farther away from the fall the view wouldn't be nearly so good. Besides, it was on private property, so that nobody had a right to go on the bridge without the permission of the owner."

"What about rails?" Terhune reminded the other man.

"Oh, yes, sir! Well, there was a rope stretched across on either side, but the detectives said that it wouldn't take any weight at all to break them."

"Was the one nearest to the fall broken?"

"Yes, sir, it was. At the inquest the detectives said that when the master became faint or giddy he must have rested his weight against the rope and so caused it to give way."

"How did they know the rope wasn't broken before the Thursday night?"

"Because I had seen it unbroken two days previously. On a nice afternoon I often spent quite a long time on the bridge."

So far, Terhune reflected, Burton had told of nothing sinister to account for his fantastic claim that his employer was deliberately murdered. As had seemed apparent from the first, he was evidently dramatizing what was admittedly a strange but otherwise straight-forward tragedy.

He tried to convey this impression—diplomatically—to the old servant.

"It was certainly a most unfortunate accident. Burton," he began.

Burton's mouth hardened obstinately. "It wasn't an accident, sir. In all the years I have known the master he has never willingly crossed the plank bridge, never when he has been alone, and certainly never at night. Every other Thursday night for more than twenty years he has come home from the *Poplars* by way of the road. Why should he have changed his usual habit and come home by the short cut?"

"We all of us do inexplicable things at times. Who knows what thoughts passed through Mr. Strudgewick's mind as he walked towards the bridge? Perhaps a sudden whim to conquer his dread of the fall made him take the short cut home just for once in his life."

"At night, sir?"

Terhune reddened. "It doesn't sound a very likely theory," he admitted. "But there is another possible explanation. Perhaps he met somebody who was willing to accompany him across the bridge and along the short cut."

A significant expression passed slowly across Burton's face. "Exactly, sir."

Then Terhune remembered something. "But, of course, you said just now that nobody had given evidence of having met Mr. Strudgewick, or of having accompanied him through the woods." He stared into the moist eyes of the old servant. "Then is it your theory that somebody met Mr. Strudgewick on his way from the *Poplars*, persuaded him to take the short cut, and pushed him over the fall as they were crossing the plank bridge?"

Burton held Terhune's critical gaze unwaveringly. "Yes, sir," he answered, firmly.

Terhune considered Burton's theory. It was not quite what he had imagined it would be—a wild fantasy, born in an unbalanced imagination. It could be admitted that there were some grounds for suspecting murder. It was peculiar, for instance, for a man of regular habits suddenly to decide upon going home by a route different from that which he had taken for more than twenty years, and that other route, moreover, one which he had feared from childhood. Certainly that aspect needed an explanation. But murder —well, to deduce murder from one peculiar happening did seem rather far-fetched! Besides, there was an alternative.

"How was Mr. Strudgewick's health at the time of his death?"

The inference behind the question was not lost to the astute Burton. "If you are thinking of suicide, sir, you can accept not only my conviction that the master's death was not a case of suicide, but the coroner's summing up. Dr. Greenstreet—the coroner—informed the jury that he had very carefully considered the possibility of suicide, but he was glad to tell the jury that, in his opinion, there was nothing to justify it. For months previous the deceased had been in the best mental and physical health: and touching upon the actual day of death, evidence had been given from several witnesses to the *effect* that the deceased had been happy and contented from the time of rising to the moment of leaving Colonel Vance's house. Colonel Vance himself had testified to the effect that during the whole of the time the deceased had spent in his company the deceased had been jovial and calm." Burton stopped abruptly. "I am sorry, sir. I can almost recite the coroner's summing-up word for word."

"Is it certain that Mr. Strudgewick fell into the lake from the fall? Couldn't he have fallen in from any other point?"

"Of course he could, sir, but there was even less reason for his being near the lake if he had not taken the short cut. Besides, the broken rope points to the likelihood of his having fallen from the plank bridge. Also there were marks on the planks which the detectives believe were made within the fifteen hours previous to their examination of the bridge. Lastly, sir, they found the master's cigarette case in the water just at the head of the fall—it had lodged itself by a large stone close to the right bank. The detectives say that it must have slipped out of his pocket as he fell forward into the water."

"Is it certain that Mr. Strudgewick had the case on him on the night of his death?"

"Yes, sir. I put it into his pocket before he left the house, and Colonel Vance accepted several cigarettes from it during the evening."

It seemed stupid to ignore such evidence, so Terhune tried a different approach.

"Where does the short cut join the road?"

"About a hundred yards from the bridge."

"You mean the road bridge at the far end of the village?"

"Yes, sir."

"And where does it lead to, besides this house?"

"Nowhere."

"So that only somebody intending to come here would wish to use the short cut?"

"Yes, sir."

"Were the rest of the household home at the time Mr. Strudgewick died?"

"No, sir. Two of the servants had their half-day off on Thursdays. They returned home about eleven-fifteen."

"Then could either of them have met Mr. Strudgewick—"

Burton interrupted with a shake of his grey, bowed head. "No, sir. They were at the *Dog and Duck*, playing darts with the proprietor and his wife in their private parlour until seven minutes past eleven. The two servants were a married couple—Mr. and Mrs. Higgs. Higgs was a gardener; Mrs. Higgs helped Martha in the kitchen."

"Is there any game in the woods?"

"A little rough shooting, sir. Mostly rabbits."

"Is there much poaching in this district?"

"A certain amount."

"Is it possible that Mr. Strudgewick surprised some poachers, who knocked him off the plank bridge in self-defence?"

Burton gestured unhappily. "That is a possible explanation, of course, sir, but it does not account for why the master was taking the short cut in the first place."

"It *must* have been the result of a sudden whim or impulse," Terhune said, decidedly.

"No, sir," Burton denied obstinately.

"But don't you see, Burton, your own evidence contradicts your theory of Mr. Strudgewick's being accompanied along the short cut. The only people likely to be using that cut would be members of the household, all of whom can be accounted for—" Terhune paused, and looked enquiringly at the other man. "I take it that is so?"

"Yes, sir. Every one can prove an alibi."

"Then who else would be likely to visit Tile House at such a late hour?"

"The master's nephew, sir," Burton answered tonelessly.

Chapter Six

Terhune started. "Ronald Strudgewick?"

"Yes, sir."

"Was he living at Tile House at the time of his uncle's death?"

"No, sir."

Terhune frowned. "Then, in heaven's name, Burton—"

"By the death of his uncle Mr. Ronald has inherited nearly sixty thousand pounds," the old chap explained in the emotionless voice he used when speaking about Strudgewick.

Sixty thousand pounds! That was quite a sum of money! Enough to excite the cupidity of quite a number of people.

Terhune began to feel more and more respect for Burton's theory. No doubt it was as full of holes as a colander, no doubt it was far-fetched. But more and more the man was proving that it was at least worth serious consideration.

Ever since he had been called over to the window he and Burton had been standing side by side, staring at the woods, at the particular clump of trees which land-marked the general direction of the plank bridge, and at Colonel Vance's home. Now he turned, and pulled a chair nearer to the window and, telling Burton to sit down, himself sat down. Then he pulled his cigarette case from his pocket and offered it to the other man.

"Do you smoke?"

Burton nodded. "Yes, sir," he admitted, but made no move to take a cigarette.

"Take one. We'll both smoke."

After a moment's hesitation Burton took a cigarette. Then he produced a box of matches and, forestalling Terhune, held out a flaming match.

"My respects, sir," Burton murmured as he lit his own cigarette and once more sat back in his chair.

"Tell me of this nephew," Terhune suggested.

"There is not much to tell. Mr. James's father had three children: Mr. James, Miss Margaret, and Mr. William, the youngest. Mr. William married in nineteen-ten, at the age of twenty-four. Mr. Ronald was born in nineteen-sixteen, two months after his father had been killed on the Western Front. He was a self-willed and undisciplined boy from very early days, and caused his mother much sadness—leastwise, sir, that is what the master used to say about him. At the age of seventeen Mr. Ronald ran away to sea because his mother wouldn't buy him a new bicycle. At that time Mrs. Strudgewick was in a very poor state of health, and the shock killed her. As a consequence Mr. Ronald inherited nearly eight thousand pounds which Mrs. Strudgewick had inherited from Mr. William, in nineteen-sixteen.

"With this money Mr. Ronald led a life of ease in different parts of the world for the next six years, but by the spring of nineteen thirty-nine every penny had been spent. As soon as he was penniless he came back to England and sponged on Mr. James—if you will excuse me using that word, sir?"

Terhune nodded. "Go on."

"Mr. James didn't care much for his nephew, but he agreed to allow him two hundred pounds per annum. Mr. Ronald wasn't very grateful for this amount; he said that his uncle was well enough off to allow him at least double that sum. But Mr. James wouldn't, and Mr. Ronald had to make the best of what he was given.

"When war was declared Mr. Ronald joined the Royal Air Force. The service suited his undisciplined nature, and he did well as a fighter-pilot until he was wounded and shot down in the English

Channel. He was rescued, but he was never the same again, because his pride had suffered from having been beaten in an aerial duel. He was grounded, and later got in trouble in connection with some mess cheques. Mr. James reimbursed the mess, but his generosity did not save Mr. Ronald. He was discharged from the R.A.F.

"For some months he lived here with Mr. James, but he could not stand the quiet country life, and when he had the offer of a war job in West Africa he took it. We did not see him again until a year ago, three weeks after his aunt and her husband had been buried. Can you guess why he came back, sir?"

Terhune thought he could, but considered it more discreet not to say so aloud. He shook his head.

Once again Burton proved his mental astuteness by correctly interpreting his visitor's silence. "Perhaps it isn't for me to say anything about what I think to have been Mr. Ronald's reason for coming back to England, but it wasn't grief for his aunt which brought him home—he and Miss Margaret had always disliked each other." He laughed—it was a grating, unpleasant laugh. "But facts are facts, aren't they, Mr. Terhune, and don't have to be proved. The fact in this case is that, after the death of Miss Margaret, Mr. Ronald became Mr. James's only living relative.

"Mr. Ronald isn't a fool," Burton went on stridently. "He knew that, while Miss Margaret remained alive, he stood as much chance of inheriting the master's money as old Higgs. The master had seen to that, for he had made a will leaving nearly everything to Miss Margaret and her husband, and only two thousand five hundred pounds to Mr. Ronald.

"As soon as Miss Margaret was killed the master tore up his will. Mr. Ronald tried to persuade his uncle to make another will in his own favour, but Mr. James refused, saying that before he left his money to his nephew he wanted to be quite sure that Mr. Ronald was a fit man to receive the money."

Burton's voice became scornful. "Mr. Ronald took this advice to heart. He became a changed man, and tried to make the master believe that he had turned over a new leaf. But Mr. James knew better. He kept putting off making a new will, and every time Mr. Ronald spoke to him about it he said: 'One of these days I will. There's no hurry. I've still a few more years left to me'." The old chap turned away. "That's where the master made a mistake," he continued chokily. "He hadn't reckoned with Mr. Ronald. Mr. Ronald got tired of waiting. Last February he made certain of it by pushing his uncle into the lake. Now he is turning everything of his uncle's into cash so that he can live abroad, and spend money like a lord. The house—furniture—these books—even the master's clothes—everything is to be sold—"

Burton's voice tailed off, and a long silence followed. Terhune stared uneasily out of the window. Certainly the other man had succeeded in making out a case of sorts against the very unpleasant-sounding Ronald Strudgewick, but it was incredibly weak, founded apparently on nothing more reliable than mere supposition, and prompted, he suspected, by personal prejudice. Perhaps if he had not been losing a home as a result of Ronald Strudgewick's desire to live abroad old Burton might have been more chary in voicing his suspicions—suspicions which might easily land him in Court on the charge of criminal slander. True, it was not easy to doubt Burton's sincerity; he seemed a nice old chap; honest, loyal, reliable—but Terhune knew that appearances could be damnably deceiving.

"Why have you told me about your suspicions of Ronald Strudgewick?" he asked presently.

Burton turned; his manner was earnest, entreating. "You are Mr. Theodore Terhune, aren't you?"

"That is my name."

"Of Bray-in-the-Marsh, near Ashford, Kent?"

"Yes."

"Then you *are* an amateur detective, aren't you, sir?" Burton questioned eagerly. "I recognized your face the moment I saw it —your photograph was in the papers some months ago—"

Terhune exclaimed his disgust. It was bad enough being treated as an amateur detective—not always politely—in his own neighbourhood, but it was becoming distinctly annoying if he were not going to be able to travel without becoming involved in the mysterious affairs of other, more distant districts. He had never wanted his photograph in the newspapers, but the Press photographers had been persistent—not to say, cunning—and in the end they had snapped and publicized him—

Cuss them! he thought, angrily.

"I am *not* a detective, amateur or otherwise," he stated firmly.

"But the newspapers said that you've helped in solving at least three murder mysteries."

"They exaggerated. The little I did any one might have done. It was mostly coincidence—the fact that I happened to be at the right place at the right time—"

"Perhaps that is what has happened this time," Burton interrupted eagerly.

"What do you mean?" Terhune challenged.

Now that he had reached the critical moment the old servant became nervous. "With all my respects, sir—I don't want to be forward—but if you would—would investigate the master's death—"

"Good lord, man—"

"Please listen, Mr. Terhune. There wasn't a finer, nicer man than the master. If he was killed in cold blood, doesn't the crime deserve to be punished?"

"Of course it does, but I am not the person to investigate the death. You should mention your suspicions to the police, who are not only the proper, but the only people capable of proving or disproving your theory."

"But I did that at the time."

"What!" Terhune stared at the other man, amazed by this unexpected item of news.

"Yes, sir," Burton confirmed uneasily. "I spoke to Detective-Inspector Longworth."

"Didn't he do anything?"

"Yes. He discovered that Mr. Ronald had spent the night at Thirsk."

In complete astonishment Terhune made a gesture with his arms that was almost Latin. "What more do you want than that, Burton? That fact knocks your theory bang on the head—at least, as far as Ronald Strudgewick is concerned."

"Thirsk is not much more than thirty miles south of Hawley Green," Burton stated obstinately.

"What difference does that make?"

"According to what the inspector told me Mr. Ronald had left London in the morning with the intention of visiting the master, but that he met a friend on the train—a Mr. — Mr. —" Burton paused, frowned, and closed his eyes. "What was the name?" he murmured. Presently he shook his head. "I forget the name, sir, but anyway, Mr. Ronald said they met on the train, and that—Mr. Tanner—that was the name—that as Mr. Tanner was getting off at Thirsk to spend the night there, Mr. Ronald changed his plans, and decided to spend the night with Mr. Tanner instead."

"Well?"

"Why didn't he let the master know that he proposed visiting him?"

"Did he usually warn his uncle in advance of his intention to pay a visit?"

"Usually."

"*Usually*! That means he didn't *always* do so?"

Burton looked miserable, and nodded his head.

"Then that answers your first question. This was one of the few occasions when he didn't give prior notice."

"Very well, sir. But why didn't he come to Tile House the following morning?"

"Didn't he?"

"No, sir. We neither saw nor heard anything of him for two days. Then he telephoned from London one night to say that he had only just received the telegram I had sent to him announcing the death of his uncle, and that he was catching the next train for Saxhawley."

"And did he?"

"Yes, sir. He was only just in time for the funeral."

"Did he offer any explanation why he failed to continue the journey here?"

"He told the inspector that Mr. Tanner had come to Thirsk to fetch a car which he was having repaired there, and that as Mr. Tanner was motoring south again the next day, Mr. Tanner suggested that Mr. Ronald should accompany him in the car to London, via Birmingham."

"To which, I take it, Ronald Strudgewick agreed?"

"Yes, sir."

"That all seems a plain and straightforward explanation."

"The car which this Mr. Tanner was picking up at Thirsk was a Lagonda, sir. The Lagonda is a fast car."

"I know that. What of it?"

"It wouldn't have taken a Lagonda very long to cover the distance from Thirsk to Hawley Green and back."

Terhune considered this statement. There was something in what Burton said. But surely a detective-inspector would not have overlooked that possibility. He said as much to Burton.

Burton sucked at his pale lips. "According to what Inspector Longworth told me, Mr. Ronald and his friend had a drink in the hotel smoking-room at eight-fifty before going upstairs. At five minutes to ten a waiter from the lounge took up more drinks to Mr. Tanner's room. At fifteen minutes past eleven both men went downstairs to ask the hotel porter whether it was possible to buy some cigarettes."

Terhune shrugged his shoulders. "As complete an alibi as any one could wish. The friend, Tanner, must have been with Ronald Strudgewick at the time of your master's death. Therefore it is not humanly possible for him to have killed his uncle."

"Unless the friend was lying," Burton persisted.

This time Terhune became really angry. "Now you are talking nonsense, Burton. If what you said were true it would mean that the two men had entered into a conspiracy to kill James Strudgewick, in which case Tanner would be found equally guilty of the crime. What man is willing to risk his own neck for the sake of helping a friend to inherit a large sum of money?"

"Suppose that they agreed to share the inheritance, sir?"

"If Tanner owned the Lagonda he was driving he cannot have been a poor man. No, Burton, I think you are allowing your dislike of Ronald Strudgewick to affect your judgment. Now I must get on with my work." He turned back to the bookshelves once more, but not before he had seen the expression of despair which passed across the other man's lined, puckered face. He felt rather a brute.

The hours passed. Round about one o'clock Terhune began to feel peckish, but when he asked whether it would be possible to obtain lunch at the *Dog and Duck*, or at any other place in the village, he was immediately informed that Martha Burton had prepared a meal for him. Despite half-hearted remonstrance on his part luncheon was served to him in the library.

And what a luncheon it was, too. He was sure he had never tasted better cooking, and rarely as good. A clear soup which had a lingering, provocative flavour he could not identify, but which excited the palate, and tasted good all the way down. Then trout, golden-brown, flavoured with butter and the pleasant tang of herbs. Next a cold, home-made meat pie, with mushrooms, hard-boiled eggs, and aspic jelly. The whole washed down with a local nut-brown ale. And, lastly, a heaped plate of raspberries and cream, a half-bottle of a very dry white wine (unlabelled), which Burton said had been in the cellar since 1938—one of a dozen lot which Ronald Strudgewick had somehow overlooked, or perhaps intended for sale with the furniture—and coffee. While in no sense a gourmet, Terhune liked food. At the end of the meal he decided that the luncheon alone repaid him for the journey north.

By mid-afternoon he had finished his inspection of the library, and was more than satisfied with his purchase. Having time to spare he decided to explore the inviting woodland which surrounded Tile House. With a word to Burton—who gave him a glance of dumb entreaty, which he affected to ignore—he left the house and made for the woods, purposely taking a direction different from that which would lead him to the waterfall. Nevertheless, as soon as he was well hidden from curious eyes he turned to his left and made for the stream which fell into the lake below.

He struck it about fifty yards away from the fall. It was neither wide nor deep, but it was picturesque. It flowed swiftly over a bed of rounded stones of all sizes from large to tiny, and had moderately steep banks out of which curved many uncovered gnarled roots of the old, lichen-covered trees which lined both banks. The stream was shaded and cool, the air seemed slightly dampish, and smelled of the moss which was everywhere to be seen, and wild flowers which flourished, unchecked, in every direction—purple loosestrife, codlins-and-cream, gipsy-wort, skull-cap.

He followed the dancing, singing stream to his right, and soon arrived at the plank bridge. This was much as he had seen it in his imagination—three wide, thick planks, the ends resting flat on steps cut in the bank, the middle supported by two uprights which had been driven into the bed of the stream. At either end and on either side of the planks stood short upright poles to carry the protective rope. Both ropes looked new, so he assumed that the old ones had been replaced after the accident which had killed James Strudgewick. In a prominent position on either bank was a notice:

> THIS PLANK BRIDGE IS PRIVATE PROPERTY.
> ANY UNAUTHORIZED PERSON USING IT
> DOES SO AT HIS OR HER OWN RISK.

He moved on to the bridge, but stopped half-way across, to admire the view. It was certainly extremely picturesque, though on a small scale. By a strange, perhaps freakish, configuration, while the water from the stream descended directly below, on either side the land sloped down to the lake-side at a much less pronounced angle. Consequently, immediately below the fall there was a long wide spit of water—a miniature lake in itself—which ran a distance of between fifty and seventy yards before joining the lake proper.

Terhune glanced down at the stream, just below the bridge, which flowed three feet or so before disappearing over the edge of the fall. He could see the bottom quite clearly: it looked no more than knee-deep.

Presently he pursed his lips. It did seem as if it needed a decided push to make any one fall in such a way as to continue the fall into mid-air. Only by falling full-length was there reason for one to over-balance and follow the water over the fall itself. Otherwise there was just enough room between the bridge and the edge of the fall for a man to save himself from going into the lake, *if he fell doubled up*.

Terhune frowned. Now that he was on the spot he could visualize how easy it could have been for Ronald Strudgewick to have pushed his uncle over the fall— Then he shrugged his shoulders, as he became annoyed with himself for wasting thought on stupid suspicions. The only man who had had any apparent reason for murdering James Strudgewick had a cast-iron alibi. No. Evidently the police had rightly concluded that a sudden, unexplainable whim had caused James Strudgewick to go home by way of the shortcut. Later, in crossing the bridge, he must have become giddy, and had leaned up against the rotten rope which had snapped under his weight and precipitated him into the stream and over the fall.

From the plank bridge Terhune proceeded along the short cut —which was little more than a series of large steps cut in the steeply sloping ground—as far as its junction with the road just this side of the hump-backed bridge which he had seen on his way to Tile House. Then he turned to his left, and walked up the hill, which comprised Hawley Green's one and only street, as far as the gates of the Strudgewick estate.

Back in Tile House he continued to ignore Burton's pleading glance, and made arrangements for the books to be crated and despatched south, leaving it to the old man to hire a carpenter to do the crating. Then, after thanking the couple for the excellent lunch they had given him, he said good-bye, and returned to the *Saxhawley Arms*.

The following morning he called at the offices of Hinchcliffe, Martin and Rogerson—he wondered how on earth such a small town could boast a firm of so many partners until he learned that Martin was the only one, having transferred the firm to Saxhawley from Darlington upon the death of Rogerson, and his own partial retirement. Terhune paid for the books and completed the formalities of sale; then, soon afterwards, caught the main-line connection.

Late that night he let himself into his rooms at Bray-in-the-Marsh, tired but immensely content.

Chapter Seven

The following morning, Wednesday, Julia telephoned, would Theo go swimming with her in the afternoon?

"I'm terribly sorry, Julie. I can't possibly go."

Always intolerant of any one or anything which interfered with her plans, she said coldly: "I'm sorry, my sweet. I thought you were usually free on a Wednesday afternoon. But as you don't want to come—"

"Don't be so darned offish, Julie. You know very well I'd love to go with you."

"Well, then—"

"I've got work to do. Heaps and loads of it. Enough to keep me busy for the next three or four weeks at least."

"Writing?"

"No, cataloguing. I've purchased that collection I was telling you about last week."

"I suppose you take time off for tea?"

He chuckled. "About ten minutes."

"In that case you can expect me about five o'clock. And I shall bring my damp costume up to your room to make you regret refusing to be nice to me."

"You have some charming ideas sometimes. Then I shall expect you at five o'clock for about ten minutes."

"You'll expect me for as long as I choose to stay," she told him, tartly, before ringing off.

Directly he had finished lunch he began his task of classifying, pricing, and cataloguing the books which appeared on Burton's haphazard list. Immersed in this labour of love time passed by unnoticed; he was quite startled when the street bell rang, and, on glancing at the clock, he saw that it was already one minute to five.

He hurried downstairs and opened the door to Julia. The guilty expression on his face instantly warned the sharp-eyed Julia that something was wrong.

"You look like a schoolboy discovered in the act of playing truant. Have you forgotten that I am having tea with you?"

"It isn't you but the time I'd forgotten. I haven't done a thing towards getting tea ready."

She looked more pleased than annoyed. "Good!" she exclaimed with satisfaction. "That will give me an excuse for staying longer. I'll give you a hand."

As he led the way upstairs he said: "Anyway, I bought some of that special chocolate cake for you before the shop closed."

"Theo, I am beginning to think that you are a hypocrite. You like that chocolate cake even more than I do—having no respect for your figure."

"But I don't buy it for myself every day. At least I like a good excuse."

He opened the door of his study. She took one quick glance at the untidy mess of paper which was strewn all over the small room and stepped back into the hall.

"We are not going to have tea in that room, my pet," she stated firmly.

"But it's cosier in there."

Julia moved on into the front room overlooking Market Square. "Maybe it is—for a bookworm. But I happen to be a normal human being who likes to eat in a tidy room. We shall have tea in here." Even while she spoke she crossed the room to the sideboard, which contained the table linen, cutlery and so on, and began to set the table.

With two pairs of willing hands at work tea was soon ready. They sat down, and began to tuck into bread and butter, spread with the special strawberry jam which Mrs. Mann made each year for her cronies, or for people for whom she had a soft spot in her heart. Terhune was one of these latter. In fact, there were very few middle-aged women in the district who hadn't a soft spot for him, for he had that youthful, shy and sincere manner which endeared him to them, and gave many an absurd desire to 'mother' him.

Presently Julia said: "By the way, Theo, my love, there's a very good second-hand desk-table at Harrison's."

"Is there?" he began.

"Don't you know that it's rude to speak with your mouth full?"

He hastily gulped down the offending mouthful, an effort which made him choke, and brought the tears to his eyes.

"The perfect lady wouldn't speak immediately after her companion had taken a mouthful of bread and butter," he gasped.

"The perfect gentleman wouldn't stuff his mouth so full as to make conversation difficult."

"All right! I give in." It was usually safer to do that when Julia was in an argumentative mood. "What about the desk, anyway? Do you want to buy one?"

"I don't, but you do."

"I? Don't be silly. I've one in the next room, and another down below in the shop."

"But you need two in the shop."

"Two!" He stared at her serene, handsome face. "Why on earth should I want two?"

"One for you, the other for your assistant."

He looked at her commiseratingly. "You should keep your head shaded when you sit in the sun, Julie. What does Miss Amelia want a desk for?"

"I am not speaking of Miss Amelia, but of Miss Quilter."

"Miss Who?"

"Quilter—Anne Quilter."

"Perhaps I'm the crazy one," he murmured.

"She's the daughter of mother's old nurse—the one who used to put me to bed every night."

"And smack your little—well, you know what."

"Don't be vulgar, Theo. It doesn't suit you. She's hard working, intelligent, quick to learn, does shorthand and typewriting, is passionately fond of books, dresses neatly, and is not *too* good looking—but good enough!"

"For a nurse your Mrs. Quilter seems to have covered a lot of ground."

"I shall become cross in a moment," she warned. "You know very well that I am speaking of Anne."

"Anne Quilter! Well, it's a nice name. But why this eulogy of her?"

"Because she's your new assistant."

"My—my—what!" He found difficulty in continuing. "Who's been spinning you a yarn, Julie. I've never heard of the girl before in my life. How could she be my assistant?"

"Because I have engaged her on your behalf."

He gazed at her. "You've—*what*!" he questioned weakly.

Julia became very earnest. "Listen, Theo, my pet. Since you opened your book-shop in Bray you have done very well, haven't you? You are doing considerable postal business with people in all parts of the world in addition to local business. Your turnover is increasing fairly rapidly, isn't it?"

"Yes," he admitted. "Fairly."

"Then is there any reason why you should not have someone to help you?"

"But I haven't given the idea a thought."

"That is no reason. Besides—did you know that Edward Pryce came in here yesterday to ask whether you had a copy of *Ordeal*, by

Dale Collins, and Miss Amelia told him that the only book on the shelves by that author was *The Woman in White*."

Terhune chuckled. "She's a little old-fashioned in her reading," he excused.

Julia exclaimed her annoyance. "And did you know that Mother came in the last time you left the shop in the charge of Miss Amelia to buy a work of some sort dealing with the Home Doctor?"

"That must have been a treat for Miss Amelia," he interposed slyly.

A dry smile parted Julia's lips. "Well, you know what Mother is like when she gets one of her fits of hypochondria." The smile disappeared. "Do you know what Miss Amelia sold her?"

"Tell me the worst, Julie."

"*Meet Doctor Morelle*, by Ernest Dudley—and you know how she *hates* detective stories."

Terhune exploded, and presently the infection of his laughter spread to Julia. But not for long.

"You must listen to me, Theo. In the two cases I have mentioned no harm has been done, for both Edward and Mother know Miss Amelia. She's a darling old soul, and I'm sure she was of help to you when you first started your library here. But you've outgrown her services—"

"Somebody said there was no compassion in business," he murmured.

She looked almost embarrassed. "I suppose it does sound awful, put into words. You are a dear, loyal old thing, Theo, but it really is time to think of yourself. Wouldn't you appreciate being less tied to the shop, so that you could travel farther afield in search of libraries, and give more time to the postal and export side of your business? At least you would be able to do your cataloguing during the day instead of waiting until after the shop was closed, and continuing to work all night."

There was much to be said in support of Julia's arguments, he reflected, as he gazed thoughtfully at her. As usual his expressive face betrayed his thoughts, and Julia knew that the seed she had sown was already sprouting. Cunningly, she did not wait for drought to shrivel the young plant, but went on quickly:

"Not only will you be freer to devote more time to buying books, my sweet, but Anne Quilter will be able to assist you in preparing your catalogues, type them out ready for the printer, type the wrappers or envelopes, or whatever you use, and, lastly, she will type your own scripts for you, ready for publication. In fact, her help will give you more time to write—"

"And go swimming with you, Julie?"

"Yes," she admitted frankly. "All work and no play makes Theo a dull boy. I don't want you to become dull, either for my sake or your writing."

He began to have doubts. "I don't know—" he began.

"I do," Julia interrupted briskly. "I have already told Anne that she begins work on Monday morning. So unless you want to make a fool of me I am afraid you will have to employ her, my pet, even if only for the week. You can give her a week's notice on the Friday if she proves unsatisfactory."

"I suppose you haven't found a wife for me as well as a secretary-assistant," he joked.

Julia turned away. There was a long pause before she next spoke. Then: "I've done enough talking. Tell me about your stay in Yorkshire," she ordered.

For the life of him he could not think why the old, sharp-voiced Julia had so unexpectedly reappeared.

I I

Monday morning brought two events which were greatly to affect Terhune's immediate future. The first was Anne Quilter.

Julia accompanied her. Or rather, preceded her, for Julia entered the shop alone, leaving Anne in the car.

"She is very shy," Julia explained. "Shy of you, I mean."

Terhune was genuinely astonished. "Of me! Good lord! What have you been making me out to be, Julie? Some sort of an ogre—"

"Don't be silly. She's shy of you because you are an Important Person, and she is not used to meeting Important People."

It was his turn to be derisive. "Now it is you who is talking rot. Important, my—my boot!"

She shook her head. "You are the author of published books—"

"One book."

She ignored the interruption. "That fact means something to a young person, Theo. In addition, you have achieved a certain amount of notoriety as an amateur detective—"

He interrupted again, with a genuine exclamation of annoyance.

"You can snort—very rudely, I might add—as much as you please, my sweet, but the fact remains that to some people you are, to some extent, famous. But all I wanted to say was this: Be nice with her—"

"I like that! Since when haven't I been nice with everyone?"

"Well, patient, then. Don't expect too much from her at first. She has never worked for any one else before."

This remark reminded Terhune, for the first time, that he had never queried Anne's age.

"How old is she, Julie?"

"Seventeen."

"Only seventeen!"

She laughed coldly. "Surely you don't think I should have trusted you alone in the shop with a sweet young thing of twenty-five? You may think of yourself as a staid old bachelor, Theo, but propinquity has been responsible for many a couple forgetting their self-imposed vows to remain celibate."

"Julie, my dear, you are talking through the back of your hat! Or have you been reading Schopenhauer? I am not in the least interested in your dissertation on propinquity, nor have I ever made a vow of celibacy—though it might not be a bad idea at that! All right—bring in your Anne."

Julia left the shop. When she returned she brought Terhune's new assistant with her—a merry-eyed but intelligent looking girl, with wind-reddened cheeks, curly chestnut-brown hair, and a most attractive dimple in her left cheek. She was neatly dressed in a quiet, pin-striped costume which emphasized her enviable schoolgirl slimness, and wore sheer stockings the equal of Julia's—not very surprisingly, for they had once been Julia's. Her manner was demurely shy.

"This is Anne, Theo. Anne, my dear, this is Mr. Terhune." Julia spoke to Terhune again. "You have not met Anne before, Theo, because she and her mother moved back to Willingham only a week ago. They are living in Mill Lane. In between times they have been living at Acton, where Anne received a commercial education at Pitman's. I have given her an outline of the kind of work you will probably ask her to do, and of her hours."

"Do you think you will like the work, Anne?" Terhune asked.

Anne raised her eyes for a moment. "I am sure I shall, Mr. Terhune."

"Good." He pointed to the second desk, which Harrisons had delivered the previous Saturday morning, and arranged—after a considerable shifting of many piles of books, and two series of bookshelves. "That will be your desk, Anne, so settle yourself there, and presently I will begin explaining how the work goes."

"Yes, Mr. Terhune." Anne approached the desk and, taking off her coat and hat, began awkwardly to inspect the typewriter, also newly purchased—from a shop in Folkestone.

Terhune turned to Julia, but before he could speak the postman entered to deliver the mail. As soon as he had gone Terhune murmured:

"Excuse me, Julie," and shuffled quickly through the bundle of letters. One of them was postmarked: 'Saxhawley, Yorks.'

He picked it out from the others. "From Saxhawley. May I?"

"Of course."

He slit open the envelope. As he had anticipated, the letter inside was from Burton.

Dear Sir,

This is to advise you that all the books were packed by Friday night, and the cases delivered at the station this morning. The stationmaster informs me that they should be leaving within the next twelve hours. We have made a good job of the work, so the books should reach you soon; and in good condition.

Since your departure I have recollected that I gave you the wrong name of the man who stayed with Mr. Ronald at the hotel in Thirsk on the night of Mr. James's death... As I do not wish to cause possible mischief to any one, I beg to advise you that the name of the friend was not Tanner, but Shilling—Mr. Robert Shilling.

Yours respectfully,
Thomas Burton.

"Good Lord!"

"Something wrong, Theo?"

"No, but read this." He passed on the letter to Julia.

She read it through, then glanced up with a startled expression.

"Robert Shilling! He couldn't be our Shilling."

"Why not? The name isn't a common one, and in combination with Robert, most unusual."

"But the coincidence—"

"Although a good writer does not make use of coincidence for his plot, coincidences do sometimes happen in real life, Julie."

"I suppose so," she agreed doubtfully.

After a slight pause Terhune went on: "If it was our Shilling who stayed at Thirsk with Ronald Strudgewick, then that fact disposes of poor old Burton's theory."

"The one about Ronald Strudgewick's being the murderer of his uncle?"

"Yes."

"Why?"

"Isn't the answer to your question obvious, Julie? Shilling may not be a likeable man—as far as you and I are concerned—but I should hesitate to class him as a type of man to risk his neck for the sake of a friend."

"Certainly he isn't the heroic or sacrificing type," she agreed.

"Furthermore, the one motive which might have made a man conspire to bear false witness for another doesn't apply in his case."

"Money?"

"Yes. A penniless man might have been willing to take the risk of being rumbled for the sake of, say, ten thousand pounds which Strudgewick might have been willing to pay; the chance of an easy ten thousand wouldn't have meant so much to Shilling, who is already probably worth several times that amount."

"I suppose so, and yet—"

"Yet what?"

"I—I don't know."

Julia's hesitating manner astonished Terhune. She was usually so sure of herself, usually so incisive.

"Don't tell me you have become infected with Burton's germ, and suspect that James Strudgewick may have been pushed off that plank bridge?"

Her glance became steadier. "Do you know, Theo, I haven't been able to forget the story of James Strudgewick's death ever since you told me about it last Wednesday."

"Why not?"

"Because I agree with Burton. Perhaps you have never lived with a person of regular habits, but I have. Poor Father was a perfect darling in most things, but he was a man of regular habits, some of which so exasperated me that I would have given much to make him vary them, even if only just for once. You know the road from our house to the church? Well, there is a second way—a short cut, incidentally; like the one to Tile House—and for some psychological reason which I was never, never able to discover, Father always insisted upon going to church on a Sunday by the short cut, and returning by way of the road.

"Nothing ever made him change this habit. It didn't matter if the short cut, which was across William Hemming's field, was ankle deep in mud, or if a thunderstorm was raging, or an east wind blowing a gale, or if Mother and I positively refused to accompany him, he would not go and return by way of the road, or even use the short cut for both journeys. No, he insisted upon using the short cut for going and the road for coming back.

"I cannot tell you how that silly habit annoyed me. Once I begged him, for my sake—because I did not want to spoil a new pair of shoes—to use the road going to church, but he refused, and laughed at me when I became quite angry with him. He told me there was nothing to prevent my using the road if I wanted to, but he had crossed the field on his way to church ever since he could remember and he wasn't going to change just on account of a stupid whim of mine.

"He had other habits of that sort, too, but I don't want to catalogue them. The only point I am trying to make is this, Theo. If James Strudgewick was anything like Father he would have died first before using *his* short cut without good reason—and this, mind you, ignoring his fear of crossing the plank bridge unaccompanied, which would probably have made him twice as obstinate."

Terhune's eyes twinkled. He could not remember ever having heard Julia talk so impulsively or at such length.

"Suppose you are right, Julie; suppose James Strudgewick didn't use the short cut without a good and sufficient reason; your argument doesn't justify calling Ronald Strudgewick a murderer and Robert Shilling a willing accomplice—to say nothing of the fact that people in the hotel lounge, a waiter, and a hall porter all gave evidence to Inspector Whatever-his-name-was which proved it wasn't physically possible for Ronald to have been at Hawley Green round about the time of his uncle's death."

"Theo, when did you last take a holiday?" Julia asked unexpectedly.

"Two years ago, when I went to the United States for Lady Kylstone. Why?"

"Would you do something for me?"

He grinned. "Go to New York again? You bet I would. Or is it to be Cape Town this time?"

"Sometimes you are not in the least funny, my pet. I want you to come away with me—and Mother, of course, to preserve the proprieties."

"Come away—leave the business—"

"You forget you have engaged an assistant so as to give you the chance of leaving it occasionally."

"You scheming little minx—"

"The idea of the holiday has only just occurred to me," she interrupted coldly.

He protested weakly: "I couldn't leave Anne so soon—just like that—"

"You could—in two weeks' time."

The temptation was one not easy to refuse. He temporized, to give him time for sober reflection.

"For how long?"

She glanced down quickly to conceal the smile of triumph which flashed across her face.

"For four days? A week?"

"A week! Leave Anne on her own to cope with Thursday and Saturday!" Thursdays and Saturdays were the two busiest days of his week.

"Well, say Sunday morning to Wednesday night then?"

He still was not prepared to decide.

"But there's no place worth going to in that short time."

"Oh, yes, there is," she assured him swiftly.

"Where?" he was weak enough to ask.

"Thirsk," she replied significantly.

Chapter Eight

Julia's suggestion was a mad one, but it was not unattractive, so Terhune gave it a moment's consideration. By doing so he was lost.

Early Sunday morning, two weeks later, Julia, her mother, and Terhune headed northward from Bray, *en route* for Thirsk. Of the three people in the car Alicia MacMunn was the most excited.

"I think this journey is *most* thrilling, Mr. Terhune," she began in her usual fluttering manner. "It was really most kind of you to ask me to accompany you—"

"Theo did nothing of the kind, Mother. It was I who insisted upon your coming with us. Otherwise all the tabby cats in the district would soon be telling one another that I had at last succeeded in seducing that nice, dear Mr. Terhune—"

"Julia! Oh, dear! Sometimes you say the most appalling things—" Poor Alicia! She was genuinely embarrassed. "Besides, I am sure that nobody would have *dreamed* of saying anything of the kind—"

"Of course they would. You know they would have, Mother, for you would have been the first to think so, even if you didn't say it."

"Julia! Upon my soul your tongue becomes worse and worse every day. I dare not let myself imagine what Mr. Terhune must be thinking."

"Mother dear, seeing that we are all to be together for several days, don't you think it would be nicer if you called Theodore by his Christian name?"

"I think it would be most indecorous. Besides, I cannot *bear* the name of Theodore; it is *so* ugly," Alicia added naïvely.

"Then call him Tommy. Everybody else does."

"Tommy is a nice name," Alicia agreed flutteringly. After a long pause she went on: "Oh dear! Now I cannot remember what I was saying; your interruption has driven the words completely out of my head." This, of course, was nothing unusual. Alicia MacMunn rarely completed a sentence that was involved, or too long, for she had the disconcerting habit of dropping one subject and almost without pause carrying on to speak of something quite unrelated.

"Don't try to remember, Mother. It wasn't of any importance."

"What a rude girl you are," Alicia complained plaintively. "It might have been something very special—"

Terhune took pity on her. "You were saying that you thought the journey quite thrilling, Mrs. MacMunn."

"Of course I was. It is very nice of you to remind me, Mr. Terhune—"

"Tommy," Julia interposed coolly.

"Oh, yes! Tommy," she repeated in a somewhat protesting voice. "But as I was saying—why, surely that was Mrs. Ford we passed just now. Whatever is she walking along this road for, so early on a Sunday morning?" Apparently Alicia did not expect an answer, for she rattled on: "Do you think you will be arresting this Mr. Burton for having murdered his cousin? I have never seen anyone being arrested. I don't think I should much care to do so —Julia, my dear, why didn't you wear your black and white—"

They drove steadily northward, not at the speed to which Terhune was used, when Julia was at the wheel—whenever she was in the car Alicia insisted upon Julia's controlling her passion for speed—but still at an average rate which assured their reaching their destination that night. In good time they turned left on to the Dover Road, and made for Gravesend. There they caught the ferry for Tilbury. Once in Essex they continued north for Chelmsford, where they turned north-west for Bishop's Stortford and, later, Huntingdon. Thence to Stamford, and north again for Grantham, Newark, Doncaster, Selby,

York and, lastly, as dusk began to spread from the east, Thirsk, where they engaged rooms at the *Crown Hotel*.

They breakfasted the following morning in the dining-room, about eight-forty-five. Alicia ate little; she said she was *much* too excited to eat properly. As was usually the case with Alicia, the less she ate the more she talked; Julia and Terhune found it difficult to slip in even an occasional word. Presently an expression of mystery transformed her. After a cautious glance in every direction —which positively reeked of genuine, conspiratorial mystery and would not have disgraced old Lyceum days—she enquired in a hushed whisper: "What is our first move to be, Mr.—er—Tommy? I am positively *thrilled*—"

"Don't be so ridiculous, Mother," Julia chided crossly. "You are acting like a child. There is no need to whisper."

"Don't you be so rude, Julia," Alicia snapped back. "Do you want me to shout so that everybody may know that we are on the track of a murderer?"

Julia glanced despairingly at Terhune. "Mother darling, we are going to do nothing more exciting than to go for a drive in the country."

"A drive in the country!" It looked as if Alicia could not decide which to be—angry or astonished. "Surely we haven't travelled all this distance up to Yorkshire just to go driving round the country?"

"Why not? Parts of Yorkshire are very beautiful."

"You assured me solemnly that Mr. Terhune wanted to visit Thirsk in order to make enquiries into a murder mystery."

"So he does."

"You are not going to make me believe he can do that just by looking at the scenery." Unconsciously, Alicia's voice began to rise, and as her voice was of the penetrating type Terhune was not surprised to notice that several pairs of eyes glanced enquiringly in the direction of their table.

He thought it high time to act as peacemaker—of the two evils her melodramatics were probably less disconcerting than her too-revealing voice.

"We have to make some enquiries first," he said, quickly, in a low voice.

She reacted immediately. "You have?" she whispered, but with a pantomimic gesture which made her two companions wince. "Of whom?"

"You will see—but you will be sure not to—er—interrupt?"

"I am the soul of discretion," she informed him, believing sincerely in her own statement. Julia laughed derisively, so Alicia added, meaningly: "When I wish to be. Who are you going to—to —interrogate—isn't that the technical word to use—first?"

"Our waiter."

"Our waiter!" Her excitement, and her amazement, increased. "Do you really think *he* knows something about the murder of that poor Mr. Burton?"

"Strudgewick, Mother."

Alicia gestured vaguely. "Mr.—I mean Tommy knows whom I mean."

"Besides, we don't know definitely that Mr. Strudgewick was murdered," Julia went on. "If you are not careful, Mother, you will find yourself the defendant in a slander suit."

"As if anyone would bring an action against *me*!" Alicia exclaimed scornfully.

Fortunately their waiter passed by at that moment, so Terhune hailed him.

"Yes, sir." The waiter was of the white-haired, ruddy-nosed, bowed-shouldered type which seems to find its way to provincial hotels as if by a homing instinct. "Some more coffee, or marmalade?"

"Not at the moment, Henry—"

"William, sir," the man corrected despondently. "The other waiter is Henry."

"Sorry, William. Is the manager about?"

"Do you mean Mr. Dunstable, sir? He is the proprietor."

"If he also manages the hotel, yes."

"Mr. Dunstable is usually having his own breakfast about this time, sir, in the private room."

"Then would you tell him that we should appreciate a few minutes' conversation with him as soon as he is free?"

"Yes, sir."

William shuffled off and disappeared through a door marked Private. Two minutes later he returned to the table.

"Mr. Dunstable will be glad to see you in the office at nine-thirty, sir."

"Thank you, William. And now, if you would like to bring that marmalade you mentioned just now—"

At nine-thirty Alicia, Julia and Terhune knocked upon the door of Dunstable's office—Julia having done her best to persuade her mother to let Terhune interview the hotel proprietor alone. But Alicia revealed the source of Julia's obstinacy by refusing positively to be deprived of one second's thrill, and insisted upon their going in a body to the office.

"Come in."

They entered.

"Mr. Dunstable?"

"Yes."

"My name is Terhune. This is the Honourable Mrs. MacMunn, and her daughter, Miss MacMunn. As you probably know, we arrived late last night, and booked rooms here."

Terhune had a purpose in stressing the handle to Mrs. MacMunn's name. It succeeded in so far that the middle-aged Dunstable became exceedingly deferential as he hastened to produce two chairs for the ladies.

"What can I do for you?" he enquired directly of Alicia.

She laughed flutteringly. "We have some questions to ask you," she whispered.

Dunstable looked puzzled. "Questions, madame?"

"Mother!" Julia exclaimed sharply.

"At least Tommy—I mean Mr. Terhune—has," she explained, with an angry glance at her daughter.

Dunstable turned towards Terhune, who was standing up for lack of chairs, or perhaps the room in which to put another one down.

"Well, Mr. Terhune?"

The moment was an embarrassing one. This fact Terhune had recognized from the moment that the project north had first been mooted. In between while he had carefully rehearsed a tactful series of questions, which now, faced by an uncompromising expression which gave one the impression it could soon turn unpleasant, he entirely forgot.

"I rather wanted—we wanted to ask you a few questions about two people who stayed in this hotel last February—"

He got no farther than that. Dunstable's expression fulfilled its promise of becoming unpleasant when the need arose, while the man himself interrupted with a sharp: "Excuse me."

"Well?"

"If it's evidence you are looking for it is no use your coming to this hotel. Nearly all the staff here are elderly; they have very bad memories."

This was an encouraging beginning, Terhune thought dismally as he glanced quickly at his companions. Both were betraying an expression of surprise, as though somebody had just smacked them on that part of the body which no lady expects to have smacked. For once Alicia was the first to recover.

"My dear man, I don't think you understand—"

"I understand only too well, madame. Ever since I have been a hotel-keeper I have made a point of trying to keep the name of this hotel out of the newspapers."

"How ridiculous! I always thought hotels like to have their names advertised."

"Mother—" Julia tried to warn Alicia.

Alicia did not intend to be quietened. "It's no use your trying to stop me saying what I think, Julia. If Mr. Barnstable does not understand that it is his duty, as a good citizen, to help justice it is time somebody told him of his responsibilities."

"I hardly think I need trouble you, madame, to instruct me in my duties as a good citizen."

"Are you being insolent—"

"Not at all, madame, and I do not wish you to construe my remark in that light. I am merely pointing out that I do not want anyone to teach me my own business—and more particularly, how to mind it!"

Alicia began to exclaim her indignation, but Julia quickly forestalled her.

"Are we to understand, Mr. Dunstable, that you refuse to help us in our enquiries?"

With the utmost respect, Miss MacMunn, I am not prepared to change a lifetime's custom."

"Then there is nothing more we can do here," Julia rose to her feet. "Come along, Mother."

For a moment it seemed as though Alicia was preparing to argue with her daughter, but a glance at Julia's angry face evidently made Alicia change her mind, for she rose to her feet, and with a disdainful glance at the impervious hotel proprietor she moved to the door and out of the room with an imperial gesture of scorn which, in other circumstances, would have made Terhune chuckle.

She was followed by Julia and Terhune. As the door closed behind them she burst out dramatically: "Keep your eyes on that man, Tommy. He has a guilty conscience. He is in the conspiracy with your Mr. Burton, and Mr. Copper. He has been bribed—"

"Please, Mother!" Julia interrupted. "Please try to be grownup. Just for once. He's just a silly, narrow-minded man who dreads the thought of the name of his hotel being introduced into a Criminal Court."

"Whatever his reason, I do not like him, and I refuse to stop another moment in his hotel."

"We are going to stop here just as long as we planned," Julia announced firmly. "He cannot turn us out—"

"I should think not."

"And as long as we are staying here we may be able to get the information we want some other way."

This possibility cheered Alicia. "In that case it might be worth putting up with his insolence." She lowered her voice. "What are we going to do now?"

"Going for that drive," Julia said, firmly.

They passed through the hotel into the garage at the back. The car, shining like a new pin, was waiting for them. Immediately they appeared in sight a young man deserted his job of work to rush across the garage to them.

"I've done what you asked last night, miss. Cleaned 'er, given 'er air and water, and filled 'er up—that took seven gallons, miss." She gave him a tip which stretched his smile from ear to ear. "Cor! *Thank* you, miss."

"Do you know Hawley Green?"

"Hawley Green!" He scratched his head with hands reeking with black oil and petrol.

"Just this side of Saxhawley."

"Cor, yes! 'Course I knows it. Are you wanting to go there, miss?"

"Yes. Which is the shortest route there?"

"The *shortest* route! That would be by way of Nellersby." He pointed to his left. "Go down the street to your left, and take the second turning on your right. That'll be the Nellersby road what will take you through Hawley Green into Saxhawley. 'Bout thirty mile I give it."

"Thank you." Julia nodded to her mother to enter the car through the rear nearside door, while she and Terhune used the front doors. As soon as they were all settled she pressed the self-starter. The engine began to purr.

As she drove along the narrow, cobbled drive which joined the garage with the road Julia said: "Take a careful note of the time, Theo, as we turn into the road."

He did so. "Six minutes past ten," he told her.

They turned into the second turning on their right, a long, twisting road which soon brought them to the open countryside. The driving was easy and straightforward, but Terhune noticed that Julia did not allow it to pass the 40 m.p.h. mark, a speed less than her normal on clear roads. This was because they were trying out the possibilities of driving from Thirsk to Hawley Green in something less than an hour in the dark—and neither Julia nor he believed that anyone doing the journey at night would have cared to risk travelling much faster than that.

All went well for some distance. At ten-forty Terhune glanced at the speedometer, to note that they had covered sixteen miles. So far so good, he thought. Evidently old Burton was right. Ronald Strudgewick could have driven from Thirsk to Hawley Green in the hour. Quite easily, in fact.

And then—a level crossing! They rounded a corner, and saw the gates closing, two hundred yards farther down the road.

"Theo—" she began.

"I know," he exclaimed. "Something has gone wrong somewhere. If Strudgewick was trying to create a false alibi he wouldn't have dared risk being held up by a level crossing. Unless—"

"Unless what?"

"If the line ahead is one of these four-trains-a-day branch lines perhaps the last train of the day passes over the crossing say about seven or eight o'clock, so that he would not have to worry about being stopped."

"Perhaps! We can find out later."

They came to a halt by the gates. The lines—a single track only —were visible for some distance either way, but there was no sign of a train to be seen; not even a trail of smoke puffing into the air. On their right was a station—or rather a halt, if the bare, trestle-like platform was anything to go by. On their left was a small signal-box in which stood a man peacefully smoking a pipe, and staring into the distance beyond the halt.

Julia tooted the horn suggestively, but the signalman ignored the sound with superb indifference. There being still no sign of a train, she switched off the engine. The seconds passed. Still nothing happened. Then more seconds, the best part of a minute, in fact. Then a bell rang in the signal-box. The signalman emerged, descended the wooden steps, walked along the lines—all this time without one glance towards the waiting car—and up the ramp on to the platform. At the same moment a shrill whistle in the distance, and a wispy plume of smoke above the trees heralded the coming of the train.

"I believe the train's going to stop at the station," Julia said, incredulously.

"I'm sure of it," Terhune agreed glumly. "Why that fool of a signalman couldn't have let us through—"

At a crawling speed the train rumbled towards the crossing, but came to a shuddering halt by the platform—empty save for the signalman who, it seemed, had meanwhile become ticket-collector, porter, and stationmaster in one. Two passengers alighted, and conversed for a while with the general factotum. Then all three walked along the platform to the engine, apparently to share a joke with the driver and fireman. The joke shared and over, the porter regretfully signalled to the guard, the guard solemnly waved his flag and whistled. Slowly, and with deep resentment, the engine puffed itself into motion, and proceeded on its way.

Having bidden the two passengers a lingering "So long," the general factotum returned to the signal-box—again seemingly unaware of the waiting traffic—and turned a large wheel. The gates swung open, and the traffic moved across the lines, Julia going northwards, and a lorry and two cyclists who were proceeding in the reverse direction.

"How long has the delay been?" Julia gasped.

"Nearly four minutes."

"I didn't know anything so incredible remained in England—"

When their laughter had subsided Julia increased the speed of the car to forty-five, but another thirty minutes passed and they were still short of their destination. Not until Terhune's watch showed eleven-twelve did they catch their first glimpse of Hawley Green, this time—as far as Terhune was concerned—from the opposite direction.

"There's the lake—there's the fall—and there—" his arm moved, "the house, Tile House. You can see its chimneys above the trees, half-way up the hill."

"Dear me! What a charming view!" Alicia gushed. "I almost think I could live here. Don't you, Julia?"

Julia did not answer. She was too busy talking to Terhune.

"Where shall we make enquiries about the train, Theo?"

"Saxhawley. I should have liked to have suggested stopping at the *Dog and Duck* for a drink, Julia, but I might be recognized."

"Would there be any harm in that?"

"If Burton were to suspect that I was doing what he asked he might let the cat out of the bag in his enthusiasm."

They coasted down the hill, passed over the hump-bridge at the bottom, and ascended the hill on the other side, through Hawley Green, and past the *Dog and Duck*.

A few minutes later they reached Saxhawley. Leaving the car in the station yard they went into the saloon bar of the *Station Hotel*, where they ordered welcome, cooling drinks. Afterwards they returned to the station, where Terhune grabbed hold of a porter.

"Can you tell me the quickest route to Thirsk?"

"Aye, sir, I can that. It be by way of Keeley Hill."

"Keeley Hill! I thought the shortest route was via Nellersby."

The porter revealed a set of broken, tobacco-stained teeth in a slow, friendly grin.

"Nellersby be the shortest route but that tain't to say it's the quickest."

"Because of the level-crossing?"

"Aye, sir. 'Tis a couple of mile more, now by way of Keeley, but if I wanted to get to Thirsk in a 'urry, that 'ould be the way I'd choose."

"Are there many trains on that line?"

"Six a day on weekdays."

"Would there be one passing over the crossing between eight-thirty and ten?"

"Aye, sir, there would. That 'ould be the last train of the day on that line, the 10.16 p.m. into Saxhawley."

"Ten-sixteen! Well, thanks, porter. Will you have a drink?"

"I will that, sir, and gladly, this warm day. Thank you kindly, sir, and my best respects." The porter touched his hat and ambled off.

After a short conference they decided to return to the hotel for lunch. As they passed over the hump-backed bridge Terhune glanced at his watch—11.51 a.m.

Two miles beyond Hawley Green the roads divided. The left arm of the signpost pointed to Nellersby and Thirsk; the right, to Keeley Hill and Thirsk. They branched off to the right. Just sixty-two minutes later Julia brought the car to a stop outside the *Crown Hotel*. She turned enquiringly.

"Well?"

"Two minutes over the hour."

She laughed triumphantly. The scoring against Ronald Strudgewick had been opened.

Chapter Nine

After the meal the three visitors from Kent entered the smoking-room and ordered coffee. This was brought to them by William, so, having made sure that Dunstable was nowhere about, Terhune determined to take advantage of the opportunity to interrogate the waiter.

"Black or white, sir?"

"All three white." Terhune waited a moment and then asked: "Have you been working in this hotel very long, William?"

"The best part of twenty years," the man answered lugubriously.

"Then you were here last February?"

"Yes, sir."

"In that case would you care to give me some information concerning something which happened here on the eighteenth—it will be worth your while—"

William's face became an expressionless mask. "February is some time ago, and my memory isn't what it used to be."

"I don't want to know much—just whether you remember serving a Mr. Strudgewick—"

"I hardly ever pick up the name of our visitors. Perhaps Mr. Dunstable could help you."

Terhune shrugged his shoulders. "All right, William. That will be all."

William departed, somewhat sullenly, Terhune believed. Perhaps he was thinking of the tip of which his bad memory was depriving him.

"It looks as though Dunstable has warned all the staff to hold their tongues. I'm afraid we have wasted our time coming here."

"Not entirely," Julia contradicted. "We have proved that Strudgewick could have made the journey from here to Hawley Green in the hour."

Terhune shook his head. "That fact is not much use on its own, Julie. Even if we assume that James Strudgewick was killed, and that his death took place about nine-fifty, if it were to be proved that Ronald Strudgewick was seen in this coffee-room at, say, nine o'clock, then his alibi is unshakeable."

"But surely Burton said—"

He interrupted with a shake of his head. "Burton's evidence is prejudiced, and therefore may not be reliable. He has only to exaggerate or perhaps minimize the actual times by a matter of a few minutes to make the impossible possible. And alternatively, the possible impossible."

Disappointment made Julia's voice sharp. "What can we do now, Theo?"

"There's nothing much we can do. As far as we know, the only people who might be able to give any information against Strudgewick are the people at this hotel, whom Dunstable has effectively silenced."

"Couldn't your friend at Scotland Yard help in some way or another?"

"You mean Sampson?" Terhune shook his head. "New Scotland Yard has jurisdiction over the Metropolitan Police Force only, They co-operate in criminal investigations only when they are directly invited to do so by the Chief Constable of whichever force seeks their aid."

"Why not ring Sampson up?" Julia urged. "There is just a chance he might know somebody up here who could put in a friendly word on your behalf with the obstinate Mr. Dunstable."

He reflected upon Julia's suggestion. The odds against Sampson's knowing any one in the local police force were long, but there could be no harm in ringing up and putting the matter to the test. Presently he nodded, and rose to his feet.

"If you will excuse me—"

There were some public call-boxes in the Post Office which was round the corner from the *Crown Hotel*. Thither he made his way. After a not unreasonable wait he found himself connected with Whitehall 1212.

"Detective-Inspector Sampson, please."

During the few seconds' interval he wondered whether he would have the luck to find Sampson in. Probably not, he thought pessimistically. Even if the detective wasn't out on a case, he was probably giving evidence at Old Bailey, or at one of the numerous police courts which ringed the Metropolitan Police area. However, luck was with him, for the crisp, incisive voice which answered the 'phone was unmistakeably Sampson's.

"Detective-Inspector Sampson?"

"Yes. Who is it?"

"Theodore Terhune."

"Mr. Terhune! How are you, sir? Quite fit?"

"Yes, thanks. And you?"

"In the pink. I'm sorry we missed each other yesterday."

"Missed—yesterday!" For a moment Terhune was puzzled, but he recollected that yesterday was Sunday, a day on which Sampson sometimes made a point of stopping at Bray on his way to the coast. "Did you call at my place yesterday?"

"Yes. About eleven. I was hoping you would have lunch with me somewhere. But didn't you get the note I dropped in the letterbox?"

"No. I—"

"You should have done. I thought you were calling me up because of it."

"I didn't return to Bray last night. As a matter of fact, I'm in Yorkshire."

"Yorkshire!" Sampson chuckled. "You've travelled a fair distance——" He paused. "If you haven't had my note then you must be calling me up for some other reason."

"I am. I want to cadge your help—if possible."

"Are you in trouble, Mr. Terhune?"

Sampson's voice sounded anxious, and it became Terhune's turn to laugh. "No, I'm still in the good books of the police. But I want some information."

"If there's anything I can tell you——"

"Not from you, Inspector, but from some people up here— private people——"

"Just one moment, Mr. Terhune." Sampson interrupted ominously. "You are not investigating another crime, are you?"

"Well, I'm not sure yet whether it is a crime or an accident."

"It beats me!" Sampson mumbled. "It just beats me! Not satisfied with having taken a hand in investigating three crimes in less than a year, bedamned if you haven't found another."

"I didn't find it. It found me."

"What do you mean?"

"Somebody recognized me as the Terhune who has been publicized in the Press, and promptly unloaded his troubles upon me."

"Ah! That's the penalty for becoming a Press Personality."

"So I've found. But would you like to hear the story of this particular case?"

"If you make it brief, Mr. Terhune. I don't want you to spend half a fortune telephoning."

As briefly as he could Terhune gave the Scotland Yard man a gist of the case which was responsible for the journey to Yorkshire. Sampson listened to the end without interruption, but as soon as it was evident that Terhune had no more to add the inspector said crisply: "Leave everything to me, Mr. Terhune. There is a man in the North Riding Police I know very well—we were in the same platoon during the war. I'll get in touch with him and ring you later on, say about ten o'clock. Would that time suit you?"

"Excellently."

"What is your hotel number?"

Terhune had to confess that it was unknown to him.

"Never mind. Give me the name; I'll get Directory Enquiries to give me the number."

Terhune gave the name of the hotel to the inspector; after a few more words they disconnected.

On returning to the hotel Terhune found Julia alone. Alicia, it seemed, had gone for her afternoon rest. But Julia was too impatient to speak longer of her mother.

"Did you speak to your Inspector Sampson?"

"Yes. He thinks he will be able to arrange matters. He is going to telephone me tonight, about ten."

"Then there is nothing more we can do before then?"

"Not so far as I know."

Julia looked more pleased than otherwise. "Shall we go for a drive—a real one this time?" she suggested.

The idea was passed unanimously.

11

At eleven minutes past ten that night William appeared in the smoking-room to inform Terhune that he was wanted on the telephone. With a hurried word of apology to his companions he followed William to the telephone, which he found in its own booth just along the passage from the office.

Following his "Hullo," Sampson's familiar voice came back with: "Sampson here. Is that you, Mr. Terhune?"

"Yes."

"I succeeded in getting hold of my friend Miller just over an hour ago. He has promised to send a man along to the hotel about ten-thirty tomorrow morning to meet you. He will question the hotel staff on your behalf."

"Thanks a lot, Inspector—"

Sampson interrupted: "There's no need to thank me, Mr. Terhune. Glad to be of assistance. I hope you don't uncover a mare's nest."

"So do I," Terhune agreed wholeheartedly.

"I'll come along to Bray as soon as I can manage to snatch a few hours for myself—I shall be interested in hearing what happens tomorrow. Meanwhile, if anything should come of your enquiries don't mind getting into touch with me again."

"I shall, and thanks again—"

But the inspector would not listen to Terhune's thanks, and with a quick "Good night" hastily rang off.

III

After breakfast the following morning Terhune suggested to Alicia and Julia that the three of them should wait in the hotel gardens for the arrival of the man from the North Riding Police. The garden was not large; for the most part it consisted of a fair-sized lawn surrounding a fish-pond, being in its turn bounded on three sides by formal flower-beds, with flowering shrubs beyond. Scattered about the lawn were some half a dozen tables beneath large, striped umbrellas, with accompanying chairs. What attracted Terhune to this spot was not only the fact that the morning was inviting in its warmth and freshness—and therefore so much pleasanter than the stuffy, over-furnished sitting-room—but more especially because the furthermost table was secluded and far enough from the hotel for conversation to be private.

Alicia immediately expressed herself content to fall in with that arrangement, but Julia was less compliant.

"The man is not due for more than an hour," she pointed out impatiently. "Isn't there anything we can do in that time?"

Mrs. MacMunn glanced at her daughter with some surprise. "Why are you so restless, Julia? It is not like you always to be wanting to be on the move. At home I have difficulty in persuading you to go anywhere."

"At home there is nowhere fresh to visit," she replied scornfully. "It's so rare for us to go anywhere farther than ten miles from Willingham—"

"If you are in one of those moods then by all means get Mr.— I mean Tommy—to take you around. For myself I cannot think of a nicer place in which to pass the time. I shall be able to finish that magazine I borrowed from the lounge last night."

So it was settled: Julia and Terhune escorted Alicia to the most convenient of the tables, and settled her with some cushions, and a selection of magazines. Then they left, after promising to return not later than ten-fifteen.

"Mind you are back by then," Alicia warned them, flutteringly. "I shouldn't know *what* to say to the man if he should come here before you were back."

Julia laughed drily. "Mother dear, there is nothing you would like more than to have the man on your own for an hour or so."

Alicia made a protesting gesture, but did not pursue the subject, perhaps because she was sufficiently honest with herself, for once, to admit the justice of Julia's remark.

The other two passed through the hotel into the street. "Now what, Julie? Do you want to buy postcards of the church, some crested china or a spoon with the town's coat-of-arms?"

She laughed gaily. "I just want to wander through the streets, looking at the shops and the people."

"Any place where you may see something different from home?"

"Yes, my love. Just that."

"Poor Julie! Can't you persuade your mother to travel more than she does? Just occasionally—for your sake—"

"I've tried so desperately, Theo. But you've seen for yourself how much visiting new places means to her. Sitting in a hotel garden— She will be quite content to leave Thirsk without having seen more than the *Crown Hotel.*" Her manner became once more gay. "Come along, my pet. Let's enjoy what little time we have to spare."

In that carefree mood they wandered through the streets of Thirsk, laughing cheerfully, talking nonsense, and even buying a few postcards of the district. All too soon they glanced at a clock and found it was time to return. They retraced their steps, and found Alicia sitting at quite a different table from the one at which they had installed her, talking energetically to a rather handsome old man of rising eighty, with a tiny white beard which reminded Terhune of Napoleon III.

Julia giggled. "Dear Mother! I thought she wouldn't be long finding somebody to listen to her gossiping. Now she will consider the journey here has been worth while."

Alicia did not immediately rejoin her daughter, but presently she revealed signs which Julia recognized as impatience.

"However much she enjoys the Admiral's company—or is he a General, do you think, Theo?—she does not mean to miss meeting our expected visitor," Julia said—and the last words had not been uttered before they saw Alicia rising to her feet, and waving the white-bearded old gentleman a fluttering farewell. As she moved across the lawn towards them a domestic came out of the hotel, followed by a tall, angular man with greying hair, keen pale-blue eyes, and a military-looking grey moustache.

"Five shillings to one this is our man coming," Terhune whispered quickly.

"Nothing doing, Theo. I don't bet against certainties."

It became a race between Alicia and the stranger to reach the table first, which Alicia won, but only by a short head, as it were, for even as Alicia sank into her chair the man approached the table and took off his formal-cut felt hat.

"Mr. Theodore Terhune?" he inquired in a voice by no means friendly.

Terhune nodded.

"My name is Detective-Inspector Longworth——" He paused, and smiled dryly. "I see that my name is not unknown to you."

Terhune indicated his companions. "Mrs. MacMunn—Miss MacMunn."

Longworth nodded to each in turn. "Morning, ma'am. Morning, miss." His politeness done, he faced Terhune again. "I have been instructed to call upon you with reference to certain investigations which, I understand, you are making at this hotel——"

Terhune interrupted. "Won't you sit down, Inspector." Longworth did so. "A cigarette?"

For a moment it seemed as if the detective intended to refuse the offer—Terhune guessed the reason for the hesitation—but then he thought better of the impulse and took one from the case. "Thank you," he muttered grudgingly.

As soon as four cigarettes had been lighted Longworth began crisply: "Now, sir, if you don't mind we'll get down to business. As I understand the matter from my superior officer, who instructed me to call upon you this morning, you are investigating the death of James Strudgewick, of Hawley Green, found drowned last February in a lake adjoining part of his property."

The inspector's scarcely-veiled antagonism did little to make Terhune feel less an interfering idiot.

"That is roughly the case, Inspector," he mumbled.

"In view of my instructions it is not for me to express surprise, but perhaps you will permit me to confess that I am at a loss to know why a matter which has already been investigated officially by the police should be reopened by an ama— by somebody not connected with the police, and from another part of the country."

Terhune appreciated the fact that he was not likely to make much progress as long as the Yorkshireman remained antagonistic.

"In plain words, Inspector, you resent my interfering in matters which do not concern me. Please speak frankly."

"Yes, sir, I do," Longworth admitted bluntly. "And as you invited me to speak frankly I will add this—that I might not object so much if I had not thoroughly investigated the circumstances of Strudgewick's death, and convinced myself that Ronald Strudgewick had no hand in his uncle's death." He paused as if a passing reflection had disturbed his current of thought. "At least, I suppose your visit to this particular hotel means that Ronald Strudgewick is the party you suspect?"

"He is."

"May I ask you a question, Mr. Terhune?"

"Of course."

"Has James Strudgewick's old servant, Burton, taken any part in making you suspicious of Ronald Strudgewick?"

"Well—yes."

"I thought so!" The inspector became angry. "It's old fools like that—" He checked himself abruptly, and the others never learned what he intended to say—although they could guess! "I wonder, now, if Burton told you the whole truth?"

"I cannot say, of course. Are you referring to any special fact?"

"I am. Did he mention anything about James Strudgewick's will?"

"Yes. He told me that Strudgewick had left the bulk of his money to a sister, but that when the sister died he cancelled the will, and refused to make another."

"That is only half the truth. Two months after his sister's death he had his solicitor draw up a draft will in which he left forty thousand pounds to various charities, five thousand pounds to his nephew Ronald, and the residue to—Burton. Did you know that?"

"N—no."

"I thought not. He didn't pass that information on to me either; Strudgewick's solicitor did that."

"Martin?"

"Yes." Longworth looked surprised. "Have you met him?"

"Yes. I recently purchased Strudgewick's library; it was while I was inspecting the books previous to confirming my offer for them that Burton told me the story of Strudgewick's death, and of his suspicions of Ronald."

The inspector's surprise deepened. "Are you a—a bookseller?"

Terhune nodded. "I have a business in Kent. At Bray-in-the-Marsh, near Ashford."

The other man frowned. "Bray-in-the-Marsh! I know that name." His expression changed. "Are you the Mr. Terhune who was mixed up in that business of the House with Crooked Walls and, later, the murder of Frank Hugh Smallwood?"

"Yes."

"So that is why Scotland Yard interfered—" Longworth checked himself once more. "Did Burton recognize you when you visited Tile House?"

Terhune grinned shyly.

The inspector nodded his head understandingly. "So, of course, he told you that Ronald Strudgewick was the murderer of his uncle, that the Yorkshire police are a pack of gormless ninnies, and no doubt finished up by persuading you to see that justice was done?"

Terhune reddened. "Something like that," he mumbled, thinking to himself that it was possible to be a little too forthright—

The explanation of Terhune's interference seemed to mollify the inspector somewhat. In a more agreeable voice than he had hitherto used he went on: "That makes matters a little clearer. I suppose I can't blame you for wanting to repeat some of your previous successes, but all the same—"

"You still blame Scotland Yard for encouraging an amateur to interfere in a matter which you have already investigated?"

Longworth smiled—and in doing so looked almost human. Then the smile faded and he asked in a voice more inquiring than aggressive: "With all respects, sir, yes. You see, what puzzles me —and annoys me even more, if you don't mind me saying so—is this: what makes you think that I am such an incompetent detective officer as to overlook anything which you may be able to discover?"

Terhune did not know how to answer this pertinent question. While he was still fumbling mentally for a reply Julia came to his assistance.

"That is my fault, Mr. Longworth," she interrupted coolly.

The inspector's thick eyebrows started jerking. "Yours, miss?"

"Yes. When he heard that the police had checked up on Burton's story he was convinced that Burton had no genuine reason for remaining suspicious of Ronald Strudgewick. I persuaded him to think otherwise."

Longworth remained silent, but his face expressed his thoughts more trenchantly than any words of his.

"You see," Julia concluded, "I happen to know Ronald Strudgewick's alibi—Robert Shilling."

"Ah!" For the first time Longworth betrayed real interest. He leaned forward slightly. "Well, miss?" he asked crisply.

"He is a man I heartily distrust."

The inspector looked disappointed. "Quite! Quite! But can you give me any reason—any concrete reason—why this man Shilling should have supported a false alibi, and so become liable to be charged as an accessory before the crime?"

"No."

Longworth shrugged his shoulders disparagingly. "Many a man

who is willing to risk a sentence of imprisonment for the sake of gain would hesitate to risk being hanged, which is the maximum sentence for which an accessory before the crime of homicide is liable. No, miss, however much I might distrust a man I shouldn't care to believe him to be an accessory to murder without very good proof, if not of the fact itself, then, at least, of a very good reason for him having been an accessory."

Julia did not like having her intuition dismissed so lightly, and stared angrily at the ground. For a few seconds there was an embarrassing silence. Then Terhune stepped into the breach.

"You were speaking of Strudgewick's draft will, Inspector. Was it never executed?"

"No," Longworth said grimly.

"Why not?"

"Because Ronald Strudgewick talked his uncle into destroying it. In doing so he deprived Burton of several thousand pounds. Now do you understand why the old man is so bitter against his master's nephew?"

And Longworth leaned back in his chair again, contented with his own reasoning.

Chapter Ten

Alicia was the first to speak. "The man has deceived us," she exclaimed querulously, but in complete disregard for her own deception in the matter of the plural pronoun. "He should have spoken of the reason for his prejudice against Ronald Strudgewick."

Longworth smiled complacently. "Old gossip-mongers like Burton, ma'am, are all the same. When they are drawing a long bow they only paint one side of the picture."

Terhune's eyes twinkled at the glorious mixture of metaphors, but the lighter moment quickly passed. "How do you account for James Strudgewick's having returned home by way of the short cut?" he asked presently.

The inspector frowned as if the question disturbed him. "I was expecting you to ask that sooner or later," he began uncertainly. "I'll begin by admitting that I can offer only one explanation—that Strudgewick acted on impulse."

"You'll never make me believe that," Julia said, abruptly. "A man, especially an elderly man, does not change a twenty-year-old habit without some better reason than impulse."

"I know it sounds weak, miss, but you've got to remember this: that you've only Burton's word for it that Strudgewick never used the short cut."

Terhune started. "Is that so, Inspector? Is there nobody else to back up that part of Burton's story? What about the rest of the servants, the villagers, Colonel Vance?"

"Well—" Longworth paused uncertainly, and flicked his cigarette stub on to a convenient flower bed. "All the evidence is negative. Everybody is quite willing to testify that Strudgewick usually went to and from Colonel Vance's house by way of the road, but none—except Burton—is ready to swear that Strudgewick *never* used the short cut. In fact, on three occasions at least he did use it—"

"By himself?" Julia asked quickly.

"No, miss. With Colonel Vance. It seems that on these three occasions the Colonel and Mr. Strudgewick were so interested in a discussion they were having that the Colonel accompanied his friend almost as far as Tile House."

"Doesn't that prove that Strudgewick didn't mind using the short cut as long as he had somebody with him?"

"Well, yes, Mr. Terhune, but that doesn't prove that he wouldn't —or didn't—sometimes use the short cut on his own. If he had only done so once in twenty-odd years then there are grounds for assuming that he did so the second time. Still, even if he did have somebody else with him on the night he died that person wasn't his nephew Ronald."

Terhune was glad to notice that Longworth's attitude was more friendly, either on account of having learned Terhune's identity, or perhaps because, despite himself, he had become interested in discussing the pros and cons of Strudgewick's death.

"Is that certain?"

"Certain," the inspector agreed emphatically. "On Thursday, the eighteenth of February, Ronald Strudgewick left King's Cross, on the four o'clock train. At least, he says so. I haven't checked up that particular fact, but it makes very little difference whether he caught the train then or later. What is the more pertinent fact— and of which there is ample proof—is that he was on that train when it arrived here in Thirsk, at eight-forty-one, two minutes late."

"Eight-forty-one!"

The detective smiled drily. "Yes, sir. Eight-forty-one," he confirmed, once again with emphasis. "I do not know the exact moment of his arrival in the hotel, but it cannot have been earlier than eight-forty-five."

Terhune nodded agreement. It might easily have taken a car longer to travel from the station to the hotel, but certainly four minutes was the absolute minimum time.

"Now, sir, Strudgewick and his friend booked two single bedrooms for the night, and were allotted rooms eight and nine respectively—"

"I am occupying room eight," Alicia interrupted in an excited voice.

"Indeed, ma'am." Longworth did not appear particularly interested. "Well, Strudgewick occupied room eight, and Shilling nine. Before going upstairs they went into the smoking-room and ordered two large beers. These were brought to them quickly— and as quickly swallowed down, it seems." This admission was grudging. "Immediately afterwards the two men went upstairs, and were not seen again for a time. Now, sir, how long would you say it would have taken the men to do all that?"

Terhune glanced at his watch, then closed his eyes and tried to visualize the scene. After what seemed to him a very long time he reopened his eyes and took another look at his watch. Four minutes and twenty-one seconds had elapsed.

"Say, five minutes," he suggested tentatively.

The inspector shook his head doubtfully. "I think that is too conservative an estimate, but let it stand. Therefore, the two men cannot have entered one of the bedrooms before eight-fifty at the very earliest. Now, sir, on the evidence of Colonel Vance, supported by another member of the family, James Strudgewick left Colonel Vance's house at 9.35 p.m. From the door of the house to the short cut is a good ten minutes' walk—I did it in nine, but I am a quick walker. Suppose we allow Strudgewick fifteen minutes. That means he would have reached the short cut at about nine-fifty. Exactly one hour after Ronald Strudgewick had entered a bedroom in this hotel, thirty-two and a half miles distant by road. I do not think he could have transported himself from one place to the other in that time."

"Why not?" Terhune asked quickly. "Yesterday morning Miss MacMunn did the journey in just two minutes over the hour."

Longworth seemed impressed with the knowledge that they had taken the trouble to test out the time. "That is two minutes less than the time I took," he admitted. "But are you not losing sight of the fact that Ronald Strudgewick would have had to do the journey at night? He could not have matched either time at night."

"He could have done it in fifty-six minutes by night," Julia said, quietly.

"Oh, no, miss—if you don't mind me contradicting—" Longworth began.

"I covered the distance in that time last night."

Terhune choked. "You did what, Julie?"

She would not meet his glance. "I reached the short cut in fifty-six minutes," she repeated in a voice surprisingly meek for her.

"But when?"

"Last night, after you and Mother had gone to bed."

"Really, Julia! What will you do next?" Alicia remonstrated angrily.

Terhune was reproachful. "Why did you leave me behind, Julie?"

"I am sorry, my pet, but you and Mother will never let me drive as fast as I can. If you had been with me I know I should have taken more than the hour."

"Tommy is quite right to restrain you," Alicia snapped. "I think it is ridiculous to risk a serious accident just to save five minutes on a journey—"

Longworth coughed discreetly. "Well, miss, if you say you did the journey in fifty-six minutes that means that Ronald Strudgewick may have been able to do the journey in much the same time. But, of course, he didn't do so, for at a quarter past eleven he and Shilling were in the smoking-room again, buying cigarettes from Mr. Dunstable."

"How long do you estimate it would take for James Strudgewick to reach the plank bridge from the road?" Terhune asked.

"About nine or ten minutes."

"Say ten. Ten to reach the fall, and eight, or even less, to return to the road."

"You are thinking of Ronald Strudgewick when you speak of returning to the road?"

"Yes. If Ronald left the road with James at nine-fifty, he could have been back again on the road at eight minutes past ten. That would have left him more than one hour and ten minutes to make the return journey."

Longworth nodded. "Agreed. But there is one item of evidence which no amount of timing or theorizing can contradict. Just about ten o'clock Strudgewick 'phoned down to the smoking-room and asked for a bottle of whisky and a siphon of soda to be sent up to his room. One of the waiters took the drinks up to room eight and found both men playing cards." The inspector shrugged. "As Strudgewick could not have been playing cards in his bedroom at approximately the very moment you are assuming him to have been pushing his uncle over the fall, it is obvious that Ronald Strudgewick is not the murderer of his uncle."

He waited for Terhune to speak, but when the ensuing silence remained unbroken he said impatiently: "Well, sir, what have you to say about that?"

Terhune glanced diffidently at the other man. "Was it William or Henry who took the whisky and soda up to room eight?"

"Does it make any difference?"

"Not much. They are neither of them bright sparks, but, if anything, William is the more dumb."

A smile twinkled in the inspector's eyes. "It was William. But surely you are not doubting *his* honesty?"

"Not for a moment. But all the same—" Terhune hesitated to put his thoughts into words.

"You would like to question the man for yourself?"

"Well—"

Longworth laughed. "You do not need to be shy of admitting that you are a doubting Thomas. We all are, about matters we haven't actually seen or heard for ourselves." He glanced at his watch. "I have some time to spare, sir, so if you would like to question William for yourself—" He rose to his feet.

"Thanks a lot, Inspector," Terhune began gratefully.

The other man shook his head. "Don't thank me, Terhune. After all, if you have the ear of somebody at Scotland Yard I should like to prove to him, through you, that we Northerners are not quite so provincial as you Southerners seem to think." If the words were pointed, Longworth's manner was not in keeping. Indeed, his smile was friendly and indulgent, such as one might expect to find on the face of a man attempting to teach the rudiments of some adult subject to a kid brother.

"And the ladies—" he murmured awkwardly.

Julia sacrificed herself. "Run along, my pet," she ordered Terhune brightly. "Mother and I will remain here. You can pass on the result of your enquiries when you return."

Terhune nodded, relieved, if the truth were told, not to have Alicia present. Nevertheless, he turned to her. "May we enter your bedroom if necessary, Mrs. MacMunn?"

"Of course you may, dear boy," she granted lazily. "And while you are there, will you bring me down that packet of cigarettes which I left on the table?"

On their way to the hotel Terhune informed the inspector of Dunstable's injunction to his staff to cultivate a bad memory, so Longworth suggested calling in at the office before looking for William. Together they entered the small room in answer to Dunstable's "Come in."

Dunstable nodded curtly at Terhune, and glanced enquiringly at the other man.

"Do you remember me, Mr. Dunstable? Detective Inspector Longworth. I visited you last February to make enquiries about two guests who had been staying here."

"Ah, yes, of course! Now I recollect you, Inspector. Won't you sit down?"

Longworth gestured protestingly. "We don't want to keep you long, but Mr. Terhune here has found your staff suffering from very bad memories, and is wondering if there is any way of curing the complaint."

The proprietor of the hotel looked at each man in turn as his surprise grew. "I don't understand, Inspector. Are you officially asking me to let *Mr. Terhune* interrogate the staff? Is Mr. Terhune a member of a police force?"

The inspector rubbed his chin. "Well, he isn't that, Mr. Dunstable, but he has—er—friends at New Scotland Yard—"

"Scotland Yard! What has Scotland Yard to do with a divorce case?"

The detective stared at Dunstable. "What's this about divorce? He is investigating a case of suspected murder."

Dunstable's face was a picture as he turned to face Terhune. "I am sorry, Mr. Terhune, I had no idea— But murder is a police job. Besides, you came with ladies, and when you spoke of two people staying here in the hotel I jumped to the conclusion that one of them was either your wife, or the husband of Mrs. MacMunn—"

Longworth roared. "That's the funniest thing I've heard in years," he gasped presently. "Your—your wife—Mrs. MacMunn's husband—" He pointed a shaking forefinger at the proprietor. "Ten to one you thought it was Mr. Terhune's wife *and* Mrs. MacMunn's husband—"

Dunstable's embarrassment was an answer in itself, but he had the grace to admit: "Well, the thought did cross my mind."

Presently, when the laughter ceased, the three men discussed business. William was sent for, and came into the office looking more lugubrious than ever—Terhune felt like asking the old chap whether he had forgotten to take his Eno's that morning!

Longworth began the interrogation. "Do you remember my coming here some months ago and asking you some questions about two guests who had been staying here—a Mr. Shilling and a Mr. Strudgewick?"

After a glance at his employer—which Dunstable answered with a quick nod—William agreed that he did remember.

"Can you also remember what happened on the night those two men were staying here?"

"Maybe! Though it's a while ago now, and things don't remain with me clear-like like they used to."

"You were on duty in the smoke-room that night, weren't you, William?"

"Aye, that I was."

"Didn't Mr. Strudgewick 'phone down to you and ask you to take a bottle of whisky and a siphon of soda up to room eight?"

"I can't remember what room it was," William mumbled. "It might have been six, 'cause that were the one Mr. Shilling was occupying."

"Mr. Shilling was in room thirteen, on the second floor," Dunstable interrupted.

"No, Mr. Dunstable, he were in room six," the waiter contradicted obstinately.

"It was during his previous visit that he occupied room six."

This time Terhune interrupted. "Had Shilling stayed at this hotel previous to the night he was here with Strudgewick?"

Dunstable nodded. "Yes, sir. He was here for two nights during the week before. He had been motoring through Yorkshire, and had had a crash just outside Thirsk. He had the car towed to a garage, and stayed here hoping to have it repaired right away. As the garage couldn't promise the car for another week Mr. Shilling went to London by train, and said he would call back for it in a week's time."

Longworth waved an impatient hand. "Let's get back to the night of February eighteen."

"One moment, Inspector," Terhune again interrupted. "Has Strudgewick ever stayed at this hotel previous to February the eighteenth?"

"No," Dunstable replied.

Terhune looked at William. "Did you serve beers to Shilling and Strudgewick immediately they arrived in the hotel?"

"Yes, sir."

"Who ordered them?"

The waiter screwed up his face in an effort to remember. "Mr. Shilling," he said at last.

"Did the two men talk much while they were in the smoke-room?"

"Bless me soul, no. They rushed in, ordered two pints, swallowed them down, and rushed upstairs."

"Very well, if you did not hear them talking how do you know that it was Strudgewick who asked you to take up the whisky and soda?"

"'Cause he said so," William replied in an aggrieved voice. "He said to me, he said: 'This is Mr. Strudgewick speaking. Will you please send a bottle of whisky and a syphon of soda up to room eight'."

"Quite! But do you know if it really was Strudgewick who spoke to you and said: 'This is Mr. Strudgewick speaking'?"

The inspector's eyebrows twitched; he rubbed his chin reflectively. William was more obtuse.

"Who else but Mr. Strudgewick would say he were Mr. Strudgewick?" he asked scornfully.

"Suppose Mr. Shilling had said he was Mr. Strudgewick, would you have known that he wasn't?"

The question took time to sink in. At last came a mumbled "No."

"But confound it, Mr. Terhune, does it matter who telephoned the order? The vital factor is this; that when William here took the order up he saw both men together in room eight, playing cards."

"That is what I want to know—did he see *both* men in the bedroom?"

The other three men waited anxiously for the answer on which so much depended. Meanwhile the waiter screwed up his face in a dozen different grimaces, he pulled at his puffy, crimsoned nose, he shuffled his feet.

Dunstable was the first to lose patience.

"Surely you can answer the questions, William," he said, sharply.

"I can and I can't," William mumbled.

"You can and you can't! What the devil does that mean?"

"It means this, Mr. Dunstable, that now it's put to me, in that there manner, I don't know that I can 'xactly say I seen both men with me own eyes though they was both there without a doubt."

"What's that?" Longworth barked angrily. "The last time I was here you told me that *both* men were in the bedroom."

"Well, so they was," William confirmed querulously. "They was both there, but I ain't *seen* them *both*. I only seen one of 'em."

"The saints preserve you, you silly old fool!" the inspector shouted furiously. "If you only saw one of the two men where was the other?"

"In the bathroom," Terhune suggested calmly.

The waiter was delighted to find an ally. "That's right, mister. That's where he was an' all. In the bathroom. They was talking to one another."

"It's time we got this situation straightened out," Longworth announced ominously. Then to the proprietor specifically: Mrs. MacMunn said we might enter her bedroom."

"Come along then," Dunstable said, promptly, leading the way to the door.

In a body the four men ascended the stairs to the first floor, and along the passage to room number eight, which they entered. There was nothing very extraordinary about the room and its furniture, except perhaps the small table which stood between the two windows which overlooked the garden. In the left-hand corner of the room farthest from the door was another door which led into the bathroom of which William had spoken.

The inspector took charge of the situation. "Try to remember what this room was like when you entered it on the night of February eighteen, where who was sitting, and so on."

William's dullish eyes moved slowly from left to right as his glance circled the room. Presently he said: "The blinds were down."

"Of course they were down," Dunstable exclaimed sharply. "It was night."

The inspector made a swift gesture to the proprietor to keep silent, and another to Terhune to pull down the blinds. Meanwhile he himself snapped on the electric light.

"What else?"

The waiter pointed to the small table—used ordinarily as a writing table. "That was in the middle of the room—"

This time Terhune did not wait for a sign from the detective. He moved to the table, bundled the things that were on it on to the floor, and moved it to the spot at which William was pointing a wavering finger.

"That chair was here, this side of the table," William went on—and if the tone of his voice were any indication of his thoughts he was beginning to enjoy his little moment in the limelight. "One of the guests was sitting on it, with his back to the door. Mr. Shilling it was."

"Would you mind, Mr. Dunstable," the inspector suggested.

Dunstable sat down.

"A pack of cards was on the table," William went on patiently. "They were playing one of them two-handed patience games, for some of the cards were laid out in front of Mr. Shilling, and the rest opposite."

"As though Mr. Strudgewick had been sitting on the foot of the bed?"

"Yes, sir. On the right-hand side of the table was an ashtray. Mr. Shilling was smoking a cigarette, while Mr. Strudgewick's cigarette, still alight, was on the opposite side of the ashtray, like Mr. Strudgewick had just put it down—like this—" and William illustrated his meaning. "I had to move the ashtray to put the tray with the whisky and soda down on the table. Like this." Once more the waiter added action to his words.

"Where was Strudgewick all this time?" Longworth questioned briskly.

William turned and stared at the bathroom door. "In there. He was washing."

"How do you know?"

"The door was open enough for me to see that the light was on, and to hear the water running into the hand-basin."

"What happened when you brought in the tray with the drinks?"

"Mr. Shilling told me to put the tray down on the table, like I said. Then he called out: 'The whisky's arrived, Ronald'."

"And then?"

"I went out again."

"Did you hear Strudgewick answer? I mean, did he say anything about the whisky, or something to the effect that he was just coming?"

The waiter shook his head. "No, sir. I didn't hear him say nothing."

"Now think carefully, William. Although you know that Strudgewick was in the bathroom, probably washing his hands, did you actually see him, or any part of him?"

There was a long, interminable pause.

"Now you come to put it like that, sir," the waiter presently answered, "no, sir, I didn't."

A startled expression flashed across the inspector's pale blue eyes.

Chapter Eleven

A s soon as the four men had re-arranged Alicia's bedroom so as to leave it as they had found it Terhune and Longworth rejoined the ladies. As they sat down Alicia asked excitedly: "Have you discovered anything important?"

The inspector answered. "Enough, ma'am, to make me apologize to Mr. Terhune—and to Burton—on the one hand, and to make me lose faith in myself on the other." Having made that announcement he went on to give an account of their experiment in room eight.

"I blame myself for not having checked up on William's story," he finished up. "But I believed Burton's theory to be so preposterous that I had no reason to suspect the reliability of William's positive assertion of having seen both men in room eight at ten o'clock."

Then another thought prompted him to continue: "Mind you, I'm still not agreeing that Ronald Strudgewick had any hand in the death of his uncle, but I do admit that that possibility is not one to be dismissed as casually as I originally dismissed it.

"The position is this," he went on. "A careful check of times shows that the only person left who can supply an absolute cast-iron alibi for Ronald Strudgewick appears to be Mr. Robert Shilling. Now, if Strudgewick was guilty of the crime it is evident that Shilling must deliberately have played a definite role in contriving a false alibi—the telephone call for the whisky, when he called himself Strudgewick; his arrangement of the smoking cigarette to make it appear as if it had only been put down a few moments previously; the running of the water in the bathroom, and the call to Strudgewick announcing that the whisky had come up! These things, if done deliberately—with malice aforethought, one might add—constitute almost a partnership in the killing of James Strudgewick; enough of a partnership, I suggest, to justify Shilling's being charged as a principal in the first degree. Technically, this is a more serious charge even than that of accessory before the act, though the *maximum* punishment is the same in both cases."

"And the maximum is that for which the criminal himself is liable—in this case, the death penalty," Terhune pointed out to Alicia and Julia.

"That's right," Longworth confirmed. "I see that you know something of our criminal laws, Mr. Terhune. Well now, sir, I ask you: would Shilling have risked being hanged just so that his friend might murder James Strudgewick presumably for the sake of inheriting about sixty thousand pounds? I don't think so, sir. To my way of thinking, ordinary friendship isn't that strong."

"'Greater love hath no man than this, that a man lay down his life for his friends,'" Alicia burbled.

The inspector smiled drily. "Not when it comes to a hanging matter, ma'am. Nothing will make me think that Shilling took that risk for nothing."

Julia spoke. "Before we speak of Shilling's risk, what about Strudgewick's risk? Would he have taken many risks, even for the sake of sixty thousand pounds?"

"What is your meaning, miss?"

"To profit from Shilling's alibi would have entailed the risk of being seen away from the bedroom, which would have completely ruined the alibi which we are assuming the two men so carefully planned?"

Longworth nodded his head. "There's something in what you say, miss, but Mr. Terhune reckons that Ronald Strudgewick could have left the hotel without being seen."

"How?"

Terhune answered for himself. "Have you looked out of the window of your mother's bathroom?"

"No."

"We did, just now. There's a shed of some sort right below it. Ronald Strudgewick could have stepped off the bathroom window ledge on to the roof of the shed, and thence down to the passage which leads from the hotel garage to the road. He could have regained the bedroom by the same route."

"What of the car he used to travel to Hawley Green—"

"I am assuming he used Shilling's car, Julie."

"I know, Theo, but presumably Shilling's car was still in the garage which repaired it. Would the people there have delivered it over to another person? If they did, and that other person was Strudgewick, then somebody at the garage should be able to identify him, and give evidence that he was *not* in the hotel at ten o'clock, because he was collecting Mr. Shilling's car."

"Mr. Terhune has the answer to that puzzle," Longworth said, a trifle despondently.

"Maybe Shilling telegraphed the garage to have the car waiting for him at the station," Terhune explained. "Perhaps that is why they reached the hotel so soon after their arrival at the station."

"And left the car in one of the street car-parks?"

Terhune nodded. "Probably the one just round the corner. He could have nipped into the car, driven it to Hawley Green, killed his uncle, and returned it to the car-park later on without any one's being much the wiser. As a matter of fact, Shilling himself drove the car into the hotel garage at eleven-thirty that night—William opened the doors for him—so it hardly seems likely he would have collected it from the repair garage at that time of night."

"I can soon make any inquiries from the repair garage that may be necessary to check your theory," Longworth pointed out. "But I am not yet satisfied that they are necessary."

"My dear man! What nonsense! Of course they are!" Alicia exclaimed indignantly. "Is there any doubt but that those two awful men conspired together to kill that poor Mr. James Strudgewick?"

Longworth smiled indulgently. "With all respect, ma'am, I come back to the question of the part Mr. Shilling is supposed to have played in the killing of Strudgewick." He turned to Julia. "You know Robert Shilling, don't you, miss?"

Julia shrugged. "*Know* him? No. He is just a passing acquaintance."

"Well, miss, would you know whether he is a poor man, now, ready to do anything for money—"

"No," she broke in. "He is comparatively wealthy—by that I mean that he was wealthy before the death of James Strudgewick."

"So there is no question of his sharing the spoils, as it were?"

"I should think it most unlikely."

"Very well, miss. Then have you seen enough of him to judge whether he has the guts—beg pardon, ma'am, but that's the word for it—the guts to risk his neck rigging an alibi for a friend?"

Julia was silent.

"Well, miss?"

She gestured uncertainly. "I can only tell you, Inspector, that Robert Shilling does not impress me as being the type of man who would do that unless he had a most urgent motive for doing so, a motive of a kind I cannot even begin to imagine."

"Thank you, miss." Longworth nodded his head as if her opinion confirmed his own.

An embarrassing pause followed, which was presently broken by Alicia.

"What are you going to do about our discoveries, Inspector?"

"Nothing, ma'am."

Alicia was shocked. "Nothing! My dear man—"

"Nothing meanwhile, ma'am, that is to say," Longworth hastily corrected. "You see, ma'am, there is nothing much the police can do as long as Mr. Shilling is ready to swear that Ronald Strudgewick didn't leave this hotel on the night his uncle died. Unless the police could prove that Shilling's evidence is not to be trusted, or produce evidence to contradict the alibi—by that, I mean, produce a witness who, for instance, would swear that he saw Strudgewick in Hawley Green round about 10 o'clock p.m. that night—unless we can do that the jury would be bound to find in favour of the defence."

"Why?" Alicia asked.

"Because it is their duty, ma'am. A man arrested for a crime doesn't have to prove his innocence; the police have to prove him guilty. So, unless they can do that beyond all reasonable doubt, the jury finds him innocent."

"Couldn't a few tentative inquiries be made as to whether any one in Hawley Green did chance to see Ronald Strudgewick?" Terhune suggested.

"I think you forget that such general inquiries were made when Burton first accused Ronald Strudgewick."

"Of course."

Again a pause. This time the inspector rose suggestively to his feet. "I think, Mr. Terhune, that inquiries can only be reopened if some evidence is produced to incriminate Shilling. For instance, if there were reason to suspect that he has a criminal record—"

Terhune shook his head. "Not a hope!" he exclaimed despondently. But this definite statement he amended. "At least, so far as I know. But then I scarcely know the fellow."

"Perhaps a word to your friend at New Scotland Yard might produce a useful result," Longworth insinuated slyly. "But now, if you will excuse me, ma'am—miss—"

To Terhune he held out his hand. "I'm glad to have met you, Mr. Terhune. You have proved to me that Burton's theory isn't quite so far-fetched as I once believed, thanks to that fool of a waiter, but

I still think that the idea of Strudgewick and Shilling conspiring to do away with the old uncle is a bit too fantastic for the police to swallow without something more substantial than theories to support it. You do understand?"

Longworth's manner was too pleasant for any one not to understand. Terhune warmly grasped the proffered hand. "Of course I do, Inspector."

"Thanks. But, of course, if anything significant regarding Shilling should turn up you will let me hear from you?"

"That's understood."

With a last gesture to the ladies Longworth departed.

II

On their way back to Bray-in-the-Marsh, Alicia, Julia and Terhune discussed the death of James Strudgewick at much length. Now that the interest of their journey north was at an end Alicia began to accept the inspector's opinion, and poured ridicule on the possibility of Shilling's having been an accessory before the fact.

"I'm quite sure that that nice Mr. Shilling wouldn't have had anything to do with a murder," she protested. "Oh! I know you didn't care for him, Julia, but if everybody you didn't like was a prospective murderer nobody's life would be safe."

Julia, wilfully obstinate, snapped back at her mother. "At least I don't go to the opposite extreme and make a bosom friend of any one who is willing to fawn and flatter one just because one is an Honourable."

"Really, Julia, sometimes you are almost coarse," Alicia remonstrated plaintively. "I do not suppose that Mr. Shilling even knew I was an Honourable. From what you say one would think that I introduced the fact on every conceivable occasion."

Julia softened. "No, Mother dear, that isn't true. You are the least snobbish person I know. My complaint is that you make friends too easily. With you new friends, not old friends, are the best, just because they are new and will let you chatter on to your heart's content. I like to know people very well before I make confidants of them. But we were talking of Robert Shilling, Mother dear, not of you. There were several people in the hotel at Las Palmas who had gone out on the same ship with us, from one of whom Shilling could have learned all about you."

"One would think he was a confidence trickster, or something of that sort."

"That is not what I mean. I think he was a vulgar little man with plenty of money who purposely sought your company so that he could boast of his friend 'The Honourable Mrs. MacMunn— daughter of the Lord Fulchester, you know?' I can just hear his nasty, soft voice saying the words."

For once Mrs. MacMunn spoke sagely. "Even if he is a snob, Julia, that does not mean to say that he is willing to become a murderer's accessory or accomplice, or whatever the word is."

Julia nodded. "I quite agree, and two months ago—if I could have remembered the nasty little man—I should certainly have denied that he had the guts, as Inspector Longworth said—" Julia laughed softly, "the guts to risk severe punishment and even death to help another man inherit sixty thousand pounds."

"Well, then—"

"When Theo and I met him again a few weeks ago I found him changed. I sensed something about him which I couldn't identify or analyse—I don't think I can do that even now—but it was something deep, something quite different from the reactions which I had from the shallow-minded man we met in Las Palmas."

"Stuff and nonsense! I believe you are developing a neurotic imagination. It's time you—"

"Time I travelled more?" Julia interrupted bitterly. "Before my brain becomes atrophied through lack of stimulation?"

"I don't know what you mean," her mother retorted crossly. "What I was about to say— Dear me! Now you've made me forget what I was going to say."

"Never mind, Mother. I still say that Shilling has changed from what he was when we first met him two years ago." She turned to Terhune. "I suppose you didn't have the impression that he had something on his mind?"

"I thought he was uncertain whether to be glad or sorry he had run into us, Julie. Beyond that—well, he struck me as being the sort of man who feels more at home in a saloon bar than in a ballroom."

"Then do you think now that Strudgewick didn't murder his uncle?" she demanded sharply.

"I don't know what to think," Terhune confessed. "Frankly, Julie, I am keeping an open mind. There are a lot of suspicious facts—theoretically suspicious—which point to Strudgewick as being a murderer, but almost as many to the contrary.

"For instance, if Strudgewick and Shilling conspired to kill the uncle, it must be assumed that they made arrangements some time beforehand—probably two weeks—"

"Why must that be assumed?" Alicia asked in a surprised voice. "And why do you think the time to have been two weeks?"

"Because Shilling's excuse for visiting Thirsk was that of collecting a car which was being repaired after a smash. The accident had taken place a week previously. Add to that the time taken to drive the car up to Thirsk, and necessary arrangements to leave his home for that purpose—well, there aren't many days left out of two weeks.

"Then, of course, the day chosen for the visit to Thirsk is significant. A Thursday! To create a reasonable alibi Thursday was the only possible day they could have chosen. If the two men had arrived in Thirsk on the Wednesday, and not departed again until the Friday, one might well ask why Strudgewick did not visit his uncle on the Thursday morning, returning to Thirsk in the afternoon. Or even this: why didn't he ask his friend Shilling to drive him the odd thirty miles to Hawley Green? Still more does this argument apply to any day in the week earlier than the Wednesday.

"One could argue this, too: that Shilling had a secondary reason for taking the car up to Thirsk, and deliberately crashing it. Not only did he want to leave the car there as an excuse for revisiting the town, but the first visit gave him an opportunity of seeing whether the *Crown Hotel* had a room or rooms of the type necessary for rigging an alibi—and two adjoining bedrooms, with a connecting door and a house telephone, would have served their purpose providing the ground could be easily reached from one of them. Alternatively, Strudgewick may have spent some time in visiting all the towns within a reasonable distance of Hawley Green in the hope of finding a hotel with all the necessary requirements."

Julia laughed softly. "Your theorizing points to the guilt, not the innocence, of Strudgewick and Shilling."

"So far. I am coming now to arguments for the defence. If Strudgewick was his uncle's murderer, why, in heaven's name, didn't they catch an earlier train from King's Cross—"

"It is the second quickest train of the day, Theo."

"Yes, but in not planning to arrive in Thirsk before eight-thirty-nine they were running time very close. Surely they would not have risked Strudgewick's being too late to catch his uncle by the short cut for the sake of saving an hour's extra train journey. The ten o'clock reaches Thirsk at three-seven. That would have given them an ample margin of several hours."

"Time enough for Strudgewick to have called upon his uncle," Julia pointed out.

"Is a nephew supposed to call upon his uncle every time he approaches within thirty miles of him?—of the uncle, I mean. My nephew doesn't call upon me even when he is less than ten miles away," Alicia complained.

"True, Mother dear, but we are assuming that Strudgewick was trying to arrange an alibi that would be beyond the scope of even a faintly awkward question. In fact, darling, he probably hoped that no inquiries would ever be made, and only arranged the alibi just in case they were."

"If he did *arrange* the alibi," Terhune warned with a chuckle. "He may be as innocent of murder as a babe unborn. But I agree with you, Julie. If it had not been for Burton, Ronald Strudgewick's name might never have been even vaguely connected with the death of his uncle."

"Go on with your defence of him, my pet."

"It is mostly based on the question of time," Terhune admitted. "That, and the fact of Shilling's mentality."

"What about his mentality?"

"As we have said before, he does not appear to have sufficient courage—spontaneously—to risk his life for his friend's gain. Still less, if the crime were deliberately planned, as it must have been. Besides, he is probably too selfish to do anything without promise of some reward—and as Longworth asked—what reward is there, for a moderately rich man, to tempt him to take such risks for somebody else's gain?"

After a long pause Julia asked: "Are you going to do anything more about solving the mystery of James Strudgewick's death?"

"What is there I can do?'"

After a still longer pause Julia replied disconsolately: "Nothing, I suppose."

Alicia laughed. "At last you are talking sensibly, my dear. Now let's change the subject. When are we going to visit your Aunt Mattie—"

III

With his return to Bray, life became once more normal for Terhune. Rather to his surprise, but certainly to his great delight, Anne Quilter proved a first-rate assistant. As quick to learn, as business-like, and as deft as Julia had promised, Anne was very soon relieving him of much of the routine work of library and shop sales, so enabling him to give more time to the postal and export side, and, of an evening, to the writing of his new book, concerning which his publisher had already given him a gentle reminder.

In the stress of work, and particularly the cataloguing of the books from Tile House, he had but little time to spare for pondering over their late owner's death. As the days went by he gave less and less thought to the mystery—if it were a mystery!—until, by the end of the second week after it, the trip to Thirsk had become no more than a very pleasant memory.

About that same time Julia and Alicia left Willingham to visit Aunt Mattie for a week or two. Ten days later he received a telegram from Julia.

It read:

Urgent you come here at once to St. Andrew's Church to stay for a few days. Have booked room hotel don't fail me.

Julia.

Chapter Twelve

Terhune made a wry face. It was all very well for Julia to send him an imperious demand to join her for a few days, but he had a business to run which, for all Anne's eagerness and capability, needed his constant supervision, advice and responsibility. On the other hand, Julia was not the type of thoughtless person to overlook the possibility that his business might suffer from his neglect, so it was to be assumed that the summons really was urgent.

Perplexed as to what her reason might be in sending for him he re-read the telegram. 'Urgent you come here at once to St. Andrew's Church—' St. Andrew's Church, where? Clyst St. Mary, no doubt, for that was where Aunt Mattie lived. He glanced at the place of despatch. Yes! The telegram had been handed in at Clyst St. Mary, 9.25 a.m.

But St. Andrew's Church now—what interest could he possibly have in the church—or was it one of two or more?—at Clyst St. Mary? Could it be that the rector—or vicar—had a library to sell? But Julia had telegraphed 'urgent' and 'come at once.' The demand for haste scarcely seemed related to a library sale. Unless, of course, an offer had already been made for the books, which Julia thought he might wish to better. But, in those circumstances, wouldn't she have made some mention of books? He was sure she would have done so. Besides, why—come to St. Andrew's Church? Why not: come to the Rectory? Or—come to the Rector of St. Andrew's Church?

The more he studied Julia's telegram the more it tantalized him. Meanwhile, it obviously called for an answer, whether the answer was to be 'Arriving on such-and-such a train' or 'Impossible to join you.'

Still undecided what to do he reached for an A.B.C.—no harm could come of looking up the times of trains. After all, he would not be committed— Or so he tried to argue with himself. Ridiculously, for he knew at heart that he could not fail Julia. Only some fact of the greatest importance would have made her send the telegram, he knew. Urgent—come at once—don't fail me. The three concise sentences repeated themselves in his thoughts, again and again.

Then he made a new discovery. Having ascertained from the A.B.C. that Clyst St. Mary was not listed, he opened out a road-rail-map to look for the nearest station. In doing so he came across the village St. Andrews Church (without the possessive apostrophe which he had mentally inserted), a mile south of Clyst St. Mary. So it was some small Devon village he was to visit, not a church at Clyst St. Mary! Far from this fact dispelling the tantalizing effect of Julia's telegram, he experienced a greater urge to answer her summons. Surely a village with such a pleasant-sounding name could be nothing but an attractive one to visit.

With characteristic impulsiveness he told Anne of his proposed visit to Devon. Although his departure would mean more and harder work for her the girl was delighted at the prospect of again being left in sole charge of the shop. Having made all the necessary arrangements he hurried round to the post office to send his reply to Julia:

Leaving Waterloo three p.m. tomorrow Tuesday arriving Exeter six twenty-two.

Theo.

I I

The train arrived on time. As it came to a slow halt he saw Julia, alone, not five yards distant. She noticed him at the same instant, and waved. A moment later they were together.

He chuckled. "Not a bad guess on your part, Julia."

She did not respond to his gaiety with her usual readiness. "Yes," she agreed automatically. "Is that your only bag?"

"It has all I want for the night. I don't think I can stay longer than that," he replied, most untruthfully. He picked it up; they started walking down the platform to the exit. "Now, Julie, what's all the mystery about? Is somebody selling his library——"

She stopped abruptly, and turned towards him with an anxious face. "You didn't think that, Theo?"

"Not really. The thought did occur to me, but I decided against it."

She sighed with relief. "For a moment I was afraid——" She resumed walking, he also. "Would you mind if I don't answer your question?"

"Well, I'll be darned! Do you mean solemnly to stand there——"

"I'm not standing."

"Walk, then——and tell me I'm not to know why I travelled nearly two hundred miles, at great inconvenience——"

"Was it very inconvenient?" she asked contritely.

"Well——not very. But all the same——"

"I want you to find out for yourself——first-hand."

Julia's words naturally increased Terhune's curiosity, but they were nearing the gates so he did not question her further until they were in her car, threading their way through the streets of Exeter. Then, by way of an introductory question, as it were, he asked: "How is your mother?"

"The darling is enjoying every minute. A week ago Aunt Mattie was rummaging in the drawers of her writing desk——*escritoire* to Aunt Mattie——and came across an old photograph of a man named Dick Merridew——Admiral Merridew to you and me, Theo."

"The hero of the first landing in Italy?"

"Yes. Well, as Aunt Mattie passed the photograph over to me she announced, very proudly, that Dick Merridew was her first beau. When she heard Aunt say that Mother said: 'Mattie! How could you tell such fibs? Dick Merridew was in love with me'." Julia laughed. "They've been arguing the matter ever since. After the third day I suggested writing to the Admiral to ask him to settle the argument."

Terhune chuckled. "I can see the dear old chap's face upon receiving a letter: 'Dear Admiral, which sister did you love best, Alicia or Mattie? Please reply by return of post. Hoping this finds you as it leaves me—'"

"Ass! Personally, from some of the confidential revelations I have since heard, whenever Mother or Mattie could get me on my own without the other's being present, I suspect the gallant Admiral of having been a very gay young spark who courted them both with equal insincerity."

"Cynic!"

"Well, he didn't marry either of them, did he? Anyway, the argument had a secondary consequence: it started a spate of reminiscing which has lasted from then till now. During the last few days I have heard stories of relations of whom I have never heard before. The scandal! Theo, my pet, you wouldn't believe the scandal which two perfectly respectable married women can remember when they begin to discuss their own past, and that of their relations and friends. On several occasions my cheeks have positively burned."

"Julie! Not yours."

"Well—almost! Anyway, I have never known Mother so happy. Nor Aunt Mattie. They are just wallowing in memories. *And* revelling in them. They have been so wrapped up in the past, in fact, that they haven't even bothered their heads about me."

"Which oversight has met with your thankful approval, I take it?"

"Of course. For a few days I have been able to do just what *I* wanted to do."

"What a change!" he mocked.

"Shut up, Theo! You know very well that I devote quite a lot of my time to acting as Mother's chauffeur."

He thought it wiser to avoid controversy. "Touching upon the matter of a certain telegram—"

"I am coming to that. During the afternoons I have been going about this district visiting—anywhere. Just where the mood took me."

The slight pause, the quickening of her voice as she spoke the last sentence, convinced Terhune that Julia had checked herself just in time to prevent his hearing something she did not want him to know. However, he made no comment, and she continued:

"Yesterday afternoon I had tea in a farmhouse kept by a Mrs. Barker. She's a dear old lady, Theo, and her home, both outside and in, looks as though it is a Christmas-card picture come to life— you know the kind of picture I mean—whitewashed walls, copper utensils gleaming like gold, antimacassars, chintz curtains, honeysuckle, roses—"

"Like the inn at Farthing Toll?"

"Even more Christmas-cardy than that, Theo. Anyway, you'll see it for yourself—"

"Why?"

"Don't ask silly questions. Anyway, I was talking to Mrs. Barker when she—she started to talk to me about her daughter Maria—"

"Maria! I thought that name had died with the Duke of Wellington."

"Maria is dead, too," Julia announced abruptly.

He waited for her to continue, but she remained silent. "Well?"

"I—I thought you might like to—to hear how she died from Mrs. Barker herself."

A horrible suspicion began to pass through his mind. "Julia," he began sternly. "Have you brought me all the way from Kent to Devon just to hear the details of Maria's death?"

"Yes," she replied defiantly.

He groaned. "And you once sneered at me because you thought I had a secret ambition to become one of those perfectly odious amateur detectives."

"I was thinking of you as a novelist," she told him in a voice unusually meek for her. "Nothing is more useful to a novelist than—than human stories—"

"Is that true?"

"No."

"I thought not. There was something queer about Maria's death, wasn't there?"

"Not—not queer. At least—perhaps. It—it depends—"

"A most lucid answer! My dear Julia, if you tempt me into investigating every queer death which takes place in the length and breadth of the British Isles the Chief Constables all over the country will petition the Government to have me exiled—or chucked into jail as a blithering nuisance—obstructing the police in the execution of their duty is the charge, I believe."

"If you are sorry you came—" she began sharply.

"I'm not, and you know it, you little devil, Julie. All right! Let's have the gory details."

She shook her head. "I am not going to say another word tonight, Theo. As I told you at the station, I want you to hear everything firsthand from Mrs. Barker. I'm taking you along there tomorrow morning."

"But tonight?"

"Tonight I am reserving you for myself," she informed him coolly.

III

Soon after ten the following morning Julia called at *The Mitre*— St. Andrews Church's one and only inn: bed and breakfast, eight shillings and sixpence. Terhune was waiting outside the inn so he stepped into the car beside her with a cheerful "Good morning," to which she replied with a welcoming smile. As the car moved off he added: "Have we far to go?"

"Less than half a mile. Do you see those chimney pots on the left above the trees? They belong to Whipple Farm."

"Is the farm a large one?"

"About a hundred acres, I believe, but Mrs. Barker does not farm it herself. She rents it to a son-in-law."

"Is she a widow, then?"

"Yes. And mother of four daughters. Two dead, one in Australia, and the remaining one married to her tenant. She is also a grandmother of two boys, aged seven and thirteen."

"Does she know the reason for my visit or are you springing that on her as you did on me?"

"She does, so you do not have to beat about the bush, my pet."

Soon they reached Whipple Farm. Julia turned off the road, and passing an open five-barred gate on one side, and a notice board on the other with FARMHOUSE TEAS SERVED painted upon it, drove a few yards to a patch of grass bordering a small orchard of mixed trees, where she parked the car. Together they walked to the house, which, he believed, he would have recognized immediately from Julia's description of it. Compact, mellowed, crooked-chimneys, gable-windows, with honeysuckle and clematis covered walls, crazy paving, herbaceous borders, picturesque out buildings, a background of pasture-land, sheep, cattle—nothing was missing to make it seem as though the scene had been pulled bodily from a calendar, or the cover of a *Special Cottage and Farmhouse Number* of some illustrated magazine devoted to homes and gardens.

The interior was in keeping with the outside. Everything shone and twinkled in the cloud-speckled sunlight, and the soft breeze which blew through the narrow, flagged passage was scented with the cloying perfume of hay, and herbs, and jam-making.

The picture was one which could so easily have been spoiled by the wrong person, but no! Mrs. Barker was no less Kate Greenaway than her home; dumpy, snowy-haired, twinkling-eyed, dressed in lavender bombasine, white fichu, jet cross and chain.

"This is Mr. Terhune, Mrs. Barker."

"Good morning, sir, good morning, my dear. It is kind of you both to visit an old lady." She spoke in the soft, rich dialect of the district. "Won't you sit down? I'll ask Elsie to bring in some cider—"

"Please, no, Mrs. Barker—it is too early—" Julia protested swiftly.

"Then a cup of tea?"

"You must not worry about us, please. I have only just finished breakfast."

"Me, too," Terhune hurriedly confirmed.

Mrs. Barker began to look a little worried. "It doesn't seem right, you coming to visit me so kindly, and me not offering you anything."

"Later, perhaps, Mrs. Barker."

The promise brought the welcome back into her eyes; she nodded her head with satisfaction, and beamed in a trusting way from one to the other.

"Would you like to tell Mr. Terhune of Maria?"

The faded blue eyes saddened and watered. "The poor, dear soul!" she murmured. "God rest her in peace!" Presently she nodded her head. "What shall I tell the gentleman, my dear?"

"Everything, Mrs. Barker. I wanted Mr. Terhune to hear everything from your own lips so I have told him nothing. Begin when Maria was a little girl."

"She was my third, the dear child. She was a sweet baby. So pretty, too. Prettier than any of the others. She was born with golden hair. Every morning when I brushed it I used to compare it with sunshine—"

Terhune looked quickly at Julia, but she gave him a warning glance and shook her head, while Mrs. Barker carried on, speaking in a low voice, as she gazed out of the window. Terhune could see that she was lost in her memories, and already unconscious of the presence of strangers.

"Maria was John's favourite, though he tried to pretend she wasn't. She was mine, too, until Elizabeth came along, some years later. But there, all us mothers are the same. We all love the youngest-born the best because they are helpless without us, and when their bonny wee fingers clutch at our hands and hold on tight it is our hearts the darlings squeeze between their little fingers, not our hands.

"Maria was five when Elizabeth was born, but she was still small and tiny like me, and she used to speak with a funny lisp which used to make her sisters laugh at her, but Maria didn't mind. She was too good-natured, the pet, and though they laughed at her they loved her more than they loved each other, the naughty children. They were always quarrelling, Dora and Charlotte. Maria never quarrelled with any of her sisters, not even when Dora stole her first beau and went off to Australia with him. But then I don't ever remember her quarrelling with anyone. She was always too quiet, too good-natured. And she was such a hard worker. Poor dear Charlotte used to try and hide from me when there was a lot of work to be done, but the more Maria worked the happier she used to be."

Terhune thought the introduction was becoming somewhat monotonous, but he had not the heart to interrupt Mrs. Barker, whose pallid lips were parted in a smile which betrayed the wistful happiness afforded her by this turning back of the pages of her life.

Presently her white fingers toyed with the jet cross. "I still remember her First Communion. The Rector gave her some chocolate drops because she had learned her catechism so well. He knew she adored chocolate drops. But the next day she gave them all to Elizabeth, because Elizabeth had fallen off a hay-stack and hurt her leg."

She paused, and gazed at her visitors with an expression which seemed to suggest that she had suddenly realized their presence.

"But there, my dear," she murmured apologetically. "You don't want to hear of dear Maria's childhood, do you? But she was so sweet and we all loved her so much that we were quite sad when George started courting her. Then Dora made George marry her instead, and we didn't know whether to be sad for Maria's sake or happy for our own. Dora and George hadn't been married a month before there was another young man hanging round the door every week-end—a nice young fellow from Pinhoe, who used to ride here on one of those nasty-smelling motor-bicycles."

She nodded her head once or twice, and a note of pride crept into her voice. "It wasn't long before we all realized that Maria was likely to do well for herself by marrying her new young man, for he wasn't a farmer's boy, like George, scarcely able to earn more than enough to keep him and his family in food and clothes. No, my dears, Maria's new beau was already worth four pounds a week working for his father, and for a young man of twenty-three to earn four pounds a week at that age, and almost certain to inherit a big business when his father died, was something to make us all hope that Maria wouldn't say no to Bob when he asked her to marry him.

"She didn't. And in April, nineteen twenty-four, her dad and me saw another of our daughters married. But Maria didn't only change her surname. Bob didn't like the name of Maria. He said it was dull and old-fashioned, and wanted Maria to call herself Marian. Maria wouldn't, but she said she didn't mind Mary. So Maria Barker became Mary Shilling, and the next year—"

"Good lord!" Terhune exclaimed impulsively.

Chapter Thirteen

Although Terhune's exclamation was spontaneous, it was caused less by astonishment than by the confirmation of what he had begun to suspect from the moment of Julia's mentioning that Mrs. Barker was the widow of a farmer. But now that it was an established fact that Julia had brought him to this part of the world in order to investigate the death of Mary Shilling he became immediately less patient, and therefore less content to listen to a long, rambling narrative of which only one word in a hundred was of any real significance.

Not that Mrs. Barker's story had been wasted, he reflected a moment later, for it had adequately portrayed Mary Shilling's personality in a manner possibly more effective than the conciseness of an impersonal description. He could now imagine, quite clearly, the sort of person Mary had been—good-natured, hard-working, retiring; a younger version of Mrs. Barker herself.

But enough was as good as a feast! If he were to allow the widow to ramble on the complete recital of Mary's death might take hours.

"Your daughter, I take it, Mrs. Barker, is the Mrs. Shilling Miss MacMunn met in Las Palmas?"

"Yes." Mrs. Barker smiled sadly. "Isn't it strange that Miss MacMunn should have come here for tea yesterday without knowing that it was my daughter she had met a few years ago?"

Strange! Was it strange? Was the meeting just a coincidence? He glanced quickly at Julia, but she was very studiously looked elsewhere. Ha! A few words with Julia—later on— seemed called for, he reflected.

Meanwhile: "So your daughter married Robert Shilling in nineteen-twenty-four?"

"Yes, Mr. Terhune."

"Then they would soon have been celebrating their silver wedding had she lived. Where did they live after their marriage? In Exeter?"

Mrs. Barker nodded. "Yes. In Edinburgh Street. Bob said that, as a married man, it was necessary for him to live near his father's office because it would give him the chance of getting business for the firm. He was very hard-working, was Bob, and he soon got so much new business that his father gave him more money. Then in nineteen-thirty Bob was made a partner in the firm. Five years later his father died and Bob came into the business.

"When that happened he and Maria moved into a bigger house in Park Avenue, although Maria wanted to move into the country, near here if possible so that she could visit me and Dad and Elizabeth and all her old friends. But Bob wouldn't listen to her at that time. He said it was necessary to live in Exeter, if he wanted to keep the business up, because there was so much competition that it was only possible to get business by mixing with important people all the time."

"Were they still living in Exeter at the time of your daughter's death?"

"Oh, no! They were living down the road, a mile from here, at Tudor House. I was coming to that, Mr. Terhune."

"Why not let Mrs. Barker tell her story in her own way, Theo?" Julia suggested.

Terhune swallowed. "Please go on," he said meekly.

"Bob and Maria were still living in Exeter when war was declared," Mrs. Barker went on. "At that time Bob was thirty-nine, and expecting to be called up any day. But when the war went on and he wasn't called up because of his age he carried on with his business. Then in nineteen-forty-two—the year Dad died—he was given a very big

Government contract, and began to make so much money he didn't know what to do with it."

Terhune thought of E.P.T. and the other safeguards which were intended to prevent this happening, and wondered how the clever Mr. Shilling had managed to keep the money away from the eager fingers of the Income Tax Collectors. However, convinced that Mrs. Barker was not likely to be able to solve the mystery—which probably had no connection with the story anyway—he remained silent.

Mrs. Barker went on: "Then, when the war came to an end, Bob got another big contract for rebuilding a bombed factory in Bristol. The day after the factory was finished Bob was hurt in a motor-car accident. His injuries weren't very serious, and after two weeks in bed he was quite well again. But he said it was time he had a real holiday, so he went to some island somewhere near Africa, and took Maria with him." She turned to Julia. "That was when you met him and Maria, wasn't it, my dear?"

"Yes. I thought Mary was a dear, sweet person."

"Thank you, my dear." Mrs. Barker's lips quivered for a few moments.

"And then?" Terhune prompted.

"They returned to Exeter the following April. At that time they were still living in Park Avenue. About a month later Maria wrote to ask me whether she could come and stay with me for a week as Bob was going up to London. I was very pleased to have Maria with me for a whole week, because I hadn't seen much of her for several years—"

"Why not?"

The unexpected interruption seemed to unsettle Mrs. Barker. She gazed at Terhune with reproachful eyes which presently became blank as though she had forgotten the question, and could not remember what it was.

"Why hadn't you seen your daughter much?" Julia asked quietly, but with an angry glance towards Terhune.

"Well, my dear, Bob didn't much care to visit us since—since —you see, we are farming folk, and Bob got to know so many big people." Mrs. Barker explained sadly.

Julia and Terhune exchanged significant glances. So they had made no mistake in believing Shilling to be a snob.

"Of course, Maria hadn't changed," Mrs. Barker went on, mumbling a little so that it was not too easy to distinguish what she said. "Whenever she came on her own she would always give a hand with the washing-up and other housework, and amusing Elizabeth's children. But Bob didn't like her to come too often, even without him, so she didn't, because Maria was not a person to upset her husband by doing what he didn't want her to do. Of course, I understood Bob's reasons—as he said, it wasn't good for a business man to let it be known that he had married a farmer's daughter."

"The swine!" Terhune muttered, but not loud enough for Mrs. Barker to hear him. He waited for the old lady to continue, but when she remained quiet, staring dreamily out of the window, he prompted: "Your daughter came to stay with you for a week—"

Mrs. Barker sighed. "Yes, my dears. Bob was in the habit of going to London three or four times a year, on business, and usually Maria went with him although she was not fond of London. But this time she came to me instead because she wasn't feeling very well." She shook her head several times and continued sadly: "If only she could have known."

"Known what?"

"I don't know," she replied vacantly.

Terhune grimaced. Julia, sensing his impatience, asked quietly: "Did something happen to Bob during that week?"

"Yes, my dear. When Bob returned to Exeter he told Maria that he was thinking of doing some business in London, which would mean him going there more often, and as Maria didn't like going there would she like to move out into the country, nearer to me."

Again Julia and Terhune exchanged glances as a similar thought occurred to each of them. Had the first meeting between Veronica and Shilling taken place during that week?

"Did Mrs. Shilling welcome her husband's suggestion?"

"Oh, yes! She was longing to get back to the open country again. She told Bob she wouldn't mind him going to London without her if she could be near me and Elizabeth. So Bob and Maria began to look for a house not far from here. They couldn't find one good enough to suit Bob until he came across Pratts Cottages. One day they were offered at an auction sale, so Bob bought all three, and rebuilt them into one house which he called Tudor House. As soon as it was all ready Bob and Maria left Exeter and moved into Tudor House."

"When was that?"

"About August."

"Last year?"

"No, my dear. August two years ago."

"I see. And once they had moved into Tudor House did Mr. Shilling begin to visit London more frequently?"

Mrs. Barker nodded. "He used to spend a long week-end there, about every third week. But Maria didn't mind him going now that she was near me, and Elizabeth and her children, and all the people she had known when she was young." Her eyes misted. "I think the few months she lived at Tudor House were the happiest she had known for many years."

"Do you mean that she was not—not happy with her husband?"

"Oh, no, my dears! I don't mean that. Maria was very fond of Bob. But she had always wanted children, and when she didn't have any of her own she doted on Elizabeth's two boys instead, and spoiled them no end."

Once more Mrs. Barker broke off to look forlornly out of the window. She seemed in no hurry to continue. Terhune glanced enquiringly at Julia.

Julia nodded. "Won't you tell Mr. Terhune of the night your daughter died?"

The old lady's lips quivered. "If he wants to hear, my dear."

"But don't you want him to know what happened?"

"I don't know. Sometimes I do—but it makes me so sad—"

"Poor Mrs. Barker!" Julia murmured sympathetically. "Please go on. It happened last September, didn't it?"

The frail, white head nodded. "On a Wednesday night. She had spent the afternoon and evening with me, and went home about nine-thirty. That was the last I saw of her—alive. The next morning—the next—morning—" She turned pathetically to Julia. "Won't you please tell your friend, my dear. I can't abear to tell of it again—so soon—"

"The next anyone saw of Mary Shilling was the following morning, about twelve o'clock. At eight-forty-five the maid rang the bell for breakfast. When her mistress did not come down to the dining-room, Ada—the maid—went up to Mrs. Shilling's bedroom and knocked upon the door. When she didn't get an answer she opened the door and went in. To her surprise she saw that the bed hadn't been slept in. Although Ada was surprised she wasn't particularly worried or alarmed—"

"Why not?"

"Knowing that Mrs. Shilling had spent the previous day here she thought that Mrs. Barker might have been taken unwell and that Mrs. Shilling had stayed the night to keep her mother company—"

"Poor dear Maria had done that several weeks before when I was taken poorly," Mrs. Barker broke in tremulously.

Terhune nodded understandingly. "Go on, Julia."

"About twelve o'clock the cook, Mrs. Tregarth, went into the garage to fetch some paraffin for the oil cooking range. There, still in her car, she found Mrs. Shilling."

Terhune's lips formed the word: "Dead?" and Julia nodded.

"You did say—in *her* car?"

"Yes. Mrs. Shilling drove a small Austin."

He was vaguely surprised. Evidently his mental picture of Mary Shilling was, in some respects, inaccurate. Had he made a guess on the subject he would have said that she was too old-fashioned in outlook to like cars, still less drive one of her own.

Something of his thoughts must have revealed themselves on his face, for Mrs. Barker said: "Maria had varicose veins. She never walked more than she had to."

The explanation satisfied his ego. He was sure she had driven a car only to save her legs, and not from inclination.

"Bob had a car, too," Mrs. Barker went on. "A big, very fast one." There was a note in her voice which made her hearers believe that she was rather proud of being the mother-in-law of a man able to afford two cars.

He turned back to Julia. "What was the cause of death, Julia? Heart failure?"

Julia shook her head. "No, Theo. Carbon-monoxide poisoning."

The answer startled him. Subconsciously he pursed his lips to whistle, but choked it back in response to a warning glance from Julia. All the same—

With a quick glance in the direction of Mrs. Barker to make sure that the old lady was not looking directly at him, his lips once more formed a silent question. "Suicide?"

Julia emphatically shook her head.

"It was an accident," she said aloud. "What must have happened is that Mrs. Shilling misjudged the distance, and caused the car to hit the garage wall with an unexpected bump which jerked her head sideways against the window hard enough to knock her unconscious. There were signs of a bruise on her forehead, close to her right temple. Unfortunately the engine of the car continued to run, and before Mrs. Shilling could recover consciousness the garage began to fill with gas which first kept her unconscious and then poisoned her."

The explanation did not satisfy him. "That couldn't have happened as long as the doors of the garage remained open."

"I know, Theo, but unfortunately the garage doors were very wide, so that it was only necessary to open one side for the Austin to get through."

"Well?"

"It was thought that Mrs. Shilling drove into the garage without seeing that the door was properly secure. While she was still un con-scious the wind must have banged the door to, and as the lock was of the Yale type it automatically secured itself."

"When you said just now: 'it was thought that Mrs. Shilling did so-and-so,' were you referring to the inquest?"

"Yes."

"What was the verdict?"

"Accidental death."

"Was the engine still running when the—when Mrs. Shilling was found in the morning?"

"No, but as the petrol tank was empty it was believed that the engine ran until the tank emptied."

Terhune frowned. "That might not have happened until early morning."

"I know."

"Do you mean to say that it was possible for an engine to run all night, or at any rate for a number of hours, without somebody's hearing it? Where was Shilling?"

"In London. He had left Tudor House the previous Saturday for a week's stay in London."

"Did neither the maid nor the cook live in?"

"Both did."

"Surely one or the other ought to have heard the car running. A stationary car can kick up quite a racket, at any time, especially in the middle of the night, and especially in a garage. The throb is a bit like that of a ship's engines—you can't get away from the noise."

"Some people can sleep through an earthquake, Theo, but it so happens that the domestic bedrooms were in a separate wing one end of the house, while the garage was a semi-detached building at the other. But you can see the house for yourself. It is still empty, and Mrs. Barker has said that we may borrow the keys if we want to look over the place."

"Yes, my dears, do please go along and see for yourselves," Mrs. Barker urged anxiously.

So it was arranged, and a few minutes later Terhune and Julia were driving towards Tudor House.

"Why is the old lady so keen for us to look over the house?" he asked.

"I am afraid that the poor old soul is not really satisfied that her daughter's death was accidental, and she is hoping that we shall confirm that it was—she has implicit faith in you, Theo."

"Damn the newspapers!" he exclaimed crossly. "But how does Mrs. Barker think Mary Shilling died, if not by accident? Surely to goodness she's not been infected by the murder bug?"

"No. Of course, she won't say so openly, but I am sure she is suspicious that Mary committed suicide."

"Oh ho! Had rumour began to reach Mary Shilling of that blonde-headed wench, Veronica?"

"A woman in love doesn't need to hear rumours to realize that her man has become infatuated with another woman," Julia moralized in a low, serious voice. "Mrs. Barker didn't intend to say anything about Mary's suspicions of her husband—out of loyalty to Mary on the one hand, and because, on the other, despite everything, I think she has a soft spot for that cad of a son-in-law. All the same, she said enough to me yesterday to make me believe that she thinks Mary Shilling killed herself."

"Perhaps she did, Julie."

"No," Julia denied sharply. "No. She was not the woman to kill herself. She had too sincere a Christian faith to kill herself, however strong the temptation. I don't mean she was a religious fanatic, or anything of that sort, Theo, but she was a genuine Christian, who practised Christian principles, and would have died before doing anything against her conscience, such as committing suicide—or divorcing her husband."

"Just what are you getting at, Julie?" he questioned, astonished by the emphasis in her voice.

"Nothing," she told him quickly. "Nothing."

"Then what—"

"I don't know. And that is the truth, Theo. All I know is, that from the first the news of Mary Shilling's death shocked me. She was so nice. So utterly simple, naïve, loyal. And so healthy. And comparatively young. When I saw the kind of woman Robert Shilling had married I almost hated him for the insult he offered to the memory of his first wife. That cheap, vulgar little chit—how can men be so beastly, and so blind? Can't you ever distinguish between tinsel and gold?"

Embarrassed by her emotion he remained awkwardly silent, so presently she continued in a quieter voice: "Of course, you have guessed that I didn't meet Mrs. Barker by accident. It's all come from that absurd argument between Mother and Aunt Millie about the Admiral. Between them they drove me out of the house. I started driving into Exeter for the sake of something to do. Then, one day, I happened to see a board: 'Repairs by Somebody and Shilling,' which reminded me that the Shillings had come from Exeter. Out of sheer boredom I decided to find out about Mary Shilling's death.

"When I found out that she had died in tragic circumstances I knew that I should be sending you a telegram sooner or later. But I thought I would find out all I could, first. And that is about all, my pet. On Sunday I met Mrs. Barker for the first time. As soon as I learned of her secret fears I didn't delay any longer. I told her all about you—though she didn't need any telling, because she already knew—and promised that you should come here and prove to us both that Mary did *not* commit suicide."

"My dear girl, how on earth am I to do that?"

"I don't know, my pet, but I am sure you will."

She spoke sincerely, with confidence, and without any hint of mockery. The genuine compliment both pleased and dismayed him. For how could he hope persistently to live up to the reputation which his first 'flukey' successes had established?

"I am beginning to wonder why the authorities trouble to hold inquests," he said, grumblingly. "Half the people seem to have no faith in the verdict anyway. You have seen something of police methods, Julie. You know that they are a conscientious body of hard-working men. Personally, if the police are satisfied that a death is accidental, so am I."

"So am I, in this instance, Theo, and Mrs. Barker wants to be, but isn't. I think she believes that the police were being generous for her sake—"

"Nonsense. However much the police might like to keep certain things secret for the sake of other people, they dare not do so. They have a duty to do—a duty to the public generally."

"I recognize that argument, of course, my pet, and wouldn't dream of contradicting it. But you cannot expect a poor old lady like Mrs. Barker to share our confidence. Now, if you investigate the death of Mary Shilling and are satisfied that it is accidental she will believe you and be easier in her mind—"

"Julia MacMunn, you are a liar and a scheming little minx," he accused. "The real truth is, isn't it, that you think Mary Shilling's death was neither suicide, nor accidental?"

"Yes, Theo," she admitted solemnly. "That is the truth."

Chapter Fourteen

H e began to lecture her on the unreasonableness of assuming that every death by misadventure was necessarily homicide, but she quickly brought the homily to an end.

"There's Tudor House," she interrupted, waving her hand in the direction of a rather rambling sort of a building which lay well back from the road at the far end of a gravelled drive, and quite a quarter of a mile away from any other house.

An inspection of the exterior, first from the road, and then from the drive as Julia drove along it towards the house, gave Terhune the impression that the work of conversion had been well done. It was difficult, if not impossible, to realize that the main building had once consisted of three cottages, for the front façade had been designed in such a way as to radiate, as it were, from the one and only entrance, which was situated in the centre of the block. But Terhune was less interested in the main building—for round about Bray-in-the-Marsh the sight of cottage-into-house was a familiar one —than in the two, modern additions which Shilling had built.

The nearer of these, as they approached from the east, was in the form of a wing, built at right angles, and standing so far back towards the rear of the main block that it seemed as if only a narrow passage connected the old with the new. Like the other part, this wing consisted of a ground floor, and a first floor, built immediately beneath a high sloping tile roof, and lighted by large dormer windows.

The second building, on the west side, was strangely incongruous. Like the converted cottages, it stood parallel with the road, but it consisted only of a ground floor, had a flat roof, and two doors which, although Tudor in design and artificially aged, remained obviously the doors of an ultra-modern garage.

Julia brought her car to a stop outside the garage.

"Shall we examine the garage first?"

He nodded. "We might as well. Have you the keys?"

She passed them to him. They stepped out of the car and slowly approached the doors. As they did so Terhune observed the two small concrete posts which had been sunk into the drive level with the hinges of the doors. Each post had a strong iron hook attached to it.

He pointed these posts out to Julia. "Do you see those, Julie?"

She nodded. "What about them, Theo? They are for holding the doors open. There are the eyes on the doors close to the ground."

"I know. If you were driving your car into the garage wouldn't you take the precaution of seeing that the doors—or at any rate the door by which you were entering—was secured to the post so that it could not bang against the side of the car as you passed?"

"I think I should, unless the day was absolutely calm."

"Yes, but if the door banged to of its own accord we must assume that the day—or night, rather—was not so calm as all that. On the other hand, I don't think we need give too much importance to that point. Mrs. Shilling might have been tired, or just neglectful, or she might have thought she had fastened the door, but didn't do so properly, so that the vibration of the ground as the car passed by caused the hook to slip out of the eye."

Julia made a non-committal exclamation, but when she kept silent, evidently not feeling disposed to argue, he opened the left-hand door. Together they entered the garage.

There was nothing about the interior to excite particular interest. The right-hand wall was occupied by a work-bench, on which stood two worn outer-covers, and one inner-tube, two empty five-gallon oil drums, a broken picture-frame, and two or three discarded household utensils. Apart from these few things—and a considerable quantity of dust and spiders'-webs—the place was empty.

High up in the north wall was a small window through which was to be seen a glimpse of formal gardens, uncared-for and overgrown. Towards the back of the left-hand, the west, wall was a door connecting the garage with the house.

Terhune stared for some time at this connecting-door. "Even if Mary Shilling had not felt strong enough to reach the outer door she might have managed to get as far as that one," he said presently.

"Not if she had had to drive her car into the right-hand side of the garage, and with her husband's car in the way to impede her."

"Was Shilling's car in the garage then?" he asked quickly.

"Yes. He usually went by train to London. According to Mrs. Barker he used to say that a car in London was more bother than it was worth."

"He's right about that. But the point is—on which side of the garage did the two cars stand? Personally I should guess that the smaller car was on the left."

"Why?"

"Because it would have taken up less room and allowed easier ingress and egress through the connecting door." He glanced at the north wall. "I think I have guessed rightly, Julie. Look at that line of chipped plaster work about a foot or so above the ground."

"Well?"

"The distance from the ground, and the length, corresponds roughly with that which the fender of a small car would have made. Probably that happened when she banged against the wall, and made herself unconscious."

"But that is the side nearer to the connecting door," she pointed out.

He nodded. "True enough! Then the bump must certainly have been a hard one to have knocked her unconscious long enough to have been poisoned by the exhaust." He gazed around. "The area of this garage isn't small, Julie. It must have taken some time to fill it—"

"It may have been running all night."

"I know, but why should she have remained unconscious for so long? On the other hand, she was inside the car, wasn't she?"

"Yes."

"Therefore the space she was in was, of itself, more or less enclosed. And with the exhaust immediately beneath—I suppose—" He broke short.

"You suppose what, Theo?"

"It was just an exaggerated notion—rather fantastic—"

"But what was it?" she demanded irritably.

"If both cars had been running—"

"Theo!" Julia gazed steadily at her companion—there was a suspicion of a twinkle in her eyes. "Are you beginning to change your opinion about Mary Shilling's death?"

"No, but if I am here to investigate all the possibilities and probabilities—well!" He gestured, at first vaguely and then irritably. "But if the two cars had been running surely somebody would have heard them." He started. "Julia!"

"Well?"

"Would you mind making an experiment?" Taking her consent for granted he went on: "Will you drive the car in here, leave the engine running, and close the door while I go up to the maids' room and see if I can hear it?"

"Shall I stay in the car?"

"Until it becomes unpleasant. You might time how long it takes for that to happen."

Among the bunch of keys which Mrs. Barker had entrusted to them he found one to fit the connecting door. He passed into the house. A depressing experience, for, like the garage, it was empty and desolate. Dust and spiders'-webs were everywhere. There was a musty odour hanging about the rooms which reminded him vividly of the time he had visited the House with Crooked Walls before Doctor Salvaterra had taken it over. His footsteps echoed weirdly on the bare boards. In spite of this, however, there was something about the architecture of the house which made him think that, furnished and cared-for, it could be a cosy, friendly sort of a place.

He passed through the house into the farther wing, which housed the kitchen, a sitting-room, and bedrooms above. There he listened attentively for the sound of Julia's car, but heard nothing. He tried both bedrooms, but the result was the same. He heard the raucous chatter of a distant tractor, the whistle of a train some way off, and nearer to, the baa-ing of sheep, the bleating of lambs, and the exhaust of a passing motor-cycle. But of the engine of Julia's car —nothing. Perhaps in the still of the night it might have been distinguishable, he reflected, but scarcely enough to awaken two sound sleepers.

He retraced his steps, and directly he entered the main building he became aware of a throbbing noise. He rejoined Julia in the garage, and found that the unpleasant smell of fumes was already hanging about to a noticeable degree, though not, perhaps, sufficiently to induce a toxic condition.

"How are you feeling, Julia?"

In reply she caught hold of his hand, turned off the engine, and hurried him to the door, which she flung open with an air of relief.

"Glad to get into the fresh air again, Theo. And you haven't been away fifteen minutes yet." She breathed in the fresh air with deep gulps. "Did you hear anything?"

"Not a sound."

She laughed sharply, unhumorously. "We haven't done much good by coming here, have we, my pet?"

He grinned. "You are impatient, Julie. Did you expect everything to reveal itself to us just by our coming here and inspecting the garage where Mary Shilling died?"

"What else is there to look for?" she asked disconsolately. "It seems to me that her death could have been accidental, it could have been suicide, or it could have been murder. Personally, I am still convinced that it was not suicide, for the reasons I have given, but are we going to be able to reassure poor Mrs. Barker's mind on that score?"

He pointed to the connecting door. "Do you know if that door was locked?"

"I believe I remember Mrs. Barker saying that this door was never locked because the maids were in the habit of using it to replenish their paraffin supply from a big drum kept in here. Why?"

"Because, if I were planning to commit suicide I should take care to see that all doors were locked so that nobody should accidentally barge in and find me before I was absolutely and truly dead. On the other hand, if I had proposed to kill Mrs. Shilling by rendering her unconscious first, then leaving her to be poisoned to death by the exhaust, I should certainly have seen to it that the door was locked, in case somebody rescued the victim before she was dead, which might result in my being exposed as a potential murderer. If the door was unlocked, Julie, then that fact points to the death as being accidental."

Her eyes shone. "Where your argument deals with suicide I agree with you. But suppose that somebody, planning to kill Mary Shilling in such a manner as to make the death appear accidental, had purposely left the door unlocked in order to avoid any suspicions of homicide being aroused, wouldn't that fact point to the murderer's having sufficient information about the household to know that, firstly, the door was usually kept unlocked; secondly, that there were only the two maids to be considered, and, thirdly, that the noise of the engine's running was not likely to be heard from their bedrooms?"

"All of which is meant to add up to—Robert Shilling?"

"Well, doesn't it?" she asked quickly. Before he could reply she continued earnestly. "Listen, my pet. You haven't forgotten your first meeting with Robert Shilling, have you? Do you remember how eager he was to talk to me until I asked about his wife? Without thinking he blurted out something about Veronica. He described her as: 'Blooming—blooming.' And then he recollected that, when he and I had first met, his wife had been Mary. Perhaps you didn't see the expression which flashed into his eyes at that moment, but I did. It made me shiver. I knew then that there was something in his past life which so horrified him that he didn't dare think about it. He blurted out something about Mary's death, and tried to hurry off before I could question him further.

"At that moment, as you know, that awful Veronica joined us. He did his best to stop her from speaking, but she was too anxious to claim her relationship with him to be quietened. She told us that she was Mrs. Robert Shilling. I could have hated him at that moment for insulting the memory of a sweet, loyal little woman by marrying that common, painted, peroxided hussy—at any rate, so soon after Mary's death. But instead of letting them go off on their own I persuaded them to make a party with us, as you know, because I wanted to hear more of Mary's death. I don't know what possessed me to do that, Theo. Intuition, perhaps. Anyway, I made the nasty little beast dance with me, I made him drink, I did all I could to make him talk about the past. But I couldn't, although when I had first met him he had done nothing else but talk of himself."

She saw Terhune about to speak, but forestalled him by hurrying on with: "I know you argue that he was probably a little ashamed of himself for having remarried so soon. I might have agreed with you if I hadn't seen his eyes when he first spoke of Mary. I thought then that he had a guilty conscience about her death, but, of course, I didn't associate it with murder. I merely thought that she might have died of a broken heart, or that he had nagged her into an illness from which she had died.

"Theo, my pet, you are an old dear, and I'm very fond of you. But you are a stick-in-the-mud, who has his head stuck either in a musty old book or in the clouds. You don't really know anything about men and women. All you can ever see about people is the nice side of their characters. You are so nice yourself it doesn't occur to you that the majority of other people are not.

"I am different—as you never stop telling me! My reactions to people work in the reverse way from yours. I begin by seeing every-body in their worst light, and finish by gradually liking them in spite of their faults—" She saw his grin. "All right, my pet, I admit that that last remark applies to not more than a dozen people in all, but I can say this: When I do like any one I like him—terribly!" She faltered for a moment, but quickly continued: "Perhaps you wonder what all this is leading up to, Theo? It is this. It amuses me to analyse a person's mind, and I do not make many mistakes. I am convinced that Robert Shilling has that type of shallow mentality which becomes an easy victim of infatuation, and which never rests until its tinsel passion has been sated. Honesty, decency, generosity—every decent quality is sacrificed to that selfish end.

"What I think happened was that Robert Shilling met Veronica during that week's visit to London when Mary went to stay with her mother. He became infatuated with her, and possibly tried to make her his mistress. But Veronica, finding out that he was a moderately rich man, was clever enough—no, cunning enough; nothing could make her clever—to realize that, as his mistress, she might last six months or a year, but that, as his wife, she could be settled for the rest of her life.

"I am not suggesting that all this happened during the first visit. I should say that Veronica allowed Shilling to think that she might become his mistress in time. Hence his reason, on his return to Exeter, for proposing that he and Mary should move out into the country.

"As we know, Shilling began to spend more and more time in London, and, no doubt, the artful Veronica kept him dangling at the end of her peroxided tresses until the crisis arrived, and she let Shilling know that she would marry him, but would not become his mistress.

"Probably, by that time, he was determined to possess her, whatever the cost. Whether he actually asked Mary to divorce him and was refused, or whether he knew her well enough to realize that she never would do that in any circumstances, we may never know, but at some time or other he must have been faced with the fact that only her death would enable him to obtain what may by then have become an obsession with him.

"Put yourself in his place, Theo, and try to think how you could kill your wife without suffering the consequences. One day it might occur to you that you could make use of the garage in causing her death by asphyxiation. You make all your plans beforehand. You go to London, but on the day you know she is going to visit her mother you return to the house, and wait about in the garage until she returns home. In due course she does so, and finds you in the garage. She may be surprised, but certainly not alarmed. She asks you why you have returned home. You make some excuse, and then, at a convenient moment, you knock her unconscious. Then you sit her in the driving seat, start the engine up drive the car against the wall, go out of the garage, and close the door behind you knowing that the fumes from the exhaust will poison her before the arrival of dawn. Perhaps you may even remain in the vicinity just to make sure of her death. In either case, you return to London and are there when your wife's corpse is found the next day."

She paused, a little breathless, and glanced at him with questioning eyes. He shook his head, doubtfully.

"You make everything sound too simple, Julie. I don't think murder is that easy. Or that foolproof. How did he get back to London in time to be there when the body was found?"

"By car, of course."

"But his car was here in the garage."

Julia frowned, annoyed by his picking upon what she conceived to be minor points in her chain of reasoning.

"He could have hired a car, Theo."

"A rather risky proceeding."

"Why?"

"The journey to Exeter and back would have registered more than three hundred miles for the return journey. In the event of investigations being made into the death, he might have been asked by the police to account for that mileage."

"He could have made the journey both ways by train."

"From what I remember of the time-table when I looked it up on Monday, the first train to leave Exeter for Waterloo in the morning was round about five-thirty, and does not reach London until after twelve-thirty. Besides, I suppose he stayed at an hotel while in London. Would he have taken the risk of the hotel staff giving evidence that he had not been there all night?"

Julia pursed her lips in aggravation. "He could have checked out of one hotel on the night before the death, and have re-registered at another following his return to London. Then nobody would have known where he stayed the night."

"Exactly. And the police might have asked him for proof of where he did, in fact, stay. Besides, would he have taken the chance of being seen in Exeter, a town where he is probably known to a good many people?"

"He might have taken a chance on that by catching a train which does not get into Exeter until after dark. The six o'clock from Waterloo, for instance, which arrives in at Exeter just after ten o'clock."

"Mrs. Barker said that her daughter left the house about nine-thirty. In all probability she would have been in bed before the train arrived at Queen Street station."

"Really, Theo, you are exasperating. Are you trying to prove that Robert Shilling did *not* kill his wife?"

He grinned. "Listen, Julie, I don't think there is anything more to be found out here. I suggest that we return to Mrs. Barker, and see if we can find out where Shilling was in the habit of staying when he was in town. If she can tell us I'll 'phone old Sampson and ask him to check up whether or no Shilling was there on the night of his wife's death. If he was, then that's that. If he wasn't, then I'll tell Sampson of our deductions. Does that satisfy you?"

She nodded, and stepped into the car. While she was reversing the car out of the garage, he relocked the connecting and garage doors, then joined her in the car. They drove back to Mrs. Barker, and having satisfied the old lady that her daughter had not committed suicide, discreetly put a number of questions to her.

In response to their questions it seemed that Shilling had not sold out his business interests in Exeter until a month after his wife's death; that he had used as an excuse the fact that he could no longer bear to live in a neighbourhood where he had been so happy with his wife; that nobody in and around Exeter was yet aware that he had remarried (not even Mrs. Barker herself); that he had not lived in Tudor House since the night of Mary's death; that, as anxious as he was to sell the house he had refused an offer which would have meant his making a loss of £300 on the sale; that he had not returned to Exeter since the day when he had concluded the sale of his business; that he had not corresponded with any one in Exeter since that time save his solicitors.

These facts made Julia more convinced than ever that her suspicions of Robert Shilling were justified, but Terhune remained cautiously open-minded: appreciating what his own embarrassment would have been in taking a new, blonde young wife to the neighbourhood where he had lived with the old one, and was prepared to believe that this disconcerting situation, added to Veronica's own ideas about where she should live, could quite easily account for Shilling's strange behaviour. Nevertheless, he telephoned Sampson that night, and asked the inspector whether he would be kind enough to make the necessary inquiries.

The following day Terhune returned to Bray, but during the rest of the week he heard nothing from Sampson. Then, on Sunday morning, just as he was finishing his breakfast, Sampson arrived, his keen, black-brown eyes smilingly contradicting the hard, menacing expression of his sharp-featured, scarred face.

"Good morning, Mr. Terhune. I'm taking the day off, so I thought I'd drop in and see you."

Terhune waved him into an easy chair, offered a cigarette and a cup of coffee, both of which were eagerly accepted. Soon they were both comfortably at ease turning the room blue with their smoke.

"By the way, I have the information you want concerning that man Robert Shilling," Sampson said presently. "Do you mind if I ask you why you wanted it?"

Terhune gave an embarrassed grin. "On that particular night his wife died rather tragically—and rather conveniently for friend Shilling. His wife's death gave him the opportunity of re-marrying —a dumb but dazzling blonde."

Sampson chuckled. "Well, I'm afraid you've drawn a blank this time, Mr. Terhune. It so happened that Shilling didn't stay at his usual hotel that week, but with a friend in St. John's Wood. On the particular night you mentioned to me the two men were playing billiards until nearly midnight. I have that straight from the horse's mouth—in other words, the valet who took Shilling his breakfast the following morning just after eight o'clock, a.m.—at that time the friend was living in a furnished service flat which he had sub-rented for six months."

"I can't say I'm really surprised at the evidence, Inspector. It's so darned easy to make two and two add up to four."

The other man nodded. "Of course, so far I have only questioned the valet. His evidence seemed good enough to me, as a man can't be in Exeter and London at the same time. But if you aren't satisfied I'll make arrangements for the friend to be interrogated by the British Consul—Ronald Strudgewick is now living abroad—"

"Good God!" Terhune exclaimed violently.

Chapter Fifteen

Sampson blew a smoke ring into the air—both an admirable example of self-control, and an admonition, Terhune reflected.

"The name means something to you?"

"It certainly does. You remember those enquiries I was making in Yorkshire?"

"I intended, later on, to ask you what happened."

"The name of the man suspected of having murdered his uncle was Ronald Strudgewick."

"Ah!"

"There is a certain amount of circumstantial evidence to prove that Strudgewick had good reason to kill his uncle James, and that, but for one vital factor, he could have done so."

"And the factor?"

"An almost watertight alibi, supplied by—Robert Shilling." Sampson stubbed out his cigarette, still only half-smoked—the sight gave Terhune a slight feeling of satisfaction.

"Let me get this affair straight, Mr. Terhune," he began slowly. "Strudgewick had a motive for killing his uncle—"

"Sixty thousand pound's worth of motive."

The inspector's thin lips parted in a mirthless smile. "More than good enough! And there would be reason for suspecting him of having committed the crime if it were not for the fact that Ronald Strudgewick can supply an alibi."

"Yes."

"And now we learn that Robert Shilling's wife died in suspicious circumstances which point to her husband as the possible murderer, but for the probability of Strudgewick's supplying an alibi for Robert Shilling?"

"Yes."

Unexpectedly Sampson banged his knee with his clenched fist. "It's fantastic—two men entering into a conspiracy in which each creates an alibi for the other for the purpose of committing two separate murders—but it's workable. By heaven, it is!" He smiled again. As often in the past, Terhune was once more impressed by the menace which a mere smile could contain. "I think it is time you told me all you know about the two murders, Mr. Terhune."

Terhune did so, but as Sampson's interest increased, so did his own doubts. By the time he had finished his face was so doleful that Sampson remarked upon it.

"Aren't you satisfied with your own deductions, Mr. Terhune?"

"Not entirely."

"Why?"

"Because if the two men had really been as cunning as I have made them out to be would Shilling have taken the risk of registering at the Thirsk hotel under his own name?"

"Why not?"

"Just in case anyone should chance to note that Shilling stood alibi for Strudgewick, and Strudgewick for Shilling. That fact alone is enough to cause suspicion in some minds where none previously existed."

"The chances of that happening were a million to one against. One inquest was held in Devon, the other in Yorkshire. The first took place last year, the second this February. The two inquests were not only separated geographically but also by time. Because they were commonplace and lacking any element of sensation the inquests were reported only in the local press. I can scarcely think of anyone who consistently and diligently reads the Devon *and* the Yorkshire local press. One or the other, but both? I doubt it.

"But did Shilling's name appear in the Yorkshire newspapers? I doubt that it was ever mentioned at the inquest. Why should it have been? At the time of the inquest neither the coroner nor the police had an reason to be suspicious of Strudgewick. I shall not be surprised to find that Strudgewick's name likewise was not mentioned at the inquest, unless as a witness to give evidence of identification. Probably that was not necessary with so many local inhabitants—what was the name of the place?"

"Hawley Green."

"So many inhabitants of Hawley Green better able to identify the body. And was Strudgewick's name mentioned at Mrs. Shilling's inquest? I doubt it. Probably Shilling gave evidence to the effect that he was in London at the time of the death, but as there was again no suspicion of homicide why should the coroner have wanted letter and verse of where he was staying?"

"Did you personally question the valet who took breakfast into Shilling on the morning following his wife's death?"

"Yes. Why?"

"Was there any doubt about his having seen Shilling with his own eyes—I mean, at that time, just after 8 a.m.?"

Sampson reflected. "No," he admitted presently. "There is no doubt. Shilling asked him whether he had an aspirin or two handy as he had a headache from having stared at the billiard balls too long the previous night." He shrugged. "I doubt whether he had a headache, as a matter of fact. Probably the question was deliberately asked so as to impress on his memory the fact that he, Shilling, was in bed at that time and on that particular morning, and had been playing billiards the night before."

"Then how could he have reached London by eight o'clock the next morning if it was he who killed his wife?"

"Quite easily. He could have done what Strudgewick did later— used his car. Exeter is less than one hundred and seventy miles from London. He could have travelled that distance in the time."

"His own car was in the garage at Tudor House on the night of the death, and we—Miss MacMunn and I, that is to say—thought that he would hesitate to hire a car in case he might be asked by the police, in case of enquiries, to account for so high a mileage."

Sampson smiled. "You may be giving Shilling credit for more fore-sight than he possesses. But it is a good point. Still, if Strudgewick has a car Shilling may have borrowed it, but even if a car wasn't available he could have returned to London by train."

Terhune shook his head. "The last train leaves Exeter at 7.40 p.m. There is not another before seven-thirty in the morning."

"Maybe there isn't—on the Southern Railway. But there is a 1.50 a.m. on the G.W.R., which arrives at Paddington just after seven o'clock."

"Well, I'll be darned!" Terhune was mortified. "I'd completely forgotten the G.W.R."

"Is Tudor House within walking distance of Exeter?"

"Three to four miles."

"Then he would have had ample time to walk to St. David's station to catch the one-fifty. By heaven! The more one examines the possi-bilities of the two men being murderers the more likely they become. The cunning devils! I'm beginning to think that the alibis which you described as 'almost watertight' are completely watertight."

"Surely they can't be, Inspector, in the light of what we suspect?"

"What help will suspicions be to the prosecution if ever the two men are put in the dock? If each man swears that the other was with him at the time of the respective deaths, no jury would dream of any verdict other than acquittal. And each man is bound to support the other in self-defence."

"Surely a jury couldn't ignore the coincidence of each man being the alibi for the other?"

"They would have to ignore it," Sampson insisted angrily. "That is, barring the production of contra-evidence. If we could find one person to swear that he, or she, had seen Shilling near Exeter on the night of his wife's death, or Strudgewick at Hawley Green on the night of his uncle's death, then the prosecution might well turn the coincidence, as you call it, against each accused in turn. But failing such additional evidence the judge would be certain to point out to the jury that no case had been made out against the accused, who was therefore justified in demanding the verdict of Not Guilty. And even if the jury ignored the judge's warning, I'm sure the Court of Appeal would reverse the verdict. I tell you Mr. Terhune, I've seen people leave the dock as free men, with everybody in the whole court knowing them to be guilty yet the police have been unable to prove that fact beyond all reasonable doubt."

The inspector paused to offer a cigarette, and light one for himself. Presently he went on: "The police will have to carry on from this point, Mr. Terhune, because obtaining the kind of evidence we want is the type of dull, monotonous routine which makes up about ninety-nine per cent of a detective's work. Tomorrow I'll report to the Chief Constable. I'm pretty sure he'll ask the North Riding and the Devon police to reopen enquiries into the deaths of James Strudgewick and Mrs. Shilling respectively. At the same time he will probably put one of our men on to checking up on the London end." His voice became apologetic. "It seems a bit hard on you, sir, taking the matter out of your hands so summarily. Especially after the work you've already done—"

Terhune grinned. "Don't forget, Inspector, I've had it happen to me before. It doesn't worry me in the slightest. My interest is in books, not crime. Now, how about a beer?"

"It's still early," Sampson murmured. "But beer's always beer—"

I I

During the week which followed Sampson's visit to Bray little happened of any real interest. On the Monday night the inspector telephoned Terhune, but only to say that he had spoken to the Chief Constable, who had agreed that a report of Terhune's findings ought to be passed on to the Chief Constables of the North Riding and Devon police forces for their attention, and that further enquiries regarding both Shilling and Strudgewick were to be made in London by the C.I.D.

The following day Julia and her mother returned to Bray. Early Wednesday morning Julia telephoned Terhune to ask him to go swimming with her in the afternoon, but she was too late—he had already promised to go walking with Helena. If the knowledge infuriated Julia she did her best to hide the fact, and went on to ask him if there were any further news of the two deaths. When he told her that there was none she no longer tried to remain amiable, and after a few caustic remarks rang off.

So to Sunday again, and another visit from Sampson. The inspector looked solemn.

"I was discussing the Shilling case with the Chief Constable this morning," he told Terhune. "The Old Man said that it might be a good idea if I visited you today to give you an outline of what has happened during the week."

His thin lips parted in a smile on seeing his companion's astonishment. "I was as surprised as you are. He doesn't usually regard outsiders—if you'll excuse the word, Mr. Terhune—with such tolerance. But he's a cunning old devil, the Chief, and I'll tell you later what he has in mind.

"But first I'll tell you of the enquiries we've made in London during the week—incidentally I was put in charge of them, with a young chap by the name of Ridley to help. Let's take Shilling first. Until the winter when he took his wife to Las Palmas, Shilling and his wife used to stop at one of those private hotels round about South Kensington way—the *Hotel Bonhomie* is its name, and I suppose I hardly need to tell you that it *doesn't* live up to its name. Its ultra-respectability needs to be seen to be believed. Not that I mean that remark in a derogatory sense, mind you, because it is kept by a couple of dear old ladies whom it's a pleasure to meet. But it is essentially the kind of hotel to which a man like Shilling would want to take a wife like Mary Shilling.

"The old ladies knew all about the holiday in Las Palmas, because as the ship sailed from London Shilling and his wife spent the two previous nights at the *Bonhomie*. They also remember Shilling's next stay at the hotel, firstly because they made him spend several hours telling them about the Canary Islands, and secondly, because he has never stayed there since, although he had been going there two or three times a year for the previous ten years or more.

"As a matter of fact there was a third reason for the old ladies' remembering that last visit of his. On the third night he went to a dance—you know, a dance with a capital D and a large exclamation mark. And the next morning what do you think happened? The chambermaid—she'll never see fifty again, by the way!—found lipstick on his handkerchief! And from then onwards his behaviour was most peculiar. Instead of going to an occasional theatre and spending all the other evenings in the lounge he went out *every* night! Yes, really. *Every* night!"

Sampson chuckled. "I needn't labour the point, Mr. Terhune. I don't think there is much doubt about what happened. He met the girl Veronica at that first dance, and she didn't waste any time in getting to work upon him. From that moment he was lost. Anyway, on the morning of his departure for Exeter, when he was paying his bill, the two dear old ladies made one or two pointed remarks about the lipstick, and the round of gaiety. The next time Shilling came to town he stayed at the *Trafalgar Palace Hotel*."

"*The Trafalgar Palace!*" Terhune grinned. "Bit of a difference between that and the *Bonhomie!*"

"You're right. And doesn't it show you what a difference a woman makes to a man? As long as he was happy with his wife— which I think he was, by the way, until that other young chit turned up—the stuffy, mid-Victorian, dull *Bonhomie* was good enough. But the *Bonhomie*, or its equivalent, wasn't good enough for the blonde wench. It had to be the *Trafalgar Palace*, with its lifts and page-boys and *à la carte* dinners and what-would-you! Incidentally, the receptionist at the *Trafalgar Palace* knows Veronica well. So much for Veronica's story about meeting Shilling for the first time a few months ago.

"Now about Strudgewick. I haven't found out so much about him. Being a wanderer he hasn't left many traces. In fact, it's a good job that Shilling's mother-in-law was able to give us the address of the flat at which he was staying at the time of his wife's death, otherwise we mightn't have learned as much as we have."

"Burton—James Strudgewick's old servant—evidently knew the nephew's address because he sent a telegram to Ronald to announce the uncle's death."

"So much the better! This Burton will be able to give us another lead. Anyway, we now know something about the service flat in St. John's Wood, which is the place which mostly concerns us at the moment. The flat consists of two bedrooms, two reception rooms, and kitchenette. Three years ago a Mr. and Mrs. Keith Rainbow signed a seven-year lease, and furnished the flat. They hadn't been installed there two years when Rainbow's firm ordered him abroad for a six months' tour of their East African offices—something to do with accountancy, I believe. Rainbow put the place into the hands of the letting office, who sub-let it to Ronald Strudgewick for six months.

"The flat is on the fifth floor of the block, next to the lift. At the far end of the passage is the fire-escape, outside the lower frame of a long, narrow window. I am especially mentioning the lift and the fire-escape because I've something to say about them both. Dealing with the fire-escape first, it is a simple matter for anyone to use it to get in and out of the building, so if Shilling did kill his wife we don't have to look far for the means he used for entering and leaving the place without being seen by the hall-porter or the lift-man.

"On the Saturday before Mary Shilling's death Strudgewick informed the hall porter that he was having a guest to stay with him for a week so would the valet take up a second breakfast-tray at eight-fifteen each morning until further notice? This was arranged, and the valet took up two breakfast trays to the flat fifty-one for the whole of that week.

"Mary Shilling died on the Wednesday, didn't she? Well, soon after nine o'clock p.m. that same night the lift-man arrived at the ground floor, after taking some tenants up to the fourth floor, and found Strudgewick waiting for him—before I go on I should add that the hall-porter goes off duty at eight o'clock, leaving the lift-man, who remains on duty until midnight, to double his own job with that of hall-porter.

"As I said, Strudgewick was waiting for him, and stepped into the lift, saying: 'Mr. Shilling is walking up, Jim, as he has to deliver a note to the Dixons'—at that time the Dixons occupied flat thirty-seven on the third floor. Jim wasn't greatly concerned with either Shilling or the Dixons, so he just said 'Okay' or something of that sort and took Strudgewick up to the fifth floor.

"Fifteen minutes or so later somebody on the fifth floor rang for the lift. Jim went up, and found Strudgewick, who said that he and Mr. Shilling intended to play a few hundred up at billiards (Rainbow had a half-size table in one of the reception rooms) and adding that they had found themselves out of whisky so would Jim like to run round the corner to buy a bottle? Apparently Jim is used to carrying out errands for the tenants, and makes more from his tips than the total of his wages—he told me so, quite proudly.

"Leaving the lift to itself—it's a press-button automatic lift— Jim went to fetch the whisky. When he got back he took the bottle up to flat fifty-one and rang the bell. While he was waiting for the door to be opened he heard the murmur of voices and the click of billiard-balls. He delivered the whisky and received a good tip for his pains.

"During the next two and a half hours he stopped on the fifth floor about four times in all. On each occasion he heard either the sound of billiard-balls, or indistinguishable voices. You can take it from me, Jim is quite convinced Shilling and Strudgewick were playing billiards together all that time."

"Strudgewick was playing by himself?"

Sampson shrugged his shoulders. "Probably, while the low voices could have come from a radio. Well, you know about the valet taking in the breakfast to Shilling the next morning—I gave you his story last Sunday. What with one thing and another there isn't an employee in the building who isn't ready to swear that Shilling spent the Wednesday night there as well as the preceding four nights. Incidentally, Shilling took care to show them the telegram from Exeter about his wife's death, which has further helped to fix the episode in their memories. 'Fair crazed with grief, he was and all,' is Jim's version."

"Had Strudgewick a car?"

"Ah! No he hadn't. We've made a few routine enquiries from the larger firms of car-hirers, also others in the neighbourhood of St. John's Wood, but none of them hired out a car about that time to anyone who can be identified with either Shilling or Strudgewick. We've checked up with Paddington and learned that the 1.50 a.m. ran that night as usual.

"What isn't so satisfactory is a preliminary report from the police at Exeter. The ticket collector who was on duty at Queen Street station in the afternoon and evening of the day Mrs. Shilling died is a distant relative of the dead woman. He knows Shilling quite well, and swears that Shilling didn't pass through the barrier on the Wednesday."

"Then I should say that it was quite certain that he didn't travel to Exeter on the Southern. He must have gone to St. David's on the Great Western."

"Perhaps, but I've suggested to the Devon police that they should check up at some of the intermediate stations within walking distance of his home. He might have changed at Honiton on to a local train."

Terhune shook his head. "I don't think he would have taken the risk of being seen at a local station, Inspector, where everybody knows everybody else who alights. A strange face would have been noted at once."

"Perhaps you are right. Then I wonder if he would have taken a bus from Honiton to somewhere."

"Very likely, but the same remark applies to local buses as to local stations."

"Humph! You are a hard person to satisfy, Mr. Terhune. I suppose you are not suggesting that he *flew* to Devon and was dropped by parachute?"

Terhune grinned. "He wouldn't have risked the pilot giving evidence against him. But what he might have done——" He hesitated. His theory seemed somewhat far-fetched now that he came to put it into words.

"Well?"

"Do you think he might have bought a second-hand bicycle, and taken it with him in the train to—well, say, Honiton, for instance. He could have cycled the rest of the way."

Sampson's eyes twinkled. "If you are as full of ideas for your writing as you are for sleuthing you oughtn't to dry up in a hurry. But, joking apart, that's an idea worth following up. He might even have bought the bicycle in Honiton so as to avoid bringing himself to the attention of the guard or a porter."

"Don't forget that Mrs. Shilling died on a Wednesday."

"Well?"

"Early closing day."

Sampson laughed with quiet humour. "For once I can score over you, Mr. Terhune. I happen to know that Honiton's early closing is on Thursdays." Sampson's face sobered up again, and he lapsed into a brooding silence.

"Any news from Yorkshire?" Terhune asked presently.

Sampson roused himself. "Nothing worth repeating. The man you met, Inspector Longworth, has taken over investigations. He has checked off times, distances and what not, and agrees that it was possible for Strudgewick to have killed his uncle. But although he has questioned every living soul in Hawley Green, and also made a few enquiries among the villagers living between Thirsk and Hawley Green, he hasn't met anyone who saw either Strudgewick or the Lagonda. Nor has he met with any success in Thirsk itself. The repair garage delivered the car at the station, as you assumed, but what happened to it between then and when Shilling drove it into the hotel garage some time before midnight nobody knows."

"How on earth are you ever going to prove that either of those two men committed murder?" Terhune asked dolefully.

"That is where you can come into the picture again," Sampson replied blandly.

Chapter Sixteen

At first Terhune thought the inspector was joking—Sampson had a sense of humour which occasionally manifested itself in a rather heavy manner—and began to grin, but a quick glance at the face opposite changed his opinion: the expression which lighted up the inspector's dark eyes was anything but amused.

"You mean—there is something I can do—"

"Perhaps. That is, if you are willing, and can spare the time— Listen, Mr. Terhune. The position is this. We believe that both Shilling and Strudgewick are murderers, but as long as they each swear an alibi for the other there is nothing the police can do about charging them with the crimes. Naturally, we are continuing with our investigations, but, between ourselves, they do not look particularly hopeful. At the moment neither in Yorkshire, nor in Devon, nor in London, have we a lead of any sort which looks at all worth following up.

"It is intolerable to think of them getting away with their damnable scheme, but as things are at the moment it looks as if there is only one possible approach to putting the two men where they belong—the dock, I mean. And that is the psychological approach, which is just about the last method an official policeman can use."

"A psychological approach—"

"I'll explain more fully what I mean in a moment, Mr. Terhune. Let me continue summing up the situation first. As far as we can judge at the moment only one of two, or possibly three, people can break the alibi. The two principal people are, of course, Shilling and Strudgewick themselves. Yet one can hardly imagine either man betraying the other, for such a betrayal would merely result in hanging a similar noose round his own neck. The third person is —the present Mrs. Shilling."

Sampson quickly held up a hand to prevent the question which he saw forming itself on Terhune's lips. "No, that does not mean that we think that Veronica Shilling was necessarily privy to the two murders. But the Old Man has been wondering whether we couldn't get at Robert Shilling through his wife.

"You see, Shilling himself is our only hope. Strudgewick is safely abroad, and apparently means to stay there. Anyway, supposing that he doesn't intend returning voluntarily, there is no way of bringing him back to this country except by applying for extradition, and it would be useless to do that without pretty good proof that he is a murderer.

"To return to this psychological approach business. Nearly every criminal has a weakness of some sort which, more often than not, delivers him to the police. Sometimes the weakness is physical. He drinks too much, and when he is drunk he talks too much. Or perhaps he is too fond of women. He deserts an old flame in favour of a new one, so the old flame has her revenge by sending an anonymous letter to the police.

"Sometimes the weakness is mental. A man nerves himself up to commit a crime, but later his nerve disappears. He becomes furtive, slinks into pubs as though he was hunted, walks a mile to avoid meeting a policeman. He can't do those things without his pals putting two and two together, and, believe me, there is usually one among them who reports this behaviour to a friendly dick— in return for half a dollar, or a pint. Then the dick begins to make inquiries. Before he knows where he is the crook is in jug, wondering how in hell's name the dicks cottoned on to him.

"Now, I'm not going to suggest that Shilling drinks too much, or that he's lost his nerve—as yet! But I do suggest that, unless he's different from all the other men I've ever met, he must have a weak chink somewhere in his armour. Suppose, for instance, we were to find out that he suffers from claustrophobia—" The inspector's eyes twinkled. He pressed the fingertips of his two hands together and gazed up at the ceiling with an innocent air.

"Well?"

"A few hours in a police cell might shake his nerve and eventually bring about unforeseen consequences."

"Quite, but how are you to get him into the police cell? Don't forget that 18B no longer exists!"

The inspector shrugged his shoulders. "Let's leave that problem to take care of itself," he answered drily. "I said 'suppose,' didn't I? And here's another suppose. Suppose that he couldn't stand receiving anonymous letters. Interesting results might come of a series of anonymous letters. Of course, I'm not suggesting that any one in the police force could send them—that would be *too, too* irregular—but the supposition makes an interesting academic argument."

"Inspector, when I first saw you in that Spanish restaurant, more than two years ago, I told myself that I shouldn't like you for an enemy. I'm becoming firmly convinced that my first impressions of you were right."

"Mr. Terhune!" Sampson tried to look shocked, but the effect was merely to heighten the saturnine quality that was so marked a characteristic of his sharp-profiled, scarred face. Then he became serious again.

"Remember that I am speaking unofficially," he went on sharply. "As a police detective, and while I'm officially on duty I am the essence of all that's legal. But I'm not on duty all twenty-four hours of the day, and when I'm off duty I'm as much a man as a detective. So let me tell you that there are some crimes so beastly that there isn't much I wouldn't do—as a man—which might assist me—as a detective—to put the criminal into the dock. But all this is strictly between you and me, Mr. Terhune, and I shouldn't like it to go any further. The Commissioner of Police might not see eye to eye with me on the matter."

Terhune chuckled. "I don't think I'd *dare* to let it go farther, Inspector."

Sampson's eyes twinkled again, but he did not pursue the matter further. "To get back to Shilling. Do you understand what I'm getting at, sir? What's wanted now is for someone to analyse the man's psychology so as to give us some indication of where his chink is—no, what it is—well, you know what I mean. And you are the only man I know who can do that effectively."

"Me! But I don't know the man. I've only met him once."

"Didn't you tell me that that wife of his wasn't—er—unwilling to renew your brief acquaintance with her?"

"She might not have been unwilling, but I can't say the same for him. He didn't have much time for me when he learned I was only a bookseller."

"Does that mean he's a snob?" Sampson snapped out.

"Yes. You should hear him when he speaks of Miss MacMunn's mother—the Hon. Mrs. MacMunn. The words just drip off his tongue—"

"By the Lord Harry!"

"What's the matter?"

"That might be a better idea. Miss MacMunn is keen to help, isn't she?".

"Keen—" Terhune's expression completed the sentence.

"Do you think she would care to have Shilling and his wife to her house one day? I take it he would accept an invitation, wouldn't he?"

"Accept! He practically begged for an invitation. As for Julia MacMunn, I'm sure she would be willing to co-operate. But I'm not so sure of her mother."

"She wouldn't be willing?"

"She would be willing enough, Inspector, but she knows sufficient about the case to let the cat out of the bag. She's a dear soul, as kind-hearted as you could wish for. But as for being diplomatic, or keeping quiet when necessary—"

"I see." Sampson spent some moments in silent reflection. Presently his keen gaze sought for, and held, Terhune's. "Can I leave it in your hands, Mr. Terhune, to renew your acquaintance with Robert Shilling?"

"Of course, but—" Terhune hesitated, and an expression of distaste passed across his face.

"But you don't like the idea of deliberately making a man's acquaintance for the sole purpose of spying upon him?"

"Something like that."

"Then remember what Shilling did. Murdered a kindly, good-hearted woman, and a loving wife, just so that he might sleep with a chit of a girl nearly young enough to be his daughter—"

"You win!" Terhune explained abruptly. "And when Shilling and I meet again—then what?"

"Are you going to co-opt Miss MacMunn?"

"Probably."

"Then tell her that I want to know the man's weakness, and let her do the rest. A woman can read a man's soul—or another woman's soul, come to that—ten times more quickly, more easily and more reliably than a man. They haven't the same loyalties— or the same notions about sportsmanship."

Terhune nodded. "If you think it will do any good."

"The odds are a hundred to one against," Sampson admitted frankly. "A devilish plot like the one which presumably killed James Strudgewick and Mrs. Shilling isn't easily exposed. But if those two murderers aren't to get off scot-free then anything which has even the faintest hope of success must be tried out. In the meantime, who knows, perhaps police inquiries may yield a more hopeful lead." But the inspector's expression was rather less optimistic than his words.

II

Usually, when Sampson visited Terhune, they spent the rest of the day together, greatly to Terhune's delight, for he knew of no one who could make himself more entertaining than the C.I.D. man. Sampson's only interest in life was in his work, off duty and on, and having spent most of his employable life in the police force he had an inexhaustible knowledge of procedure and courts, and a fund of fascinating stories of crime, crimes and criminals.

For once, however, the inspector had to hurry off on business, so having seen Sampson's car disappear in the distance Terhune returned to the shop and telephoned Julia.

"Hullo, Julia," he greeted when he heard her voice at the other end.

"Good morning, Theo," she answered coldly—evidently she still had a grudge against him for having gone out with Helena the previous Wednesday.

"Would you like to take me for a drive this afternoon?"

"I have accepted an invite from Reggie Blye to play golf this afternoon. Did you want to go anywhere in particular?"

"Tunbridge Wells."

"Tunbridge Wells!" she repeated in a faintly surprised voice. "Would some other afternoon do as well?"

"If it must, it must, but I'm very busy."

"Then shall we make it Wednesday—or are you already engaged?"

"You haven't forgotten that the Shillings live at Tunbridge Wells, Julie?"

"The Shillings!"

He knew by the excited note in her voice that she had not realized the significance of his request, so he went on: "I've just had a visit from Inspector Sampson."

"Theo! There is news—"

"None. That is why he asked whether you would like to help. But, of course, as you have fixed up for this afternoon—"

"There are times, my pet, when I could smack you. We'll go tomorrow. What time shall I call for you? Two-thirty?"

"I don't want to upset any of your plans—"

"I'll call at two-thirty," she said with finality.

III

"What were you saying on the 'phone about Inspector Sampson's wanting my help?" Julia asked as she went round Market Square and headed west.

He gave her a précis of his conversation with the inspector, and finished by repeating, verbatim, Sampson's remarks concerning her. He watched her face, and was astonished by the enthusiasm which it revealed.

"Is your inspector a bachelor?" she asked, surprisingly.

"I believe so."

"Then he knows much too much about women."

"Are you willing to do as he suggests, Julia? It will mean—well something like spying upon Shilling. That's a detective's job, not a woman's."

"Don't be childish, Theo."

So that wise old owl, Sampson, was right in his analysis of a woman's character, Terhune reflected ruefully. Julia—Julia, of all people!—was not only willing but eager to worm herself into Shilling's confidence, although she detested the man. She was willing to take his salt, and his life, with equal indifference.

His thoughts must have communicated themselves to her, for she went on: "Robert Shilling didn't mind betraying his wife's love and trust. She cannot repay him for that treachery, poor soul! but if I, another woman, am given the opportunity of doing so on her behalf I shall take it. Gladly!" Her voice had rarely been more expressive; it was passionate with an icy-cold, impersonal hatred.

"Would you have been so anxious to help the police if Shilling had killed a man instead of his wife?"

"No," she admitted presently.

He was strangely glad to have her assurance on that point, and laughed with relief. "So you are a feminist at heart, Julie."

She shook her head so vigorously that her hair waved in the wind, and its blue-blackness reflected the fitful snatches of sunshine tempered by an overhanging mist.

"No, my sweet, it's not even for the sake of another woman. It's for Mary Shilling. I did not see very much of her," she went on earnestly, "but she was so gentle, so selfless that any man who could hurt her for the sake of a stupid, common little nincompoop like Veronica hasn't the right to expect honourable treatment."

He did not continue the argument because he could not think of a suitable reply. Yet it occurred to him that the longer he knew Julia the more he discovered new facets of her always enigmatic character. She was mostly impatient with people of little character and as far as he could discover Mary Shilling had not possessed much character, certainly not of the kind to appeal to Julia. Yet now, it seemed, she was preparing to act contrary to her own high code of ethics because a woman, for whom she had obviously not possessed any deep liking, had been killed by a man infatuated with a rather common young woman with blonde hair and scarlet fingernails. Strange!

"You know," she went on, "I think it might not be a bad idea to ask the Shillings to dine with us one night—if all goes well today, of course."

"Sampson had the same idea, but I told him that it would never do."

"Why not?" she asked sharply.

"I don't want to be rude about your mother, Julia, but do you think it is possible for her to spend two or three hours in the company of the Shillings without letting out something which would put Shilling on his guard?"

She laughed softly. "I am afraid you are right, but I wonder if that might not be just the kind of psychological approach for which your inspector man is looking. I know what I am going to suggest at today's meeting—"

"If we have one."

"Naturally. If we are lucky enough to find the Shillings at home, and I am able to confirm some of my impressions of that gentleman, I think it would be a good idea to have a dinner-party of six."

"Six?"

"The two Shillings, Mother and I, you—and Inspector Sampson! Of course, we shouldn't let the Shillings know that he was a detective, but there's no knowing how much he might learn from Shilling's face if Mother should blurt out something to the effect that the police suspect Strudgewick of having killed his wife."

"A remark like that, from out of the blue, should certainly put the wind up him. I wonder!" Presently Terhune shook his head. "I don't think the shock would help. It isn't the absolute certainty that Shilling is a murderer which Sampson is after—he's pretty well convinced of that now. What he wants is proof. How is the mere fact of—what shall we say? Shilling's face turning green or white or goose-pimply, or whatever might happen—how would that fact help to incriminate him? Of course, if it made him write out a confession then and there—"

"There's no need to be funny."

"I wasn't meaning to be funny, honest, Julia. I was more or less thinking aloud, wondering if the fear of being arrested might not prove more effective in making him confess than the actual arrest."

"I think it might, and I am sure that this is what Inspector Sampson had in mind when he spoke of the psychological approach. Tell me,

Theo, do you think that Veronica knows or suspects that Shilling killed his first wife?"

"I should say, no. I don't think she has the courage or the acting ability to be normal with a secret like that hanging over her head."

"I should not have thought that Shilling had the courage either. Perhaps that is why he drinks more and talks less than when I first met him. But I agree with you about Veronica."

"Had you any special reason for asking?"

"I was wondering what Shilling's reaction would be to the possibility of his wife's learning that he was a murderer."

"He might hurry her and himself abroad before that possibility became an actuality."

"Couldn't the police stop him doing that?"

"I can't be absolutely certain—the police have so many trump cards up their sleeves which they can use when necessary, laws that were passed three hundred years ago, and long forgotten but never repealed. All the same, I fancy Sampson wouldn't be too pleased to hear that Shilling was planning to go abroad."

"Then they mustn't be allowed to meet Mother," Julia said drily.

They passed through Tenterden, and soon turned north for Goudhurst. Not long afterwards they reached Pembury, where they turned south-west for Tunbridge Wells. Later they found themselves near the Pantiles, and stopped to inquire the whereabouts of Sussex Crescent. First right, first left was the answer, so they turned first right, first left, and found themselves in a road consisting of huge Georgian houses, many of which had been converted into flats. Not so the third house on the right—Regent House. This residence bore all the hall-marks of a recent, lavish expenditure of money.

They drove into the curved, well-kept drive, stopped the car, and ascended the wide, stone steps to the solemn, ornate entrance. Terhune pressed the button of an electric bell, which started a chime of four notes echoing rather delightfully from the other side of the glass-panelled door. A few moments' silence was followed by the slither of soft-soled shoes. The door opened, to reveal a trim house-maid in brown uniform.

Terhune inquired for Mr. and Mrs. Shilling.

Another breathless, anxious pause.

Then the maid opened the door wider, and, stepping on one side, invited them to enter.

They did so, relieved to learn that their impulsively-conceived journey was not, so far, in vain.

Chapter Seventeen

W hile they waited the maid disappeared up a wide staircase to announce them to her employer, and Julia and Terhune glanced about them. They were in a reception room on the left of a wide, square hall, shaped roughly in T fashion. Five doors opened inwards from the hall, and as three of them were open, including the door of the room they were in—the maid had omitted to close it properly, and a draught had swung it open—they were afforded a comprehensive view of much of the ground floor.

Their first impression was of wealth and—unexpectedly—taste. The general scheme, the furniture, the ornaments, the colour of the paintwork, the few water-colours all looked as though they had been designed and chosen by an artist. Yet this first impression was quickly dispelled by a more critical inspection. Hung starkly and incongru-ously between two Matisses was a photograph of a blousy, blonde woman whose face bore just enough resemblance to Veronica's to make it certain that she was Veronica's mother. Elsewhere, a pot of crimson geraniums occupied a delicate porcelain vase the colour *motif* of which was mauve. Other photographs in silver frames stood on the mantelshelf above what looked like a genuine Adams' fireplace. A home-made rug, depicting a Wedgewood blue Chinese dragon curled up against a background of Turkey red, shrieked at the soft green, Chinese carpet. A hand-worked cushion, with an oriental *motif*, rested uneasily against the faded tapestry back of a Sheraton armchair. Two issues of a trade magazine and a copy of *Esquire* littered an occasional table.

Terhune found it easy to guess who was responsible for the disfiguring incongruities. Veronica, without a doubt. Certainly it could only have been she who selected the site for her mother's photograph, while the rug and the cushion cover were probably her own work, or her mother's. But whose was the taste, the touch of the artist? Not Shilling's, surely? Not that ostentatious vulgarian?

Julia was quicker in solving the puzzle.

"Interior decoration by Liberty," she murmured.

Terhune grinned. Of course, that was the answer. Shilling had handed over an empty house, and a cheque. Liberty's had done the rest, by creating a delightful home, which the Shillings, lacking any sense of artistic values, or culture, were already doing their best to spoil.

The visitors did not have long to wait. Through the open door they heard and saw the Shillings hurrying down the wide staircase. They arrived at the bottom with Veronica leading by a short head, but in between the staircase and the door of the reception room Shilling caught up and passed his wife.

"My dear Miss MacMunn," he said loudly as he advanced towards Julia with both hands outstretched, "this is an unexpected and very welcome pleasure. Isn't it, darling?" he added, turning with rather less enthusiasm to Terhune, and offering a flaccid hand.

"Yes, and isn't it lucky we hadn't left for Lady Vencey's garden party." The visitors were sure that Veronica's voice was even more affected than when they had first heard it. "Dear Lady Vencey! She works so hard for charity, and she sent a *special* letter asking us to go to her party—"

"Yes, yes, my dear," Shilling interrupted, sensing rather than appreciating the vulgarity of his wife's attempt to create an effect.

"We do apologize for dropping in upon you without warning," Julia said hastily. "I am afraid it was my idea, and all because I saw a signpost marked Tunbridge Wells. You must not let us keep you—"

Terhune was a little shocked that any one could lie with so much sincerity.

"Nonsense, Miss MacMunn, we should not dream of letting you go so soon. Now that you are here you must stay for tea." Shilling winked at Terhune. "And a snifter later on, perhaps. We don't really want to go to the garden party; we were only going because we hadn't fixed up anything better to do. Isn't that right, my dear."

"We shouldn't even have thought of going if Lady Vencey hadn't written a *special* letter—"

"For goodness' sake shut up about that letter. Besides, it was a kind of circular letter anyway."

"It was signed by Lady Vencey," Veronica pouted.

Shilling made an impatient gesture and glanced anxiously at Julia. "You are not in any hurry, are you, Miss MacMunn? I'd like to show you the house and the garden."

"We'd love to stay if it's not really inconvenient."

He was delighted. "It's a treat to have somebody really worth while dropping in on us like this. Between you and me, the people who live round about here—" He expressed his scorn with a gesture. "The Rector called the other day for about five minutes, but that was only because I sent him a cheque for ten guineas for his pet charity."

"I suppose we couldn't all go to the garden party, Bob. The Rector will be there, and he might introduce us to some of the other people—"

"No, we can't all go," Shilling snapped. "Miss MacMunn didn't come to Tunbridge Wells to go to a charity garden party."

Veronica began to pout again as she glanced quickly in Julia's direction. Terhune was sure that she was trying to decide which was the more to be appreciated, the bird in hand, as represented by the granddaughter of a Baron, or the two birds at the garden party, to whom the Rector might be inveigled into introducing her.

Then Terhune had a brainwave. "I have a weakness for bun-fights. If Mr. Shilling doesn't want to go to the garden-party, and with his permission, would you let me take you, Mrs. Shilling?"

A smile of admiration glowed warmly in Julia's eyes. A smile of a different kind flashed into Shilling's eyes, and made Terhune regret his impulse.

"That's an excellent idea," he boomed jovially. "Would you like Mr. Terhune to take you, my dear?"

Veronica nodded quickly, her eyes sparkling with pleasure. "Yes, Bob darling. Especially as I shall not want to stop there long. Just long enough to—" She paused, and all her hearers, knew that she was thinking—just long enough to meet some of the classy people who will be there. But aloud she finished tamely: "To buy one or two things for the sake of the charity."

Shilling produced a wallet from which he extracted a five pound note. This he passed over with ostentation. "Spend this, darling, on something for yourself." Then he wagged a facetious fore finger. "I'm not so sure that I can trust you alone with a nice young man like Mr. Terhune, so don't go putting ideas into his head."

Veronica giggled. "What things you do say, Bob!" She turned to Terhune. "I shall only be a few minutes, Mr. Terhune."

While they awaited Veronica's return the other three exchanged trivial conversation. Shilling's manner was impatient; apparently he was getting anxious for his wife and Terhune to be gone. Terhune, on the other hand, was beginning to feel blue, having a pretty good notion of what was in Shilling's mind. Julia, alone, remained her usual cool, serene self. Except, perhaps, for the twinkle in her eyes caused by her realization of what was passing in the mind of both her companions.

Presently Veronica reappeared. Terhune winced, and hoped sincerely that he would not run across anyone he knew. He was sure no one would believe his story. Then he wondered what the

Rector would think, and anticipated a rather amusing game of hide-and-seek.

Shilling, however, was satisfied. "Ah! So you've got your glad rags on, my dear. That's right. I'll bet you won't see anyone there with a better fur than yours. Now run along, sweetheart, and I'll try to keep Miss MacMunn amused until you come back."

She presented her face for his lips, so he kissed her with a cloying lewdness which made Terhune feel squeamish, and playfully smacked her as she turned away.

"If you can't be good be careful."

"There's no fun in being careful," she called back as she waved to Terhune, and flounced towards the door.

Terhune had previously arranged with Julia to borrow her car, so Veronica and he stepped into the front seats and drove off for the garden party. Annoyed with himself for not having anticipated Shilling's reaction to the idea of his taking Veronica to the garden fête, Terhune found that conversation wasn't rising readily to his lips. He sought, rather desperately, for something to say. At last he blurted out: "Do you drive, Mrs. Shilling?"

"No. I want to, very much, but Bob won't let me."

"Doesn't he like the idea of women-drivers?"

"Oh! It's not that. Dear old Bob isn't as old as he looks. He's only just reached middle-age, and he's not in the wee-est bit old-fashioned, but he refuses positively to let me own or drive a car. Of course, I shall get my own way one of these days, but so far I haven't been able to shift him."

"But he owns a car, doesn't he?"

"Oh, yes. A lovely car. Ever so fast it is."

"Then why won't he let you have a car?"

"You know that I'm not Bob's first wife, don't you?"

"Yes. Julia told me."

"Well, you see, Bob's first wife died through having her own car, so that's why the old dear is so afraid of letting me have a car of my own, or drive his. Isn't it silly." She giggled. "I often tell him that lightning never strikes twice in the same place."

It was by sheer chance that the conversation had so quickly touched upon the subject of Mary Shilling, so Terhune determined to make the most of it.

"How did the first Mrs. Shilling die?"

"The first Mrs. Shilling!" She giggled again. "How funny that sounds! Wasn't there a play with a title like that many years ago? But I don't know how Mary—that was the name of Bob's other wife—died. Bob won't talk about it. He says our marriage is too happy to be spoiled by discussing sad things. I think she ran into a tree, or something of that sort."

Veronica's artless chatter convinced Terhune of one fact, that Veronica was not a party to her husband's crime. Not directly. Indirectly, perhaps, by refusing to give herself to him except in legal union, but was she to be blamed for making that condition? Yes and no, Terhune thought. No, because it was her woman's right to preserve her honour. Yes, because a truly honourable woman, aware of his existing marriage, would not have bargained for her happiness at the expense of the wife's—although such a high sense of rectitude was, perhaps, asking rather too much of the average human being! Yes, again, because she had not married Shilling for love, but for material gain. At least, that was his opinion, for it was hard to believe that the feather-brained doll who sat beside him in the car was capable of sincere, genuine love for a man very nearly twice her age.

While Terhune was wondering how best to continue speaking of Mary Shilling without making his companion suspicious of his motive, the opportunity was, for the time being, lost to him. Speaking with naïve excitement she said: "The second gateway on the right—where the car in front is turning in."

Terhune followed the other car and also a line of arrows pointing to *Car Park*. 2/6 *per car*. The park was small, and already almost filled, but he manœuvred the car into what little space was left, and paid over the half a crown due to the fluttering lady of uncertain age and unwedded state who welcomed them with a nervous giggle. As they walked away from the car park Veronica slipped her hand into the crook of his arm, and glanced at him with coquettish eyes.

"Does it shock you?" she asked. "I mean, me being a married woman, and you having your Miss MacMunn?"

He was on the point of sharply informing her that Julia meant no more to him than any other woman when it occurred to him that the information might prove undiplomatic. Perhaps—or most probably—she was the type to whom stolen fruit tasted better than produce of one's own garden. A flirtation with her did not appeal to him as a pastime worth encouraging, but, just the same, something good might come of a flirtatious intimacy with her.

"No," he said, with just sufficient hesitation to keep her interested. 'I—I don't think so."

She squeezed his arm—very slightly. "It's rather fun. Of course I love Bob, he's such a dear, but that doesn't mean that I can't enjoy the company of another man now and again. May I call you Theo?"

"I prefer Tommy."

"So do I—Tommy. And you may call me Veronica." They came within sight of the Rectory lawn, bright and colourful with striped tents and tea-tables with large, coloured umbrellas for shade, and be-flagged stalls, and bunting, and gay dresses, and the uniforms of the Youth organizations.

She laughed happily. "Thank you for bringing me, Tommy." Then she added, anxiously: "I wonder which is Lady Vencey? We must look out for the Rector—"

I I

Through the window of the reception-room Shilling watched the car disappear from sight, behind a line of trees, before turning round to Julia.

"I'm glad you didn't want to go to the garden fête, Miss MacMunn."

"Why?"

"Because I shall be able to show the house to you myself. I'm rather proud of it, so I love showing it to friends. But this is a special occasion."

"Why?" Julia asked once more.

"Well, you see, Miss MacMunn, you are different. You have taste. Most of my friends—I mean, many people haven't. It cost me a lot of money to have this house furnished and decorated, but it is worth every penny, don't you think?"

Julia looked round dispassionately. "Yes," she agreed, without enthusiasm.

He pursed his lips. "You don't really think so, Miss MacMunn. Why not?"

"Really, Mr. Shilling—"

"Don't mind being frank. I want you to be. Really I do. You see—"

"Well?"

"You know more about furnishing a house than Veronica does."

"Every woman has her own ideas about furnishing her home."

"Of course. I know that. But Vee—she's a darling, but *she's* still young—"

Julia smiled drily at the back-handed compliment to her which was implied by Shilling's accentuating the pronoun. She gazed critically at the wall which contained the photograph and the two Matisses.

"Those two water-colours—" she began.

He mistook her meaning, and did not wait for her to finish. "I said from the first that they were not suitable for a room like this," he said angrily. "I know a schoolgirl who can paint better pictures than those. They'll come down first thing tomorrow morning, blowed if they don't."

"I was not going to suggest your taking them down, Mr. Shilling. They are by a very well-known French painter."

"Oh!"

"It is the photograph which is out of place. It scarcely harmonizes with the Matisses."

Shilling shrugged his shoulders. "That's Vee's Ma. Vee insisted upon hanging it where it could be seen. I didn't like to refuse her."

"Of course not. And those other photographs on the mantel—"

"Are they out of place?" Shilling seemed genuinely astonished.

Julia hesitated before replying, her dark eyes wavering with indecision. The opportunity was hers to weave the first strand of a rope intended to hang the common little man who was staring at her with such anxiety. But now that the moment had arrived to put her plan into action she hesitated to make the first, irrevocable move. Not because of any scruples, or on account of any personal feeling about ethics and honour—of those she had none, for she felt only pitilessness towards the murderer of the kindly, gentle Mary Shilling. If he were, indeed, her murderer! But suppose that her own, and Theo's, and the inspector's deductions were wrong, and that Shilling was not a murderer? The move she intended was indeed irrevocable and would lead, inevitably, to the ruin of Shilling's conjugal happiness. Dared she take the risk of committing that most despicable of wrongs?

By his own impatience Shilling forced a decision.

"Are they?" he repeated. "Isn't it done in the best circles?"

Her dark eyes filled with a friendliness of which he had not previously been conscious.

"I think *you* know the answer just as well as I, Mr. Shilling. You are only pretending you don't, because you love your wife, and want to be loyal to her." She went on quickly, to prevent an interruption: "You are a man. Men are so much more instinctively *comme il faut* than women. That is why a man should be so careful about the woman he marries. She pulls him down to her level instead of trying to raise herself to his."

She turned carelessly away, to hide her excitement. If he has an ounce of decency in him, she reflected, he will bundle me out of this house neck and crop for insulting his wife like that. He is frowning. Is he going to tell me that I am the most insulting guest he has ever had the misfortune to have in the house? If he does I shall respect him a little. I may even begin to wonder whether he is the cold-blooded murderer all of us believe him to be.

But Shilling's frown was not directed against her. "It's quite true," he mumbled. "Vee does not adapt herself as easily as I do to—to new circles." He gazed at her with a new, strange light in his eyes. "You're different, if you don't mind me saying so, Miss MacMunn. You're so—so—"

"Adaptable?" she suggested.

"That's the word. I'll bet you're at home anywhere."

"It's nice of you to say so."

"I mean what I say. You are the kind of person any one should be proud to have around." Then he continued quickly, as though to convey the meaning that he had not meant to be too forward: "Tell me what else is wrong?"

"It is not fair on Mrs. Shilling. A home should be as the wife wants it, not as her guests think it looks best."

Julia looked away unhappily, squirming mentally at her own, vile meanness to the absent wife. True, she had not even the vaguest friendliness for the other woman, but what she was doing to Veronica was spiteful, treacherous, slimy. Surely Shilling had to speak now: surely he must feel some respect for the woman on whose account he had committed murder.

Shilling spoke. "Please tell me," he insisted.

"That Chinese dragon rug—"

"Vee made it especially for this room. And the cushion cover, to go with the rug." He glanced quickly at Julia's face. "I told her that they didn't go with the room."

Julia was sure the man had lied about what he had told Veronica. And Sampson had spoken of men's loyalties! Loyalties to whom? Not to their wives apparently. She began to loathe Robert Shilling with added fervour, now not solely on Mary Shilling's account, but also on behalf of her sex.

"Aren't you going to show me the rest of the house, Mr. Shilling?" she asked, smiling falsely.

III

They went through the house, Julia and Shilling. Room by room. Wherever they went slow poison dripped from her tongue. A sly dig, a scornful shrug, a reference to people of importance, to members of Society (with a capital S), to the County (with a capital C). Without saying so in actual words she led him to realize that his wife was solely to blame if the people of Tunbridge Wells, the important people, had neglected to call and pay their respects to the Shillings. She let him believe that he, of course, was in a different category, for there was no reason why, when unaccompanied by his wife, the people of Tunbridge Wells, the important people, should not accept him as one of themselves.

There were so many differences between men and women, she commented sincerely, but with insincere purpose. Work and travel had the result of giving men a veneer and a polish. A successful man was acceptable in himself, whereas the wife of a successful man often was not. Women had the unfortunate habit of betraying their lack of breeding and deportment. But men, intelligent men, never seemed to make that mistake.

This homily Shilling absorbed with the smooth greed of a sponge absorbing water. When Julia spoke of Veronica his eyes frowned, and his thin lips tightened ominously. When she spoke of the adaptability and social qualities of a successful man his eyes and his thin lips smiled alike, and she could sense the mental preening in which he indulged, assuming quite readily that she was referring to him.

This tour, with its many pauses, proved a lengthy one. Towards the end of it he glanced casually at his watch.

"It's past six," he muttered sharply. "Vee said she wouldn't be long."

"Don't worry about her, Mr. Shilling," Julia said, smoothly. "I am sure she is having a thoroughly good time with Theodore. Theo is a dear boy, and has such a charming way with women."

Thin lines of displeasure betrayed his thoughts as he stared down into the street. "If I had known they were going to be away so long—"

"But, Mr. Shilling, how ungallant you are," she taunted.

He continued to stare through the window. "What do you mean?" he asked coarsely.

"Has the time we have spent together seemed so long?"

He turned. "My God! No!" He was quite sincere. "Not a minute too long as far as I am concerned. I wish Vee—" He broke off, abruptly, and turned towards the window again. "All the same, I don't like the idea of my wife spending so much time with another man. I shouldn't have thought you would have liked the two of them going off all this time either."

"Why not?"

"Well, he's your young man, isn't he?"

"Good heavens, no!" Julia contradicted violently.

"Then isn't that young fellow tied up in any way?"

She laughed softly. "No, Mr. Shilling. He's just a free-lance where women are concerned. But such a charming one!" And she laughed again as she saw the expression of smouldering fury which settled on his face. She was quite sure, now, that she had discovered the chink in his armour, his Achilles heel.

Chapter Eighteen

Terhune was not to blame for their protracted stay at the garden fête. Veronica was the guilty party, with the Rector and Lady Vencey as unintentional accomplices.

To begin with, it required more than an hour to catch up with the Rector. What with the crush of people on the lawns, on the paths, round the stalls and booths and tents, at the shaded tea-tables—in short, everywhere—it was not easy to recognize anyone among the restless, ever-changing crowd, or to reach any particular destination without steering a slow, tortuous course. Even so, on three separate occasions Veronica's eager eyes spotted her quarry, but in each instance at the far side of the lawn; by the time she had dragged her reluctant escort to that spot, the Rector had vanished, so the search had to begin all over again. Terhune had more than a suspicion that the Rector's eyes were as sharp as Veronica's.

Eventually luck deserted the Rector. As they rounded a rather massive rhododendron he met them face to face.

Veronica laughed happily. "At last, Rector! I have been trying to find you for more than an hour."

"Good afternoon, Miss—er—Mrs.—yes, Mrs. Shilling, I believe. How nice of you to come to our little gathering. It is most successful, is it not? Most successful. I do not remember a year when we have had more people here. I wish as many came to Church each Sunday. And now, dear, young lady—" He made a movement of departure, but Veronica quickly caught hold of his sleeve.

"There is something I want you to do for me, please, Rector."

The unfortunate man tried to act cheerfully. "Dear me, Mrs. Shilling, you sound very serious. Naturally, if there is anything I can do for a member of my flock—"

The slight emphasis on the last few words caused Veronica little or no embarrassment. "Of course, my husband and me are not *really* members of your flock Rector. We haven't much faith in the Church. But still, as long as Bob—that's my husband—isn't expected to attend the services he doesn't mind doing what he can for the Church— the Church of England, of course. As we belong to the Church of England we wouldn't dream of helping Non-Conformists, or Roman Catholics."

"But can you really claim to belong to a church which you never attend, Mrs. Shilling? But there, my dear, young lady, what service is it you wish me to perform?"

"Well, you know we haven't been living in Tunbridge Wells very long," Veronica gushed. "We haven't made many friends, and I do so want you to introduce me to some really nice people—"

"*Nice* people?"

"You know what I mean. Classy people. Like Lady Vencey. She wrote me *such* a nice letter about this fête."

"Lady Vencey is very busy," the Rector murmured unhappily. "But I'm sure you would like to meet Mrs. Playford—and Miss Spain—and Mrs. Read—"

These introductions followed. Veronica greeted them with gushing exuberance, which the three dear ladies returned, while Terhune stood aside, feeling just a little sorry for Veronica, for the Rector had seen to it that like met like! Veronica, however, was happy to meet the others, and during the fifteen-minute gossip which followed pressed a tea invitation upon them which they accepted with as much eagerness as it was given.

"Now we must find Lady Vencey," Veronica said, firmly, as the five people parted company.

Terhune tried to dissuade her, but she remained obstinately determined to meet the woman who, she was convinced, was so anxious to meet her. She stopped an inoffensive man who was passing by.

"Can you tell me where Lady Vencey is?" she asked in a loud, affected voice.

"She was in the Rose Garden a few minutes ago."

"Thank you. Coming, Tommy?" She hurried along the neat, gravel path in the direction of the Rose Garden, which they had seen earlier on.

The chase did not come to an end in the Rose Garden: Lady Vencey had moved on, it appeared. But Veronica had the bit between her teeth, and at last Lady Vencey was definitely identified, snatching a morsel of tea, and surrounded by a handful of people badgering her with questions, queries and problems.

Veronica resolutely joined the others.

"Lady Vencey."

Lady Vencey looked up. Her expression was harassed. "Yes, yes? What is your trouble?"

"I wanted to thank you so much for your frightfully nice letter to me—"

"Letter! What letter?" Her gaze sharpened as she stared at Veronica. "Forgive me if I do not recognize you."

"I'm Mrs. Shilling—Veronica Shilling. Your letter—"

"What letter, Mrs. Shilling? I do not remember having written to you?"

"The letter about making this fête a real success."

"The circular letter! Oh, quite! Thank you for coming along, and please spend all you can—the cause is such a good one." Lady Vencey turned away. "Well, Amy, have you put the notice up where I suggested? And please, please, Mrs. Green, use your initiative about refilling the sixpenny dip—"

"Cat!" Veronica exclaimed sullenly as she moved away from the busy table. "Who does she think she is, anyway? You would think we weren't much better than dirt."

"Isn't it time we returned home?" Terhune suggested hopefully.

"I suppose so," she agreed. And then: "Look, Tommy! A fortune-teller! I never miss visiting a fortune-teller ever since a woman at Putney told me I should one day marry a rich widower."

"There's a queue half a mile long."

"Never mind. I must have my fortune told."

"But I'm sure Mr. Shilling expected us back sooner than this. It's already past five."

"Bob must wait. Tea can be served at any time."

They joined up at the end of a queue of eight people. Fortunately the people went in and out of the tent more quickly than Terhune had anticipated, and soon the woman immediately in front of Veronica went in. Veronica took off her wedding and engagement rings.

"I always like trying to deceive fortune-tellers," she whispered to Terhune. "If they find me out then I know they must be good." She squeezed his hand and giggled. "You must come in with me, Tommy dear; it may make her think that you are my sweetheart, and she'll try to tell us that we will be married some time during the next six months."

Terhune was silent. Through a momentary gap in the restless crowd he could see people having tea under the striped umbrellas; the sight reminded him that he was both hot and thirsty. He glanced at his watch, and grimaced. It was not surprising that he was thirsty. Five-forty-one! What were Julia and Shilling going to say when they returned?

Presently the woman who had preceded Veronica came out of the tent smiling to the depths of her gold-filled teeth. She paused for a moment and rested a pudgy hand on Veronica's.

"She's marvellous, my dear. Everything she told me about the past is true. She says I have a wonderful time in front of me—lots of money, another husband—"

"Next, *please*," called out a sepulchral voice from inside the tent.

"Good luck, my dear," the woman said, as she moved on. "I hope your future is as good as mine."

The hand which was holding Terhune's tightened as Veronica led the way in. Inside sat the inevitable garden fête palmist, dressed in a hotch-potch costume meant to be gipsy, and sitting on a rustic chair before a rustic table and a second rustic chair.

After a searching glance at Terhune the palmist waved a long-fingered hand at the chair.

"Will you please sit down? Your friend must stand, I am afraid. Now place both your hands on the table, palms uppermost."

Veronica did as she was told. The palmist stared intently at the two hands for a few moments before lifting her head and staring into Veronica's eyes. She smiled drily.

"Why aren't you wearing your wedding ring? A few months is too short a time in which to regret a marriage."

Veronica was gratifyingly astonished. "You know that I am married?"

"It is written in your hand."

Terhune grinned. The imprint of the ring was indented on Veronica's third finger.

Veronica nodded. "I wanted to test you."

The palmist smiled, and resumed her contemplation of Veronica's hands.

"Before you married you worked for your living. In an office I believe, probably as a shorthand-typist, a private secretary to one of the directors."

Veronica nodded excitedly. "Yes," she breathed.

Terhune grinned again. It hadn't taken the astute palmist long to identify Veronica's category.

The palmist went on: "The young man by your side is not your husband. You married a man older than yourself? Much older," she added with more confidence as Veronica's hands revealed, not by their lines but by a convulsive start, slight but enough for the sensitive fingers of the palmist to feel.

Not a very miraculous guess, thought Terhune. Any woman could see that Veronica's clothes and jewellery, though in bad taste, were expensive, and beyond the salary of the average young man. Besides, Veronica's flashy prettiness was of the type to appeal to an older man.

"I think your husband is a stranger to this district. And perhaps you also. Oh, yes! *You* also. You come from London, but your husband—" this time Veronica did not react to the pause. The palmist began to guess.

"I think—mind you, I'm not quite sure on this point—that he comes from—the—the north." Lacking any reaction she added quickly: "No, not the north. I can see now that I am wrong. It must be the west—not very far from South Wales."

"That's right," Veronica breathed. "From Devon."

"You have not known him very long. A year, maybe. No, nearer two, I should say."

Veronica nodded her head, and the twinkle vanished from Terhune's eyes. Nearer two years than one! So she had known Robert Shilling well before the death of his first wife!

"But your husband was not your first love, was he? I don't need to study your hands to guess *that*—your pretty face is evidence enough. You have had several beaux fluttering round you since your emergence from the chrysalis of girlhood into the beautiful maturity of womanhood."

Terhune thought the subtle inference to a butterfly existence was neat; his respect for the palmist increased.

"But there is a line I see—one man in particular—? *Yes.* one man in particular. Had it not been for meeting your husband you might have married him?"

"Yes, but he was too—"

"Too poor. I can see it in your hand. He was too poor to give you all the things in life you wanted, and indeed, you deserved. Perhaps I can tell you his initial. Your hand says—"

The palmist paused abruptly. Veronica's thoughts flowed on along the lines cunningly started by the palmist. "R.S.," Veronica breathed, unaware that she was speaking her thoughts aloud.

"R.S." the palmist repeated quickly in a decisive voice.

"Oh! How clever you are. Please tell me more."

Terhune grinned. This time the palmist had been too clever. R.S.! Robert Shilling! The result should prove amusing.

"I seem to see an ordinary Christian name. A name like Ralph — Robert—no, I am wrong. It is not quite so commonplace. I wonder if it could be Ronald—"

"Ronald. Yes, yes. Ronald Strudgewick."

"That is right. Ronald loved you very dearly—"

The palmist rattled on, but Terhune no longer listened to her clever probings. Ronald Strudgewick and Veronica. Veronica and Ronald Strudgewick. Strudgewick had been in love with her before Shilling had come on to the scene. Surely those facts added up to something—somewhere—.

He was startled out of his reverie by a cry from the palmist.

"What is the matter?" he asked in bewilderment.

The palmist looked shaken. "That is all. I can read no more," she said, abruptly. "Five shillings, please."

"But you've seen something in my hands. You must tell me, you must."

"I prefer not to," the palmist said unsteadily. "Please go."

The obstinate streak in Veronica's nature, which Terhune had already noticed that afternoon, once again revealed itself.

"I insist upon knowing. It's my right to know what you've seen in my hands. I won't give you the five shillings until you tell me."

"The money is for charity," the woman said, still keeping her gaze upon the table.

"I don't care. I won't pay it."

The woman shrugged her shoulders. "Then it's your own fault. Remember that. What I read in your hand is tragedy—a horrible tragedy that doesn't come to one in a million people. More than that I can't see, I can't tell you. Except this," she added with sudden violence, "that tragedy has something to do with the man who stands behind you." And the palmist looked at Terhune with a genuine horror which convinced Terhune that the woman was speaking with absolute sincerity.

Veronica was in a chastened mood as they walked back towards the car-park.

"Tommy, I feel frightened. What is going to happen to me? What do you think the tragedy is? I don't want to die. I'm too young. I haven't started to lead my life yet. Why should anything happen to me? I haven't done anything wrong to anyone—"

He tried to comfort her. "Don't take any notice of what that silly woman told you, Veronica. Didn't you see the notice which said *For Amusement Only*. She was just trying to be spectacular. She can no more read a palm than I can."

"But she was so clever. Look at all the true things she told me about myself."

He chuckled. "She told you nothing. You told her. Don't you know that a wedding ring always leaves its impression—the deeper the impression the longer it has been worn. She could see that you had been in an office because your hands are well-cared-for, and haven't callouses and corns and ingrained dirt, and so on."

"How did she know I had once worked for a living, and hadn't always been a lady of leisure?"

He did not attempt to answer that question, but went on: "She guessed you had married a rich man by your clothes, and as few young men are rich it wasn't hard to guess that your husband is middle-aged. As for the other men in your life—well, doesn't a pretty girl expect to have a selection of sweethearts?"

"She even guessed Ronald's initials."

"She didn't. You told her. You whispered them without realizing what you were saying. That's true, Veronica. As true as I live."

This information shook her, but she remained unconvinced. "What shall I do to prevent the tragedy happening, Tommy? I must stop it. I can't bear unhappiness and pain and suffering. And why did she speak about you? How can you cause a tragedy in my life?"

"Exactly! How?" he said, drily—but with a horrible feeling of guilt, for was it not a fact that he was doing his best to precipitate a tragedy in her life by helping to deliver her husband to the hangman?

During their short return journey he did his best to wean her from the despondent mood into which she had fallen, but his efforts met with very little success. Silent and brooding she entered the house without a word to the maid who opened the door to them and announced that the master was in the garden. Followed by Terhune she passed through the house into the garden, and there was greeted by Shilling's explosive anger.

"So you've come home at last. Not before it is time. Where have you been all this while? What have you beer doing? Don't you know it's long past tea-time?"

"Please, Bob—"

"Don't please Bob me," he shouted. "I know what you are trying to say—that I shouldn't make a scene before other people: Well, I'm going to, see, because I know Miss MacMunn understands why. What do you think Miss MacMunn has been thinking of a hostess who leaves her guest for four hours—"

"We weren't away three hours—"

"Three hours is bad enough. And don't tell me you have been at that damned garden party all the time—"

"That is just where we have been, Bob, and nowhere else. And if you don't believe Tommy and me—"

"Tommy!" he thundered.

She faltered. "That's Mr. Terhune's Christian name."

Shilling glared at Terhune, but he did not pursue the matter. "What if I don't believe you?"

"You can ask Lady Vencey," she explained triumphantly. "It was after five when we were talking together. I thanked her for sending me her letter."

"Oh!" The name acted like magic in mollifying him to some extent. "What have you been doing since five o'clock?"

"We were just on our way home when I saw a palmist's tent, so I waited to have my hands read."

"My God! As if you haven't had your hand read a hundred times already in the past twelve months. Fancy paying good money just to be told that you are going to have a rich husband and two children, going to inherit money from an old aunt when you are forty-five, going over the water in the next six months—"

Veronica's lips trembled. "She didn't tell me any of those things, Bob dear. All she said was—" she faltered. "All she said was—"

"Well, go on. What did she say?"

"That a terrible tragedy was to come into my life before very long. Oh! Bob! She frightened me so."

"A tragedy!" Shilling's mouth betrayed his sudden trepidation. With a shaky hand he pulled at his collar which was tight round his red, over-fleshy neck. "What—what kind of a—tragedy?" he questioned hoarsely.

"She wouldn't tell me."

"Damn you! Why didn't you make her tell you?" Shilling shouted uncontrollably. Then he seemed to realize what he was doing, and made an effort to recover his self-control. "Well, never mind," he rasped. "Forget the affair, Vee. You know I don't believe in palmistry, fortune-telling and all the other rot. It's all just a money-making racket, a means of making a fat living out of a pack of hysterical women. Anyway, if the woman frightened you it's a damn good job. Perhaps you'll keep away from them in future. Here's the tea at last," he finished disagreeably. "And not before it's time. I'm thirsty enough to drink a bucketful. I'll bet you are, too, Miss MacMunn." He turned round to Julia, and his frown changed to an ingratiating smile.

Chapter Nineteen

The visit of Julia and Terhune to Tunbridge Wells was a protracted one, despite its unpropitious beginning, and the time was getting on for midnight when they began the return journey to Bray. Before this, however, following an embarrassing tea Shilling had first suggested, and then insisted upon, his guests promising to accompany him and his wife to a roadhouse some miles north of Tunbridge Wells; where, he guaranteed, they would be served with a meal comparable to any obtainable in town, and dance to the best dance band in the Home Counties.

Terhune wanted to refuse the invitation, but Julia forestalled him by a quick acceptance. With the prospect of a gay evening ahead Veronica enthusiastically backed up the suggestion, and made efforts to shake off the despondency which had begun with the palmist's prophecy of tragedy, and had been heightened by her husband's ill-humour. Shilling, on the other hand, reacted more slowly to his own idea. For some time afterwards his mood remained brooding and distraught, which convinced both Julia and Terhune that the prophecy of tragedy had deeply affected him. An expression of strain shadowed his eyes, and remained there. His round, plump face became drawn. His attention persistently wandered, and whenever it was recalled, mostly by his mystified wife, he started, and joined in the conversation with unnecessary urgency. From the moment the tea things were removed from the table he glanced frequently at his watch, each time with increasing impatience. It was no surprise when he jumped abruptly to his feet with a hoarse: "It's time for a drink."

Veronica remonstrated with him. "It's still early, Bob darling. Why not wait until we reach the club?"

"It's no use going there for another hour at least. Why wait until then?" And he hurried into the house, to return, some minutes later, wheeling a cocktail cabinet. He seemed scarcely to possess enough patience to ask the others what they would take, but having served them he poured out a stiff whisky for himself, to which he did little more than show the siphon, and with a hoarse, "All the best," he drained the glass.

During the next hour he drank, not heavily, but certainly enough to give him courage to shake off his black devil. He became loud-voiced, and more common than ever. Besides changing his mood, the alcohol had the secondary effect of making him lose all sense of propriety and caution. Practically ignoring his wife and Terhune he paid increasing attention to Julia until soon he was monopolizing her.

For a time Veronica tried to ignore this slight to herself, but she was too inexperienced to keep up diplomatic unconcern for long. Presently she turned sullen, but as this pose had little or no effect upon her husband, she, too, began to drink, and later became recklessly defiant in trying to pay her husband back in his own coin: she slipped her arm through Terhune's and loudly informed him that it was his turn to see the house. With that she led the uneasy Terhune into the house.

The evening continued as it began. They went to the club in two cars, Veronica and Terhune in Julia's, Julia and Shilling in Shilling's Lagonda. They started off together, Terhune leading, but at the first convenient stretch of road Shilling roared past, with the horn blaring loudly in derision. Veronica urged Terhune to give chase, but he refused, so it was not long before the red tail-light of the other car disappeared. For all that Veronica and Terhune were the first to arrive at the club, and nearly twenty minutes elapsed before the other two made an appearance. Terhune thought Julia was looking a trifle ruffled, and had the notion that Shilling had either kissed her or had attempted to do so. The idea choked him; he clenched his fists and looked belligerent. A sign from Julia would have precipitated a fight then and there, but Julia gave no such sign. On the contrary, she looked at Terhune with twinkling eyes and smiling mouth, so he relaxed, remembering that Julia was perfectly capable of dealing with any man, even Robert Shilling, and that, in any circumstances, she would resent being compromised by a roadhouse brawl. As a matter of fact, Julia's eyes twinkled because she had never seen Terhune in a belligerent mood, and had not realized that his soft, studious eyes could look quite so dangerous. Only Helena Armstrong knew that the overgrown schoolboy called Theodore I. Terhune could be a first-class scrapper if necessity demanded. She had seen him sail into a gang of thugs who were attacking her, she had also seen, flashingly, the damage he had done to them before being overcome by superior numbers.

The four people shared the same table at the club, but rather as two separate camps than four friends. Occasionally Shilling flung a word at his wife, occasionally at Terhune, but most of the time he monopolized Julia. He had every dance with her, too, bar one, and that one Julia danced with Terhune only because Terhune managed to speak first, for once. But Shilling did not dance with his wife, he didn't even trouble to sit beside her. He just drank steadily, and gazed at Julia with a stare which Terhune, at any rate, was unable to classify.

All four drank heavily. Julia and Terhune because Shilling insisted unpleasantly that they must keep him company, Veronica because she wanted to, and Shilling himself because he was trying to drown the devils which plagued and tortured him.

At eleven-thirty it was decided to bring the unhappy party to an end. Not by Shilling's wish. He seemed passionately eager to keep it going all night long—there was a night-club in town which carried on through the night, he urged. Or they could return to his house: there was enough drink in the cellar there to keep them going for a week or more. But Julia, pale and black-eyed, was adamant. So they had one final dance, said good night, and departed on their separate, unsteady ways.

Presently Terhune laughed thickly: "Whatta night!"

"Don't talk yet—please—"

He struggled to restore balance to his airy, bemused thoughts— Julia's voice had sounded damned strange—

"Ish—ish—is—anything—wrong—Julie—old—girl?" He tried to speak slowly so that he could enunciate every word.

"Theo dear, I'm not fit to drive. I think I want to be sick."

"Shtop—stop the—the car," he ordered.

She swerved violently, but succeeded in bringing the car to a safe stop on the edge of the ditch. He scrambled out.

"Come along, old girl. I'll hold your head."

He held her head while Julia disgorged the erupting contents of her unhappy stomach. Then Terhune spotted a duckpond not far off. With one arm slipped round her waist they pursued an erratic course to the edge of the pond where he kneeled down and plunged all he could of his head into the cold, soothing water.

When he had done this two or three times he made her kneel down beside him so that he could bathe her forehead and face with a wet handkerchief. Afterwards they sat down on the grass verge, and remained there for a while without exchanging a word. Cars flashed past every now and again, lighting them up in the glare of the head-lamps, but if the occupants of the cars were curious to know why two people were sitting forlornly by the roadside at midnight their curiosity was not powerful enough to cause them to stop and make inquiries.

At last Terhune said: "Feeling better, Julie?"

"Yes, Theo dear," she acknowledged shakily. Then: "Oh, Theo!"

"What is the matter?"

"I feel contaminated—beastly—"

"For having had a little too mush—too *much* to drink?"

"Partly."

"Cheer up, Julie. We all of us have a little too much once in a while."

"It isn't only the knowledge that I'm—I'm tight—"

"You're a long way off being that."

"Well, almost tight," she compromised. "It's the thought of having demeaned myself by pretending to be friendly with that beastly man. Theo, he's unspeakable!"

"He—he kissed you, didn't he, Julie, oh the way to the club?"

"Only on the back of the neck, Theo. He wanted to kiss me on the lips, but I wouldn't let him. Not because the idea of his slimy, nasty lips on mine was too revolting—which it was—Ugh!—but because I believed it was the time to finesse."

"Finesse?"

"Yes, Theo. Surely you haven't forgotten that we had a reason for visiting the wretched man. Your inspector wanted to know the chink in Shilling's armour. I'm sure I know it—or them. He has two chinks, Theo. His ridiculous snobbery, his overwhelming ambition to be on terms of intimacy with people of title, that is one chink. The other is his jealousy of Veronica. He is insanely jealous of her because he has just enough sense to realize that her shallow, little soul isn't capable of genuine love and affection. He knows that he is nearly old enough to be her father and that if the day ever comes when he has to compete with a younger man she will betray him just as readily as she takes his money.

"I don't mean that she will leave him. She won't sacrifice luxury for love. He knows that well enough. But he also knows that, if it is humanly possible, she will do both; she will take his money, while giving her kisses secretly to a younger man."

"He was rather asking for trouble, tonight, wasn't he, Julia, the way he monopolized you and left her in the cold?"

"It wasn't all for my sweet sake he did that. He was determined to punish her for calling you Tommy, and for having preferred to have three hours of your company rather than his. I think he hates you, Theo."

Terhune grinned. "He should know what I really think of her."

"You know why Shilling was drinking so heavily?"

"I know why I think he was drinking so heavily," he corrected.

"I have no doubts left about his guilt. If ever a man looked terrified he did when Veronica spoke of an impending tragedy." Julia wet the handkerchief again and held it to her forehead. "Did the palmist really warn her of a tragedy, I wonder?" she said, musingly. "Or does Veronica suspect the truth?"

"The palmist said that, right enough. I was there. As a matter of fact, she said more than that. She said that I had some connection with her tragedy."

"Theo!"

"I was just as startled, Julie. I thought she was just one of the usual charity fakes—and come to that, I still think so. Yet she must have had a sudden, sincere inspiration. You know, like the man who faked the power of performing miracles, and one day actually did perform one."

"It's uncanny! Why should she have picked upon you, of all people?"

"I've something else to tell which I think may surprise and excite you, Julie. Veronica was in love with Ronald Strudgewick before she met her present husband."

"I don't think that really *surprises* me. But why should it excite me?"

"Sampson wondered if there were any way of getting at Shilling through his wife. If Shilling is as jealous as you think he is—By the lord Harry!" he exclaimed unexpectedly.

"What have you just thought of, Theo?"

"I wonder if we could get Shilling to come over to your place by himself."

She laughed softly. "It is already fixed up for him to do so. He is coming today fortnight—or rather, yesterday fortnight, seeing that it is now Tuesday morning. I let him know that Mother would be glad to receive him, but not his common, little wife. And the hateful man accepted. But why do you want him on his own?"

"Listen, Julie——"

II

The following morning Terhune 'phoned through to Scotland Yard in the hope of contacting Sampson. He was unlucky; Sampson, it appeared, was out, and was not expected to report back until late afternoon. But Terhune left a message for the inspector, and just before 6 p.m., as Terhune was about to close the shop, Sampson telephoned back.

"There's a message on my desk saying that you 'phoned this morning, Mr. Terhune."

"Yes. Miss MacMunn and I visited Tunbridge Wells yesterday afternoon."

"Ah!" The exclamation was brief, but it revealed the inspector's deep interest.

Terhune gave the inspector a full account of the happenings at Tunbridge Wells. Towards the end of the story his words were punctuated by loud guffaws of laughter from the other end.

"Good work, Mr. Terhune!" Sampson congratulated presently. "I'll be glad to do as you suggest. Meanwhile, I have some news for you. Do you remember suggesting that our man might have taken a train as far as Honiton, and cycled the remaining distance home?"

"Yes."

"Well, no cycle arrived by passenger train at Honiton on the day in question, but police inquiries in that town have disclosed the fact that two second-hand bicycles were sold that afternoon, both to men.

So far the Devon police have been unable to trace either buyer. One of the bicycles was sold to a man with light hair, who spoke with the local burr, and who gave the shopkeeper the impression of being a farm labourer. I think we can take it for granted that he wasn't the man we're after.

"The second sale was so quickly over that the seller's memory of the buyer is too vague to be of any use to us, particularly in view of the fact that the sale took place nearly a year ago. But until there is good reason to think otherwise I am prepared to believe that the man who purchased the second bicycle was our man from London."

"What about the return journey, Inspector?"

Sampson laughed. "Thanks to the Somerset police I think I can answer that question satisfactorily."

"The *Somerset* police?"

"Yes. It wasn't any use his returning to Honiton because he couldn't have got back from there to London in time to establish his breakfast alibi. On the other hand, he didn't want to risk going into Exeter in case he was recognized. Do you know what the cunning devil did? He rode the twenty odd miles into Taunton, where he abandoned the bicycle in the town, walked the rest of the way to the station, and caught the 2.39 a.m. train, which arrived in Paddington at seven-five. I had a call from the Chief Constable of Devon, two days ago, to say that the bicycle which was found abandoned, in Taunton, some hours after Mary Shilling's death, has been positively identified as one of the two which was sold in Honiton less than twenty-four hours previously. That is good enough evidence for me that your theory is a reasonable one.

"And here's some more information for you to prove what a fox the man is. You remember Strudgewick's telling the lift-man-cum-hall-porter that Shilling was walking upstairs in order to deliver a note to some people by the name of Dixon, who were occupying flat thirty-seven on the third floor? Well, a note *was* delivered there, enclosing two theatre seats from Shilling for Mrs. Dixon and her daughter. Mrs. Dixon told the valet so the next morning."

"The note with the tickets was not delivered personally?"

"No. It was dropped through the letterbox."

"By Strudgewick?"

"Probably, but Mrs. Dixon was apparently convinced that it was Shilling who did so, and from what I have heard of the good lady she is the type who would be quite prepared to go into the witness stand and air her opinion—for what it was worth, of course!"

"Any further news from Yorkshire?"

"No."

"Then there is still not evidence enough to put either man in the dock?"

"There certainly is not," the inspector agreed emphatically. Then he added: "Not yet."

The strange inflection in Sampson's voice excited Terhune. "You have another clue?"

"I don't know yet, but your visit to Tunbridge Wells wasn't wasted. It is helping me to add two and two together."

"And what do they add up to, Inspector?"

"The Dixon girl," Sampson replied enigmatically.

Chapter Twenty

At one minute to seven p.m. on the night of Shilling's visit to Willingham Manor, Julia came down from her bedroom and entered the long narrow drawing-room which overlooked the charming vista of lawns, flower-gardens and wooded slopes which lay at the back of the MacMunn home.

She was not the Julia known to the inhabitants of Willingham and Wickford and Bray-in-the-Marsh. She was quite a different Julia, one at whom all her friends would have given a second, astonished glance, for the young woman who awaited the arrival of Robert Shilling was dressed deliberately 'for a killing.' Generally Julia could be said to represent the epitome of good taste, and even those who disliked her most were usually ready to agree that she was the best-dressed woman for miles around. Tonight, however, she had ignored her invariable rule of simplicity.

Her blue-black hair, usually so severely *chic*, had been dressed in a style calculated to catch and hold the attention of her expected visitor, for its foremost curl swept across her high intelligent forehead in a mischievous and not unbewitching wave. Her face remained untouched, for her warm, brown, wind-swept cheeks had a natural bloom which cosmetics could only have ruined. Her lips, in contrast, were deep crimson, while from her ears, usually unadorned, hung two ruby ear-rings which not only emphasized her gipsy-like appearance, but matched to perfection the shade of her lips.

Her dress, of emerald green and old gold, was a new one; she had purchased it for this especial occasion, and was resolved never to wear it again. It was in keeping with the fashion, yet, at the same time, was a thing of flounces and frills and artificial lines. It was also of a more *décolleté* style than her usual, being low over her perfect shoulders—really far too lovely to be hidden—and low enough over her bosom to have exposed the first swell of her tight, lovely breasts, had she not tempered modesty with provocativeness by wearing a spray of jewelled flowers.

Upstairs in her bedroom she had already surveyed herself many times in the cheval mirror. Even so, as she moved across the drawing-room to a cool corner she caught sight of herself in a large Empire mirror which hung on the wall opposite one of the twin-bay windows. She stopped, and looked once more at herself, and because she had as a background the reflection of flowers, and woods, and distant white woolly lambs, and a dappled blue sky the effect was to make her, in her own estimation, more vulgar than ever. She grimaced at herself, and then grimaced again as the distant echo of an electric bell informed her that somebody was at the front door.

She was sure it was Shilling already. It would be just like him, she reflected, to be dead on time, as though he were keeping a business appointment. Alicia, she knew, was not likely to be down for another twenty minutes at least—she made unpunctuality a habit —which meant that she, Julia, would have to entertain the nasty little man by herself for that length of time.

She heard Phillips opening the door, and Shilling's voice: "Miss MacMunn."

So he hadn't even the manners to ask for his hostess.

"Will you please step in, sir? What name shall I say?"

"Mr. Shilling. Ah! Yes, sir. Mrs. MacMunn is expecting you. Will you please come with me?"

The two men approached the drawing-room. Phillips opened the door. He seemed surprised to see Julia, but quickly recovered himself.

"Mr. Robert Shilling."

Shilling brushed by Phillips, and hurried towards Julia. As he did so his eyes shone with a light of appreciation which comforted her in the knowledge that her sacrifice was not in vain.

"You don't know how anxious I've been for tonight to arrive, Miss MacMunn," he began eagerly, breathing the unpleasant aroma of whisky about her, and gripping her hand in his own, which was warm and flabby, and holding on to it as long as he dared. "For the past two weeks I've been feeling like a schoolboy before his first party." He glanced round. "And your mother——"

"She always takes *so* long to dress. She will be down soon."

"Not too soon, I hope," and his lecherous lips parted in a meaning smile. "Would you consider it an impertinence to tell you that you look charming, charming."

"Surely no woman could think it impertinent of you to call her charming," Julia responded archly. "I am afraid you are rather a lady-killer, Mr. Shilling."

The tone of conversation having descended to his own level there was no holding him back.

"I'm not going to say that I don't like the ladies, but as to being a lady-killer——" he began to smile deprecatingly, but the smile died, stillborn, as its place was taken by a grey expression of horror.

Startled by the abrupt, unexpected transition Julia spoke. "Mr. Shilling! What is it?" Too late, she realized the extraordinary coincidence of her own remark, and his denial. *No lady-killer!*

"It is nothing—much, Miss MacMunn," he gasped hoarsely. "Just a spasm—heart, you know! Would you think me rude if I—I asked for a drink——"

"Of course not."

She rang for Phillips, and while she awaited his coming, told Shilling to sit down. He did so, heavily, and stared across the room with haunted eyes. In this trance-like state he remained until Julia flourished a whisky before him. He snatched the glass from her hand, and swallowed the liquid in one gulp.

"Another?"

"Please." His none-too-steady hand passed the glass back to her.

Julia refilled the glass, which she handed back to him. He took another deep swallow, then looked at her apologetically.

"Aren't you having anything, Miss MacMunn?"

She nodded. "A sherry." She poured one out.

The colour began to return to his face. "Here's to—us," he toasted. "May this be the beginning of a long friendship."

Julia forced herself to drink the toast.

"Did you tell your wife that you were coming here tonight?"

He shook his head. "I did *not*. What the eye doesn't see, the heart doesn't grieve over."

"But wasn't she surprised at your going out without her?"

"No. She thinks that I'm in London, on business. Besides, I've taught her not to ask questions, or to expect explanations. I believe in a married man having some degree of freedom."

"And your wife—is she allowed a similar latitude?" Julia asked drily.

"She is not! What's sauce for a husband isn't sauce for a wife."

"Oh!" Julia gazed at her sherry. "But how do you know that she hasn't taken advantage of your absence?"

"For one thing I didn't say anything about leaving her until an hour before it was time for me to leave the house, so she wouldn't have had much opportunity of fixing anything up. Besides, I know everything that goes on in my absence, anyway."

"One of the maids?"

He laughed boastfully—he was apparently recovering. "Yes."

"But maids can be bribed—by both parties."

He stared anxiously at Julia. "My God! You don't think Vee would do that to me, do you, Miss MacMunn?"

"One never knows what pretty young women of her type will do when they have the opportunity," Julia said, carelessly.

Shilling's thin lower lip began to protrude. "If I should ever catch her doing that—"

"Come, come, Mr. Shilling, you must make allowances for youth."

"Damn it! I'm not so old as all that—"

"Of course you are not," Julia murmured, placatingly. "But she is young for her years, and very attractive to men."

"Let's not talk about Vee," he said, roughly.

"Then—"

"Let's talk of you," he went on boldly.

She shrugged. "I have lived all my life in this house, and in this village. What could there be interesting in such a life?"

"But surely you have travelled a lot? Your mother—"

"If Mother visits friends in Hampshire she says she is travelling. Mother and I have really travelled—by which I mean abroad—three times in my lifetime. The last time to the Canary Islands. I am sure your past must be far more interesting."

An agonized expression revealed itself.

"Not the past," he appealed. "The present—yes. And more particularly—" He paused, and stared boldly at her. "The future. I am hoping—" He paused again, this time more uncertainly.

"Well?"

"Not now. Another time. When I know you better."

"You are very mysterious!" she mocked.

His breathing became laboured, his glance lecherous. "Are you very keen to travel?" he asked thickly.

"Very."

"Then why shouldn't you do so—in the winter—the West Indies, or South Africa, or Egypt—I've always wanted to go to Egypt."

"*You* have wanted to go to Egypt, Mr. Shilling? I don't understand."

"I—I—" His stammered beginning ceased abruptly as the door opened to admit Alicia. She sailed across the room with a regal air— she was always regal, was Alicia—and welcomed her guest with an exaggerated warmth which caused Julia quiet amusement—Alicia had been given a part to play, which, in her eagerness, she was over-acting, and would doubtless continue to over-act.

"How nice to see you again, Mr. Tanner, after all this time. Why didn't you come to see us before this? We have often spoken of you both, and wondered whether we should meet you again. You have not changed much," she rattled on. "Except perhaps— yes, indeed—I declare, you are looking more youthful than ever." She sighed dramatically. "How lucky men are. They grow older so much more slowly than we do, don't you think so, Julia, my dear?" Alicia sailed on towards a Chesterfield, sat down on one cushion, and patted the other. "Sit down beside me, Mr. Tanner, and tell me all about yourself."

"Mr. Shilling, Mother dear."

"Mr. Shilling!" Alicia stared at her daughter, at the door, and once more at her daughter. "Do you mean to say that Mr. Shilling has just arrived? How inconvenient, just at this time. Can't you warn Phillips to say that we are engaged?"

"Mother dear, Mr. Shilling is already with us," Julia explained patiently. "Mr. Shilling, not Mr. Tanner."

Alicia was not in the least disconcerted. "How stupid of me!" she chattered on. "Of course, you are Mr. Shilling, aren't you? It is the fault of that silly man, Burton, for having called you Mr. Tanner in the first case—"

"Burton! Who is Burton?" Shilling asked sharply.

Julia tried to give her mother a warning glance. "Please don't take any notice of Mother," she told Shilling. "She talks such a lot of nonsense, sometimes."

"Really, Julia, is that the way to talk of your mother? Now, what was I saying—"

"You were inviting Mr. Shilling to sit down beside you."

"That is right. So I was. Do sit down on this Chesterfield, Mr. Shilling." He did so, eagerly. "I have so much I want to ask you. But first give Mr. Shilling and me something to drink, Julia darling. I am sure Mr. Tanner must be thirsty after his long journey."

"Oh, come, Mrs. MacMunn, it is not a long journey from Tunbridge Wells to here," Shilling said, speaking in a voice which was, at the same time, both deferential and familiar. "It is only about thirty-five miles, you know."

Relative distance was a subject which had no meaning for Alicia. If she had never visited a place it could be as far off as Timbuctoo. She dismissed his statement with a careless wave of her hand.

"I'm afraid I think of it as being farther even than Exeter."

"Exeter!" he exclaimed sharply.

"Isn't that where you were living when we met at Las Palmas?"

"Yes."

"Poor Mr. Shilling!" Alicia became sympathetic. "I do not blame you for leaving a town where you had been so happy with that dear Mary of yours. I cannot tell you what a shock it was to me to hear of her sad death."

"It was a shock to me, too, Mrs. MacMunn," he said hoarsely. "I would rather not talk of it."

"But you must. You must be brave. Don't you know that it is *so* much easier to bear sorrow when it is shared? It is *so* bad for a person to be intro—intro—what is that word, Julia? I never can remember it?"

"Introspective."

"Thank you, dear. Yes, indeed, Mr. Shilling, it is one of the things which psychologists warn us against, while strongly advising us to consult psycho-analysts who can often help to cure the evil."

"I do not dwell upon her death, Mrs. MacMunn. I try to forget it," he said meaningly.

"That is the right course to take," she approved. "But you must not forget the nicer memories, but only the sorrow of the parting. You must treasure up your happiest memories of her, remember her as a sweet, dear person—"

"Please!"

Instead of faltering, his agonized appeal inspired Alicia anew. "She was such a credit to you, the dear soul. Loyal, faithful, hard-working. She was a wife in a thousand. With Mary by your side there is not a door in the kingdom which would have remained shut to you both, Mr. Shilling."

"Mary—"

Alicia patted his hand. "Nobody could help loving her. Before Julia and I left Las Palmas I made her promise that you and she would spend a week with us here, but she never wrote to me to tell me what date was convenient to you both. Now, alas, it is too late!"

Alicia lied with a convincing sincerity that was born not of any natural aptitude, but from a careful coaching which had so impressed the story upon her unreliable memory that she herself had come to believe that the fiction—which Terhune had invented—was, in fact, nothing more or less than the truth.

Shilling, at any rate, had no doubts about its veracity.

"Mary said nothing about that invitation."

"She was *so* shy and modest—such a delightfully simple woman." Alicia shook her head sadly. "Oh, dear! What a tragedy her death was! I wonder why God takes the good, the kind, the generous and leaves—the others!"

Shilling's hand tightened round the whisky glass which Julia had passed over to him—she almost expected to see his grip shatter it.

"For God's sake leave Mary out of the conversation," he shouted harshly, and quite regardless of the fact that Alicia showed no signs of touching the sherry for which she had asked he swallowed down the whisky with the same greedy haste as he had shown in tossing off the contents of the first glass.

"Poor Mr. Shilling! Of course, we won't talk of her any more if you really would rather we did not." She turned to Julia. "Surely, Julia dear, it was less than two weeks ago when we discussed the idea of going to Palestine on the s.s.—I never can remember its name, but never mind—"

"The trip Freddie was taking?" Julia suggested.

"Yes, my dear." She turned back to Shilling. "Freddie is such a dear man—the Duke of Doncaster, you know—that I like going away with him if I can arrange to do so. He had made up a party of four; the Earl and Countess of Droby, Freddie's wife Elizabeth and himself, and he suggested my doing the same, and joining up with them. I suggested our writing to Mary, to ask whether you and she would join us, but Julia reminded me that Mrs. Shilling had died." Alicia's lips trembled, tears gathered in her eyes. "I was so sad, thinking of her tragic death, that I decided not to go at all."

Shilling gazed despairingly at his hostess. "The Duke of Doncaster—the Earl of Droby—" Exasperated by the thought of what might have been he clasped and unclasped his free hand, and gazed about the room with desperate, grasping eyes.

"Mrs. MacMunn—"

"Well, Mr. Shilling?" she asked in a kindly, sympathetic manner.

"I am still married—I have a second wife—" he pleaded with pathetic hope.

With a precision that was nothing more than innocent ingenuousness, Alicia rubbed the salt into his open wounds.

"The second Mrs. Shilling!" she said carelessly. "Certainly not, dear Mr. Shilling. Elizabeth is very particular." She turned away. "Julia, dear child, isn't it time that that Mr. Sampson arrived? And where is Mr. Terhune? He is usually not so late." So the conversation was neatly turned away from Mary Shilling, and for the next four minutes was confined to trivialities. But there was no concealing the effect which it had had upon Shilling. His face was transformed into an unsmiling mask, but there was the haunting despair in his eyes of a man who had sacrificed the substance for the shadow.

Then Terhune arrived, and, with him, Sampson.

"Mr. Terhune and Mr. Sampson," Phillips announced.

Terhune took Sampson across to Alicia.

"This is my friend Sampson of whom you have often heard me speak," he began casually.

Then came Alicia's moment. She laughed shrilly.

"Why, you silly boy! As if I couldn't help recognizing the man who arrested that horrible Gregory Belcher—" Then, too late, she faltered unhappily into disconcerting silence.

Chapter Twenty-One

J ulia was the first to recover. "Mother dear," she began coolly, "Mr. Sampson didn't come here to talk shop. He is visiting us as Theo's friend. However—" She turned to Shilling with a smile. "In view of Mother's indiscretion you might as well be introduced to Mr. Sampson by his formal title. Detective-Inspector Sampson, of the C.I.D.—Mr. Robert Shilling."

Incapable of movement or speech, Shilling stared up at the inspector. Sampson nodded genially at the other man.

"Glad to meet you, Mr. Shilling," he said crisply, as though he was unaware of anything strange in Shilling's behaviour. He turned back to Alicia. "I'm very grateful to you for your invitation here tonight, Mrs. MacMunn, though it's an imposition on you, my turning up with Mr. Terhune like this."

"I won't have you saying that, Mr. Sampson," Alicia retorted sincerely. "We love arranging informal little dinner parties, don't we, Julia dear? It prevents our quarrelling with each other too often. Besides, any friend of Mr.—er—Tommy's is a friend of ours, isn't he, Julia dear?"

"Yes, Mother. What will you drink, Mr. Sampson. Whisky, gin and anything, rum, sherry—"

"It may be a queer taste, Miss MacMunn, but I'd love a rum, with some lime juice, sugar and water."

"One of sour, two of sweet, three of strong, four of weak. Isn't that a Planter's Punch, Mr. Sampson?"

"It certainly is, and a fine drink too, even on a warm night."

Julia waved her hand at the silver salver. "Everything is there. Mix your own. Theo, my pet, I suppose you want your usual Manzanilla? Mr. Shilling, whisky?"

The tension passed off as the conversation became general and lively. In the absence of further menace, and the fairly obvious evidence that the inspector had, apparently, no ulterior motive in visiting Willingham Manor, Shilling slowly recovered from the shock caused by the unexpected presence of a detective inspector from the C.I.D. Moreover, the stimulation of alcohol presently took effect. He began to wear an expression of bravado which at least three of the other four present had no difficulty in translating. What have I to fear—the expression challenged—it isn't likely that I should be suspected of killing Mary after this length of time. And even if I were to be, there's no evidence against me. I have a perfect alibi. Why should I worry because a detective from Scotland Yard has accidentally dropped in. The only reason he's here is on account of his being a friend of that damned Terhune fellow.

Ten minutes after the arrival of Terhune and Sampson, Phillips announced that the meal was served. The five people moved into the dining-room, where Alicia, at the head of the table, isolated Shilling on her right, with Sampson and Terhune opposite him, on her left, and Julia at the other end.

The meal proceeded easily but slowly. Julia had arranged this beforehand, with fell design, so as to give Shilling ample time to empty his glass at frequent intervals, and Phillips the opportunity of refilling it with a young, and quite potent, Chambertin. Before long Shilling's laboured correct behaviour began to reveal cracks in its false façade. His conversation became rambling, his words a trifle slurred. He began to boast recklessly of his business acumen, his ability to overcome obstacles, his own pleasing personality.

"I think the plum will soon be ripe for the picking," Sampson muttered to Terhune. "A nasty piece of goods, by George! And as guilty as hell."

"You think so?"

"I'm as sure of it as I am of my own name. I've seen too many men suffering from guilty consciences not to recognize the symptoms." Shilling, too, was muttering. He was sprawling across the table on his elbow, mouthing something in a low whisper to Julia which tightened her lips. "I think he's had about enough drink for our purposes," Sampson went on. "We don't want him to pass right out."

"I'll give Phillips a hint to hold off." Terhune was able to do so almost at once, and Phillips discreetly withdrew the bottle which he had just brought in. "I hope our plan succeeds."

"He's off his guard," Sampson said, but not with a great deal of confidence. "If it doesn't succeed—" His gesture was eloquent.

"Is it the only chance of putting him in the dock?"

"Yes. There isn't a capful of evidence against him. Just before coming here today I telephoned Inspector Longworth. He told me—"

Terhune did not hear what Longworth had to say, either then or later, for Alicia broke into their conversation.

"I suppose you must do a lot of travelling, Mr. Sampson, in the course of a year's work?"

The question was quite meaningless, but nobody had spoken to her for three or four minutes, and she felt aggrieved.

"Why, I wouldn't say that I do, Mrs. MacMunn. Unless you call moving about within the London Metropolitan area travelling. But, of course, there aren't many parts of London that I don't know well. I dare say you travel about the rest of the country far more than I do."

Julia laughed drily. "Mother never moves far from this house if she can possibly do otherwise."

"How unfair of you, Julia," Alicia began, complainingly. She looked at the inspector. "It so happens, Mr. Sampson, that Julia and I have twice left home in the past few months and each time for a distant part of the country."

"Yes, yes," Sampson said, loudly. "But then why should you leave this lovely house?" Fearful of what Alicia might say next, he went on quickly: "I think the view from the other room is one of the loveliest I have seen for quite a time."

Alicia was not to be silenced. "I don't know whether you have any children, Mr. Sampson——"

"I'm not married."

"Then I suppose you haven't any; in which case you have been spared a great deal of unnecessary exasperation, not to say a most distressing absence of gratitude. It really is surprising how ungrateful children are to their parents."

Julia sighed with an exaggerated gesture. "Don't prolong the agony, Mother dear. Tell Mr. Sampson the worst about me."

"I was speaking generalities, and not referring particularly to my child."

"Of course not."

"But there are times when I feel that she could show——"

"A little more respect?" Julia mocked. "A little more gratitude? A little more filial love?"

"A little more——a little more——now you have made me forget exactly what I was going to say. It was something to do with our journey to Yorkshire——"

"Shall we go into the other room for coffee, Mother?"

"Coffee! Coffee!" For a moment Alicia's expression was a little vague, but she soon recovered. "Why, of course. We always have coffee in the drawing-room, Julia. But as I was saying——"

"Phillips, serve the ice-pudding at once," Julia ordered.

"Yes, Miss Julia."

Sampson turned quickly to Alicia. "Speaking of ice-puddings reminds me of an arrest I once made, in one of the London milk-bars——"

The story was a short one, but it was long enough to make Alicia forget what she wanted to say about the journey to Yorkshire, and the others breathed more easily when, the inspector having finished his tale, she began to question him on criminal matters. For the next ten minutes Sampson continued to hold the stage, while he related one anecdote after another meanwhile, leading from crimes of greed and avarice, with which he began, to crimes of love and passion. With deliberate cunning each one of these emphasized, not the more usual story of man's infidelity to his chosen woman, but precisely the reverse.

"It makes me smile when I hear people speak of women who sacrifice themselves for love. Half the time it isn't themselves they sacrifice but their husbands or lovers as the case may be. I tell you when a woman is really mercenary the average man can't hold a candle to her for sheer treachery—"

"Oh, come, Mr. Sampson, aren't you being just a little prejudiced?" Julia remonstrated mildly.

"I'll prove that I'm not, Miss MacMunn. Listen, I'll tell you another yarn. Three years ago—"

"Shall we hear the story in the drawing-room, Mr. Sampson. We shall be far more comfortable there. You men can settle yourselves comfortably with a cigar and a brandy. I'm sure you will be able to make the story twice as interesting."

"*Twice* as interesting," Sampson agreed emphatically.

The five people returned to the drawing-room. Shilling walked somewhat too deliberately, and the expression on his face was strangely at variance with itself for, while his thin mouth wore a loose grin, his eyes were once again filled with doubt and uncertainty.

They grouped themselves round the coffee-table which awaited them. Shilling collapsed into his chair with a flop which made one of the springs twang, and stared at the brandy bottle. Presently Terhune placed one of a nest of tables by the side of Shilling's chair and on it the coffee which Julia had just poured out.

"Brandy, Mr. Shilling?"

He croaked something which Julia construed as "Please," or perhaps "Yes"—more likely "Yes" she thought—and poured out a stiff brandy. This Terhune placed beside the coffee.

As soon as they were all settled Julia reminded Sampson of the story he had proposed telling them. The inspector told it. Like the others it was about a woman who had betrayed to the police the bank cashier who had loved and trusted her, and for whom he had robbed his employers of several hundred pounds.

When he had finished Julia shook her head reprovingly. "I think you are a woman-hater, Mr. Sampson, and that you are really teasing us by exaggerating the shabby faithlessness of a few bad women."

Sampson pulled lingeringly at his cigar before he answered. "I'm sorry to disappoint you, Miss MacMunn, but I haven't. And if Rudyard Kipling were alive today I'm sure he would agree with me. He knew his women."

"'For the female of the species is more deadly than the male.'" Julia quoted softly.

"And, by George, they are, too! Why, it's not many months ago that a case was brought to our notice of a woman who encouraged a man to plan a murder so that he could become rich, and then I'll be darned if she didn't go and marry some other fellow instead."

"Well—" Terhune urged.

Sampson shook his head. "Mrs. and Miss MacMunn have heard enough about the misdoings of their sex. It's time I dropped the subject."

"No, please," Julia said hastily. "We have very broad shoulders, haven't we, Mother?"

"Broad shoulders!" Alicia shook her head. "Of course I haven't. Nor have you, Julia. I think broad shoulders on a woman are unbecoming. But do please tell us the story, Mr. Sampson. It sounds fascinating."

"If you insist." Sampson snuggled more closely into his chair. "It began in Yorkshire—"

"In Yorkshire!" Alicia interrupted unexpectedly. "Why, we know something about a murder in Yorkshire—"

"Mother!"

"Your mentioning Yorkshire reminds me of what I intended to say during the meal—"

"Mother, will you *please* allow Mr. Sampson to finish his story first. Now, Mr. Sampson—"

Sampson continued quickly: "Some weeks ago we received a letter addressed from a small place in Yorkshire called Hawley Green—"

Shilling's glass did a somersault into the air, and landed on the carpet with a thump which shattered the delicate glass. The remains of the liquid splashed Terhune's socks and the ends of his trousers.

Alicia breathed a shocked "Oh!" as she glanced at the floor. Terhune sank on one knee and began to collect the scattered fragments of glass.

Shilling himself seemed unaware that his curled fingers no longer gripped the stem of a glass. He sat stiffly motionless. A dark vein in his forehead began visibly to throb. His lower lip protruded, and a suspicion of saliva oozed from a corner of his mouth.

With no more than a quick glance at Shilling's face the inspector continued: "The letter was written by an old servant of a man who had died this spring from drowning. Apparently the old servant had got the idea firmly fixed in his mind that his master had been killed by a nephew, the only surviving relative."

"Why should the nephew have killed his uncle?"

"Well, there was a pretty good reason, Miss MacMunn, because the old man died intestate, so the nephew inherited a sizeable fortune. Just the same we didn't think there was anything serious in the accusation—we receive too many in the course of a year, and mostly false alarms at that, for any one of them to cause much excitement.

But, of course, we had to investigate the matter, so we passed on the accusation to the police on the spot. They investigated." Sampson paused deliberately.

Shilling's anxiety took the form of a gasping hiss. The saliva dribbled down his chin, and on to his tie.

Terhune asked casually: "What did the investigation disclose?"

"That the nephew was in Yorkshire on the night his uncle died."

"You mean—he was guilty?"

"Bless my soul! You do jump to conclusions, Mr. Terhune. At the time of the uncle's death he was staying at a town thirty miles away, and had as good an alibi as any one could wish."

Shilling relaxed. His shaking fingers pulled a handkerchief from his trouser-pocket, and with it he wiped his chin dry. Then he felt for his brandy glass, but failing to find it at once he turned his head and looked at the table beside his chair. When he saw that the glass was missing an expression of perplexed surprise momentarily displaced the previous glassy fear. Then he saw the pieces of the glass on the coffee tray, and he appeared abruptly to recollect what had happened, for his manner became fearful again, and he glanced furtively at the inspector as though asking himself whether the other man had noticed anything amiss. But Sampson's geniality reassured him, and Shilling breathed a deep, long sigh of relief.

The others took their cue from Sampson. "But I thought you said something about a woman," Julia said casually.

Shilling's eyes echoed the question. A woman!

"I'm coming to her, Miss MacMunn. The North Riding police reported back to us that this nephew fellow seemed innocent enough, but as he usually lived in London would we mind checking up on his past just to make sure he had no record.

"That job was passed on to me. It didn't give me any trouble. I soon found out that as far as police records were concerned the man had a clean bill of health. But there was something about him which I unearthed, and that was his fondness for your sex, Miss MacMunn. And one girl in particular. Her name doesn't matter, but she played merry hell with the poor devil, encouraging him one moment to believe that she was in love with him, and telling him the next that she didn't want anything to do with him. As a matter of fact, as far as I can make out the only reason which made him unacceptable to her ladyship was the fact that he wasn't well enough off for her—at that time he was comparatively poor, and not being a seer she didn't foresee that he was shortly going to inherit a small fortune. At any rate, it seems that she told him quite frankly that she had made up her mind to marry only a rich man, but, in the meantime, she didn't mind him hanging about her if he didn't ask for more than the pleasure of her company. I think she was as fond of him as she was capable of being fond of anybody but herself.

"Well, things went on like this for some months. Then, one day, this man introduced her to a friend of his. A foolish thing for him to have done, for the friend was pretty well off. You can guess what happened. The girl set her cap at the friend, and hang me if she didn't succeed! He fell for her, hook, line and sinker. There was only one drawback. He was married. But she wasn't going to let a little thing like that stand in her way. She told him that she would marry him if he could get his wife to agree to a divorce.

"Whether the wife agreed or not I don't know, but I have found this out: two weeks after she had promised to marry the friend as soon as he was free, this chit of a girl, convinced that she had arranged a satisfactory future for herself, coolly betrayed her future husband by becoming the mistress of the other man—the one she had refused to marry because he was too poor. I'd like to have the opportunity of telling that girl what I think of her. And, by George! one of these days when I have nothing better to do I'll see if I can't find out where Veronica Dixon has gone to—"

"Veronica!" Shilling rose unsteadily to his feet, and stood by Sampson's chair, swaying. "You damned liar!" he mouthed. "You blasted lying swine!"

Alicia was shocked. "Mr. Shilling—really—"

Shilling ignored everyone save the inspector. "Veronica was never anything more to Ronald Strudgewick than a friend, damn you."

A dry smile parted Sampson's thin lips. "Are you the R. Shilling who stayed with Ronald Strudgewick at the hotel in Thirsk on the night of his uncle's death?" he asked, apparently in surprise. "The same Shilling who married Veronica Dixon last year?"

The question shook Shilling. Besotted though he was he had just enough intelligence to comprehend that he had spoken rashly. Many expressions chased across his face; it was apparent that he was suffering every emotion in turn. Finally defiance became predominant—the leering defiance of artificial courage. He staggered back to his chair, and again made its springs twang as he sank heavily into it.

"All right, I'm the Shilling who stayed at Thirsk with Strudgewick. What of it?"

"Nothing, nothing, Mr. Shilling," the inspector hastily assured the other man. "I was only thinking that Strudgewick ought to feel grateful to you. If you hadn't spent the night with him at the hotel the police might have suspected him of murdering his uncle in order to inherit sixty thousand pounds. But thanks to you Strudgewick has nothing to worry about. *He's* safe enough!"

"Whatdyou mean, *he's* safe enough?" Shilling asked unsteadily.

"Just what I say. Strudgewick is safe enough. *He* took care to have a cast-iron alibi. But in your case, Mr. Shilling—"

Shilling tried to conceal his alarm. "Whadyou mean—my case? The valet saw me, didn't he, when he brought up the breakfast. Everybody knows that *I* never left the blasted flat. And you're a damned liar to say that Veronica and Ronald Strudgewick—a damned liar! That's whad I shay, and I don't blashted well mind who hears me say that to your face." He leered at the others in turn.

"Really, Mr. Shilling—your language—" Alicia began nervously, for she was becoming affected by the increasing tension of the scene.

"Mother!" Julia exclaimed in a sharp whisper.

Shilling laughed jeeringly. "Don't pretend to be so shocked, Mrs. Mac—Mrs. Mac—" He could not twist his tongue round the name, so he left it alone. "I'll bet they swear just as much in the upper ten as everybody else does. Don't think I haven't heard the story of the Duke of—the Duke of—" He hiccoughed loudly, then laughed coarsely. "That to the Duke of What his name."

"Do you remember the night your wife Mary was killed?" Sampson asked unexpectedly.

Shilling squeezed himself up against the back of the chair. "You leave Mary's name out of this, blasht you!" he shouted. Then the precise meaning of the inspector's words appeared to sink into his consciousness. "Damn you! She wasn't killed. She died achiden—achidentally—"

"I know how she died, Mr. Shilling, but *your* alibi isn't cast-iron. You see, your sweet innocent Veronica Dixon chose that night of all nights to welcome her lover Strudgewick to flat thirty-seven while her mother was playing bridge with some friends in the same building."

Shilling's glazing eyes stared at the detective. "Goddam you!" he shouted thickly. "I spent that night playing cards with Ronald Strudgewick. Ask him for yourself—"

"If I were to ask him he would tell me that you were playing billiards," Sampson retorted drily. "Which was it, Shilling? Cards or billiards?"

"What the hell does it matter. I was with him every minute of the night—"

"But you were not—we have proof—"

"You're a damned liar—"

"Proof, Mr. Shilling, from an independent witness, Mrs. Raymond, who lived in flat thirty-nine. Mrs. Raymond saw Mrs. Dixon leave the flat to go and play cards, she saw Ronald Strudgewick admitted into the Dixon flat at 10.30 p.m., and she saw him leave again at ten minutes past twelve, five minutes after the return of Mrs. Dixon. So much for *your* alibi, Robert Shilling. Strudgewick won't suffer for his crime, for you played your part loyally and faithfully at Thirsk, but you will suffer for yours, because your fellow conspirator took advantage of your absence to share Veronica Dixon's embraces for which you were paying such a high price."

"Damn you!—damn you!—damn you!—" Shilling tried to say more, but his confused, drunken mind seemed incapable of sustained reasoning.

"You know that what I say is true," Sampson persisted swiftly. "You can recognize the truth because you know that Veronica Dixon was in love with Ronald Strudgewick before she met you. You know that before that time she wouldn't give Strudgewick what he wanted because he was too poor to keep her as she wanted to be kept. You know that she wouldn't give you what you wanted unless you married her. So you, poor fool, believing that you could only get Veronica by getting rid of your wife, conspired with Ronald Strudgewick in order that you might murder Mary Shilling and marry Veronica, and he might murder his uncle to obtain his uncle's money. And if you had only played your cards properly you could have kept your Mary, and have had your Veronica, too. You could have had Mary and society, and Veronica and her kisses. But you killed your wife, and your chances of mixing with society, and even as you killed her your friend Strudgewick was holding Veronica in his arms and sampling freely that for which you were paying so highly—"

Shilling's arms thrashed the air, and strangled noises that were unintelligible came from his drooling mouth.

The inspector went on: "Ronald Strudgewick is the only one to come out of your conspiracy a winner. Strudgewick has everything —his life, his uncle's money, and the memory of Veronica's kisses. You are the loser, Robert Shilling. The only loser. You lost Mary, you never won Veronica, and you will eventually lose your life. Is that a fair distribution of the spoils?"

"My life——" He pulled at his collar, loosening it. "I was with Strudgewick the night Mary died—you can't prove otherwise——"

"We *can* prove otherwise. Veronica can prove that *you* were not with Strudgewick because *she* was." Sampson laughed drily. "And by giving the evidence which will hang you, Mr. Shilling, Veronica will inherit your money, which is what she really married you for, and as soon as she has it she will go abroad and join her lover, Ronald Strudgewick— It was a marvellous scheme, for those two!"

"No! No!" Shilling's voice rose in an incoherent scream. "Why should Ronald Strudgewick get off scot-free——"

"He won't—if you sign a confession. Nor will Veronica—and you could will your money to Mary Shilling's family——"

"Oh, God! Paper—pen——" Shilling staggered to his feet, tottered over to the brandy bottle, lifted it to his lips——

II

Sampson discreetly went into another room while the blubbering, drunken Shilling wrote out and signed a confession which not only implicated himself and Strudgewick, but also supplied slight, but sufficient evidence to prove his guilt in the event of a subsequent retraction. Sampson went elsewhere to avoid any charge of compulsion or coercion, so he never knew—officially—that it took the combined efforts of Julia and Terhune, as well as Shilling himself, to produce the confession: Terhune, to hold the other man upright and keep him from falling into a stupor; Julia, to guide his unsteady hand.

Sampson then rang through to the Ashford police, and shortly afterwards Terhune's old friend, Detective-Sergeant Murphy, came along with a police constable formally to arrest the murderer, and take him away.

Still later the four who remained behind gathered once again in the drawing-room.

"Oh, dear! Oh, dear! I *am* so glad that perfectly dreadful scene is over." Alicia shuddered. "I know I shall dream about it for months and months."

For once Julia was in agreement with her mother. "It wasn't very pleasant," she agreed, white and shaken.

"I never did like detective stories," Alicia went on. "Now I never shall. I'll never read another, in case it reminds me of tonight. Not even one of yours, Tommy."

"So that's my reward for helping the police—to lose a prospective reader," Terhune bewailed.

Sampson did not respond to Terhune's smile. "I think that the knowledge of the help you have given in the arrest of as nasty a piece of mankind as I've met for many years is reward enough."

"So it is, but I think the credit for securing the confession is all yours, Inspector."

"The *idea* was yours, Mr. Terhune."

"Maybe it was, but it wasn't I who invented that peach of a story about Veronica's receiving Strudgewick in her flat at the very moment Shilling was murdering his wife. Of all the macabre twists—"

"I didn't invent that story either," Sampson interrupted quietly.

"What? Then who did?"

"Nobody. It happened to be true. I heard the details from Mrs. Raymond a few days ago."

"Good lord!"

The information silenced even Alicia, and in the end it was Terhune who spoke first.

"Then Veronica, the woman for whose sake Shilling killed Mary, is equally responsible for making him pay the penalty for his crime?"

"Yes. Sometimes life can play some queer tricks."

"Queer—"

Alicia laughed, somewhat unsteadily. "But if you knew Veronica could upset Mr. Shilling's alibi why did you trouble to trick him into making a confession, Mr. Sampson?" she asked, flutteringly.

"Why?" Sampson's heavy eyebrows twitched. "Perhaps you forget, Mrs. MacMunn—as Shilling himself fortunately forgot, thanks to being well-oiled—that Veronica could not have given that evidence in court."

"Why not?" the puzzled Alicia asked.

"Because the law cannot force a wife to give evidence against her husband," the inspector explained, helping himself to soda water.

THE END

CPSIA information can be obtained
at www.ICGtesting.com
Printed in the USA
BVHW032042060622
639058BV00021B/244